THE CYRUN

Janilise S. Lloyd

The Cyrun

Copyright 2019 by Janilise Lloyd

For more information or to contact the author, please visit

www.janilisewrites.weebly.com

ISBN 9781794183223

For Ryan, whose enthusiasm and encouragement gave me the desire to keep writing.

CONTENTS

PROLOGUE

Though she was terrified, the woman who sat on the last row of the light rail couldn't help but feel some relief. It wasn't often she was able to go somewhere with absolute freedom, though it can't truly be considered absolute when on a deadline, she realized. She sighed, staring out the window into the dark night as rain scuttled down the glass in frantic lines that raced each other to the bottom of the pane.

She had relaxed some, knowing that if she'd been followed, she likely would have been confronted by now. There was still the possibility, however, that the person sent to tail her was biding his time, waiting to see what she was doing so far from her usual home.

The other passengers on the train kept shooting concerned glances at the woman, checking to see if the baby bundled in her arms was okay. There was something different about the way she clung to it, like a husband holds the hand of his dying wife—with desperation, panic, and immeasurable love. As far as anyone could tell, the baby seemed fine. She didn't cry or make any noise besides a happy giggle as her mother nuzzled her face into the child's tummy.

The light rail slowed. "Next stop: Cheshire Street, Route 109 North," a cool, female voice called over the speakers.

The woman held the baby more tightly to her chest. "Only

three more stops, darling," she cooed, as she stroked the baby's wisps of auburn hair. The color matched the mother's exactly. She fought back the tears that had threatened to spill over every day since the baby was born six months previously.

With every passing stop, the woman grew noticeably more anxious. She glanced from her baby, to the window, to the crowd of passengers, then back to her baby, repeating the cycle compulsively.

The light rail slowed once more. "Next stop: 204 North Church Street," the voice announced. The woman tensed, hardly able to breathe. Mechanically, she stood, holding her baby more tightly. Her breaths came in shallow gasps as she stumbled toward the door.

A hand shot out into the aisle, grabbing the woman's forearm. She let out a small scream, her eyes darting to the face of the gentleman who had touched her. She didn't recognize him. He had dark skin and a soft expression. "Are you okay, Miss?" the stranger asked, concern etched on his face.

"I'm fine," the woman mumbled as she continued toward the door, feeling foolish at her reaction to the kind stranger.

The train came to a stop and the doors opened. The woman filed out along with a small group of passengers, the rain pelting her exposed face. She tucked the blanket up around the child's head, protecting her from the cold.

She thought she'd feel more comfortable once she was out of the bright glare of the train lights, but she had been wrong—the inky blackness of the stormy night had her jumping at any small disturbance as she walked briskly toward her destination.

Finally, she saw it—a small, deserted park ahead, empty of children due to the hour and weather. She ducked underneath the large, twisting slide, waiting for the man she'd come to meet. She fervently hoped he'd understood her cryptic message. She bounced the small child on her hip, trying to keep her calm despite the cold storm that swirled around them.

"Rose?" a voice called out from the darkness. "Is that you?"

The woman took a deep breath, gathering her courage, and stepped out from the cover of the slide. "Yes, it's me," she replied, drinking in the face before her. She could hardly believe she was seeing him again. His golden hair, tan skin, and brown eyes hadn't changed since she saw him last. She choked back the flood of emotion that threatened to escape. "Thank you for coming."

The man stood before Rose, stunned at the sight of the woman and child. "You knew I would," he finally stammered.

Rose smiled. "I didn't, actually. But I hoped."

The man shifted uncomfortably. "Is this the girl?" he asked, clearly changing the subject. He took a step closer to Rose, then briefly pushed the blanket back from the child's face to take a look.

"Yes, this is Avalon," Rose replied. The tears she'd been holding back finally came to the surface as she took in the man's kind expression toward the child. "I don't have much time. They could be on their way right now. Please tell me, Mike. Will you do it? Will you take her?"

Mike looked at the baby and then at the woman's tearful green eyes. "I don't know the first thing about kids, you know," he hesitated. "But yes, of course. Anything for you." He gave the woman a half smile. She sobbed in response.

"Come here, Rose." Mike grabbed the woman into a tight hug, the baby pushed between their chests. "You can stay here with me. You don't have to go back." He paused. "Please don't go back." His voice broke at the end.

"You know as well as I do that isn't an option," Rose said darkly. She stepped back. "Please, just promise me that you'll take care of her."

"I promise," Mike said quietly.

"And promise you won't tell her where she comes from. She can't know—for her own safety."

"I know. I promise."

Rose took one last look at her child. "I love you, Ava. Forever and always," she breathed. She kissed the baby on the head before handing her over to Mike. He took the girl awkwardly.

"Thank you, Mike. This means everything to me. I don't deserve it, I know. But thank you." Rose stood on her tippy toes and pecked him on the cheek.

"Please, not again, Rose. I can't take it," Mike choked, grabbing her arm.

"I'm so sorry," Rose cried. "Goodbye."

She ripped her arm away from Mike and ran into the night.

Mike stood there in the pouring rain, looking after her, his mouth open in shock.

The baby in his arms began to cry, bringing him to his senses. He looked down at the tiny child, then ran off in the opposite direction of Rose.

CHAPTER 1

TRAPPED

.

Vigilante justice is not all it's cracked up to be.

I've spent the last four evenings in the dumpsters of La Sefoya Seafood attempting to scope out the bank across the street. Seafood is bad enough when it's fresh—eight plus hours later and it's definitely puke-worthy. At this point, I was certain the smell would be permanently ingrained in my nose.

A noise down the alley caught my attention—footsteps. Yikes!

I ducked down, my back sinking into a poorly closed garbage sack. I could feel unidentified juices soaking through to my elbow, spreading down my forearm. I fought the urge to simultaneously scream and vomit, forcing myself to stay quiet.

The footsteps drew closer; there were two sets of them. I held my breath, waiting for them to pass.

"Hey, Lani!" a male voice called out. "Close up those garbages before you take off tonight, will ya? Someone's been leaving 'em open the past few nights. We don't need some bum rummaging through our trash."

This was not good. This was really, really not good. I tried to think of a way out, but the footsteps drew closer, approaching the edge of the large dumpster where I hid. There was no time.

An arm reached up, swinging the wide metal lid up and around the top. I was plunged into darkness. I heard a rustling of chains and the click of a lock. The footsteps continued on, growing faint as the man left the alley.

I slowly stood into a crouch, tentatively pushing the metal lid covering me. It moved up a little, then stopped abruptly. I poked my eyes up over the edge. Just as I thought, a chain looped through a hook on the lid and a hook on the bin. A simple padlock held it in place. The lid would only lift as far as the small chain would allow. It wasn't even enough space to poke my arm through.

I took a deep breath, trying to calm myself. Bad idea—the smell made me gag.

This was fine. I'd been in tighter spots. In fact, this garbage can should be no problem for me. I'd moved right through solid walls before. A little metal tin like this? Piece of cake.

I tried to clear my head—using my abilities unfortunately required a lot of focus. I pushed out the disgusting smells, the panic, the claustrophobia, focusing on making myself feel the music. That was the best way I could describe using my powers— it was like directing a song that only I could hear.

After a few moments of intense focus, I pushed my hand against the dumpster's walls.

Nothing. No response, no give.

I remained calm, returning my focus to the music.

I tried again, pressing my hand forcefully against the metal sides, willing it to push through. Still nothing. It was as solid as ever.

"Useless powers," I breathed, shaking my head.

I took in another long breath and exhaled, forcing myself to focus even harder on the music as it ran up and down my skin; I was practically tingling with it. This was the time. It was going to work. I shoved my shoulder forcefully into the side of the bin.

All I got was a sore shoulder.

"You idiotic piece of junk!" I growled, kicking the side of the bin. Ouch!

Nice, Ava, I thought wryly. Add a sore toe to the list.

I sunk back down into the pile of rotting food, feeling defeated. I shouldn't be all that surprised. The ability to move through solid objects was my most recently discovered power, and my abilities were always temperamental, especially when they were new.

I'd discovered the talent completely by accident about three weeks ago. It was stupid, really. I was in a rush to get to school and was grabbing breakfast hurriedly. Without thinking, I went to grab the milk without actually opening the fridge door. I looked down to find my arm reaching through the door, holding the handle of the milk on the other side.

It's a weird feeling, seeing your arm half gone, sunken into what should be a solid object. I've been surrounded by weird things most of my life—the kinds of things that would only be seen in a movie as a result of special effects—but that one

8

definitely threw me for a loop.

It was hard being stuck in this very non-magical human realm. I'd get into human mode—go to school, hang out with friends, blend in—and then come home to a dad who could control animal life and was telekinetic. Not exactly a smooth transition.

Idly, my mind wandered to my dad. He would not be happy if he knew where I was and what I was doing. We tried to keep a low profile. We'd been doing a pretty good job lately. We hadn't had to move in over four years. But I couldn't just sit by when I knew something bad was going to happen here, so I'd been sneaking out every night after he went to sleep to watch the bank.

That was another ability I had—precognition—though the useless thing was almost as faulty as my ability to move through objects. I'd get feelings about certain things, places, or people, but not know any details about what was going to happen. It was all very vague. I'd feel like something good was going to happen to someone and then they'd get engaged the next day. Or I'd feel like something bad was going to happen at a certain place and someone would end up dying there. It was actually really terrible. If there was any ability I wish I didn't have, it was this one.

A few days ago, I came into town with Dad and we passed 25th Street Bank. That was when it happened—I knew something awful was going to happen here, at the bank across the street. That's why I'd been watching it. But it had been four days since then and nothing had happened yet. Usually my heightened intuition was a little more accurate on the timeline.

Really, the issue was that I was in the wrong realm. I didn't belong here and neither did my powers, which is why they didn't work well. There wasn't supposed to be magic in the human world—only in Cyrus. Of my four abilities—speed, telekinesis, precognition, and moving through objects—only my speed was consistently reliable. Even still, I was fairly certain I'd be even faster if I lived in Cyrus. Only problem was Cyrus didn't exist anymore. It had been destroyed. Dad and I were lucky enough to escape to this realm. Most Cyruns had died in the destruction.

Three gunshots rang out through the night in quick succession, bringing me swiftly to my feet. I smacked my head on the dumpster's lid in my hurry to get up. Ow!

This had to be it—the terrible thing that was going to happen at the bank—and I was stuck in this hunk of metal, surrounded by rotting fish. Some hero I was.

I slammed against the side of the bin again and again, but nothing gave. Stupid, erratic powers.

Then, without warning, the lid of the bin suddenly lifted. I straightened up, glancing around. The figure of a boy was running around the corner of the alley, away from the trash can. I caught the slightest glimpse of the side of his face. He was young, probably about 18 years old, tall, with a medium build. I don't know why he didn't want to stick around after rescuing me, but I was grateful for his help. Perhaps the gunfire scared him off.

I scrambled awkwardly out of the dumpster and crept to the edge of the alley, peeking around the corner to the street. This road was typically full of bustling people, but considering the late hour, there were only a few out and about. Those who were there stood staring at the large white building across the street that was the massive bank. Many had their phones out, presumably calling 911.

More shots rang out through the air. This time, I saw the sparks from inside the bank. They were coming from the second floor.

My mind ran through its options. As far as I could figure, I could do one of two things: wait for law enforcement to arrive or use my speed to get over to the building and check things out for myself. The sensible thing to do was wait for law enforcement, obviously. But I wasn't exactly known for being sensible.

The traffic light to the north changed to green, sending a slew of traffic through the road directly between myself and the bank. The opportunity was perfect. I could weave in and out of the traffic using it as cover. Any bystanders shouldn't be able to spot me. I was fast and all, but not so fast I became a blur—at least not in this realm.

I left the cover of the alleyway, pushing my legs as fast as they could go. I darted in front of and behind cars, nearly getting hit about six different times. A few horns blared, but nobody seemed to be able to get a clear look at what exactly had run in front of them.

In a matter of seconds, I reached the back side of the bank. Every set of doors was protected by bars that had likely lowered as alarms were tripped inside. The windows, too, were barred.

"Okay, powers. Don't flake out on me now," I breathed as I inched along the side of the wall toward the back entrance. I took a deep breath, prayed, and then walked directly into the bars that protected the glass.

I hit my head for the second time tonight. Hard.

Seriously? What good was it to be able to move through objects if all it ever allowed me to do is grab the milk in the fridge without opening the door?

I stepped back and took another breath, trying to refocus. More gunshots—not helpful when I'm trying to be calm.

I walked confidently toward the barred doors, focusing on the music that was my abilities coursing through me. This time, my body passed effortlessly through the bars and glass doors as if they were nothing but smoke. I grinned. Then I almost got shot.

"Hey! How'd you get in here?" I turned to see a large man, dressed in black, with a mask over his face running toward me, gun in hand. As soon as we made eye contact, he started firing.

"Oh shoot!" I screamed, running down a hall away from the man and his bullets. *No wait, don't shoot!* I thought wryly. *That was just an expression!*

With my speed as an advantage, I lost the man with ease, ducking behind a large potted plant a ways up the carpeted hall that surrounded the main lobby. I watched as he turned the corner at full speed, surprised when I wasn't a few yards ahead of him as he expected. He slowed down, checking any potential hiding spots where I may have ducked.

It wouldn't take him long to get to me. Better get moving.

I could see a staircase at the end of the hall that would lead up to the second floor where I'd seen shots fired earlier. I needed to get up there to see if anyone was hurt.

A glance down the hall told me the guy was busying himself checking out a janitorial closet. This was my chance. I straightened up out of my crouch, sprinting toward the staircase at the end of the hall. I reached the stairs without incident and cautiously climbed them to the next level.

The second level of the bank was entirely comprised of office space that branched off a large balcony which circled the full perimeter of the main lobby below. An ornate marble banister allowed a clear view of what was happening on the main floor. Four men dressed identically to the man who'd chased me stood with large rifles in their hands. At their feet sat five security guards who had been bound and gagged.

One of the burglars held a phone in his hand and was talking as he paced a small circle around his prisoners. "I have five hostages in here with me, Officer," he said into the phone. "If you do anything I don't like, they each get a bullet through the brain, you understand?" He paused, listening.

"Don't tell me to stay calm!" he shouted. "Do exactly as I say and these five men live. Do anything different and you can hold yourself personally responsible to their grieving wives and children." He paused again.

"Oh, the manager says there should be six guards? Yes, well, I'm afraid it's too late for one of them." He laughed coldly.

My stomach churned as I looked down the long hall and noticed the sixth guard lying facedown, a pool of blood spread around him.

I glanced around to make sure the coast was clear—the floor appeared to be vacant. I dashed over to the guard, arriving by his side in half a second. Carefully, I rolled the man to his back, dreading what I might find.

The bullet wound appeared to be in his upper abdomen, but not so high that it would have punctured his heart. I'd had only basic EMR training in a class I took last year in high school. Treating bullet wounds certainly wasn't covered, but I at least knew how to find a pulse.

I put my fingers to his neck. Blessedly, there was still a faint rhythm there, but I knew it wouldn't last long, not at the rate he was losing blood.

I glanced around, frantic. There was absolutely nothing nearby that I could use as a bandage. I looked down at my own clothes. I wore black pants, a black long-sleeve shirt, and a gray jacket. The jacket was covered in crap from the dumpster, but my shirt underneath might be relatively clean. I was no expert, but exposing an open wound to rotting fish didn't seem like it would be advantageous to his health. I swiftly unzipped the jacket and pulled off my shirt. I put the jacket back on, zipping it up to my neck. The rose necklace I always wore was cold against my skin.

After a quick examination, I decided my shirt was clean enough that it probably wouldn't cause any infection. Ultimately, I didn't know if it would even matter at this point—he might be too far gone. I quickly wrapped my shirt around the man's torso, pulling it as tightly as I could manage. I secured it with a knot and applied pressure over the wound as I continued to observe the men below.

"I want you to arrange a private flight out of the Denver airport to depart in 30 minutes, no pilot necessary—I have my own. I'll also need an unmarked police SUV gassed and ready to go in fifteen minutes to get us there on time. After my team and I have safely entered the car, I'll release three of the guards. Two of them stay with us as we ride to the airport to ensure you don't try and stop us on our way. I'll release them after we've successfully boarded our plane. I expect a call in ten minutes to confirm you have that all arranged. If you're even a minute late, I will kill one of the guards. Another one dies every five minutes after that." He hung up the phone, stuffing it into his pants' pocket.

Fifteen minutes? This man did not have fifteen minutes left to live. Something had to be done.

I searched the pockets of the guard, finding what I was hoping for—his cell phone. I didn't want to use mine because I fully intended to get out of this mess without anyone knowing I was here. Far too many questions would be asked with far too many answers I couldn't provide without sounding like a crazy person or becoming the next microbe under a scientific microscope.

Making a phone call was too risky. Text-to-911 was the better option here so that I wasn't overheard. I sent off a text that read, *I'm the security guard at 25th Street Bank the burglars think is dead. Send me the number of the person in charge of the operation so that I can communicate with him.*

The response was immediate. *467-555-2429, Police Chief Rollins*

Chief Rollins, I wrote, *I'm the security guard at 25th Street Bank the burglars think is dead. I'm injured and need assistance. What is your plan? How can I help?*

We are currently working on a plan. What are the positions of the burglars and hostages? We can't get a visual, Chief Rollins replied.

I checked the pulse of the guard. It was barely palpable. We didn't have time for all this back and forth. If Chief Rollins didn't have a plan, I'd come up with one myself.

I shoved the guard's phone into my pocket and left his side, creeping over to the banisters to get a better view. Obviously, the best option was to disarm the burglars, but my telekinesis wasn't strong enough to rip an object out of someone's hand. Somehow, I had to incapacitate them, preferably all at once. If only Dad was here. He was so much better at using his telekinesis than I was— an advantage of having actually grown up in Cyrus.

Without any kind of actual plan in place, I slipped into an office and made a call to the Chief. He picked up before the first ring ended.

16

"Chief Rollins speaking."

I did my best to sound manly and like I was in pain. It was a rather pathetic effort. "This is the guard you've been texting. Send your men into the building in exactly two minutes. There are five burglars as far as I've seen. They are in the main lobby with the hostages bound and sitting on the ground. I am on the second level. The burglars will be unarmed for your men to come in."

"Now hang on a minute," Chief Rollins said. "How do I know I can trust you? How do I know you're not one of them, laying some trap for my guys. I'm not going in there blind."

"You're just going to have to trust me," I wheezed. "All our lives depend on it. Two minutes, starting now." I hung up and turned the phone off, not wanting him to call me back.

I opened the office door and was met by two thugs. Oh boy!

"Told you there was a girl in here!" one of the oafs exclaimed. "I saw her earlier."

"Shut up and grab her already!" the other one demanded.

He lunged for me, but I dodged out of the way, moving much quicker than he anticipated. "What in the—?" he said, confused.

The other burglar wasted no time and shot at me. I hoped that wouldn't cause Chief Rollins to come storming in here. *Please wait two minutes!*

I used my telekinesis to redirect the bullet. It lodged in the ceiling. Both thieves looked up at it, confused. I used their momentary distraction to rip a handgun out of the nearest thug's hand. Fortunately, Dad and I often spent our weekends at the

17

shooting range. I directed a shot at the other man's thigh, hitting him right on target—Dad would be proud. The man doubled over, gasping in pain as he clutched the bleeding spot. The other burglar took his cohort's gun and began firing again. I moved swiftly in the small space in a zigzagging pattern, avoiding the spray of bullets.

The thieves blocked my path to the door, so that was not an exit option. Deciding to trust my faulty abilities, I launched myself directly at the wall, hoping my powers would work for me. To my intense relief, they did. I melted through the wall with ease, circling back around and shutting the office door from the hallway. I took a chair which sat next to the door and wedged it underneath the door handle like I'd seen done in the movies. I had no idea if it would actually work, but judging by the banging at the door and the fact that the two thugs didn't come tumbling out after me, it appeared to.

Evidently, our altercation had not gone unnoticed. A shout down the hall drew my attention to another burglar headed directly for me. I searched around frantically, grateful he hadn't decided to shoot—yet. His malicious grin grew wider as he closed the distance between us.

Out of other options, I decided to do the obvious. I used my telekinesis to pick up a large vase which stood slightly behind the charging man. I hurled it forward. As the vase came in contact with the unsuspecting thief, it cracked over his head. The man staggered, his eyes rolling back, as he fell into the pile of shattered porcelain, a grisly wound issuing a fair amount of blood from the back of his head.

"How did you do that?" one of the two remaining burglars shouted from the first floor. The other didn't seem to care. He began firing at me immediately. I dove behind one of the large pillars, desperate for a plan. My two minutes had to be about gone.

My brain—flaky as it was—seemed to be moving in slow motion right when I needed it most. How was I going to disarm the two guards below? The bullets continued to hammer the other side of the pillar. I desperately wanted to get a visual of beneath but didn't dare peek around with the bullets flying as they were.

I made a split-second decision to run for it, hoping a new vantage point would allow me to see below. I sprung up from my crouch and darted around half of the upper balcony.

"She's moving!" one of the thieves shouted. "Did you see that? Where'd she go, Lars?"

"I don't know," growled the man who had been on the phone earlier, "but she's fast."

My breathing was heavy—not because of the running, I could do that with ease—but because of the adrenaline. I chanced a glance around the new pillar where I ducked. Just as I hoped, the men were facing the other direction, looking around the area I'd been hiding before. They didn't expect me to be on the other side of the building already.

After a momentary pause to try and calm my racing heart, I sprinted back down the staircase to the main floor, where I threw myself behind the reception desk. Slowly, I stood, peering over the edge of the counter. The men were no more than fifteen feet from where I stood. Both were still looking around the upper balcony, their backs to me.

Hurriedly, I scanned the contents of the front desk. The only weapon was a pair of scissors. Though they'd be painful to be stabbed with, they would hardly incapacitate either thief. Besides, I was exhausted and unsure my telekinesis would still work to hurl them forward. Everything except my speed tended to wear out easily. Officers would soon be storming this building, and I couldn't bear the thought of one of them taking a bullet after I said the burglars would be unarmed. I decided to trust my purely human abilities with the handgun rather than risk using my telekinesis and failing.

Taking a chance, I stood up swiftly, aiming one shot at the back of Lars' thigh. It hit him perfectly, causing him to collapse forward at the unsuspecting pain. I sprinted forward and grabbed the rifle as he dropped it in favor of holding the back of his bleeding thigh. He fell sideways to the ground, gasping.

An intense pain ripped through my left side just as every door on all four sides of the bank burst open. At least fifty officers in full gear stormed the lobby, guns at the ready.

"Someone get to the guard on the second floor!" A portly man shouted as he emerged from the crowd of officers. I assumed that would be Chief Rollins.

Using every ounce of strength I had left, I willed myself to run. I didn't know where. I had no plan. All I knew is that I couldn't be found here. Too many questions.

I reached the outskirts of the main floor before the pain in my side became unbearable. I gasped as I gripped the area that hurt. I felt wetness—blood, spilling out of me.

I'd been shot.

I stumbled backward, the pain crippling me, until I landed on the floor with a thud. Everything from that point was a blur as I faded out of consciousness.

I heard someone shouting commands I couldn't comprehend.

I felt hands grab my shoulders tightly—too tightly. It hurt.

And then I was gone.

Chapter 2

Busted

I woke up to a pounding headache but no confusion. Well, some confusion. I remembered the events from the bank perfectly clear, right up to being shot and passing out. Everything from that point was completely gone from my memory.

And I had no clue how I got where I was.

I sat up from the dirt strewn ground where I'd been lying, looking up into the curtain of tree leaves above. This wooded area was familiar—it was on the west side of my house.

Sure enough, through the thinning trees to my right, I could see my small, yellow home, Dad's car still parked in the driveway.

It seemed to be early morning. The air was crisp after a long night's rest from the sun. I could see my breath as I exhaled.

A noise caught my attention. A few yards away, deeper into the woods, a boy stood, peering out at me from behind a tree. I recognized him. At least I thought I did.

"Hey, you're the guy who let me out of the dumpster last night, aren't you?" I said, standing up quickly—too quickly. A wave of nausea washed over me. I grabbed a nearby tree trunk for support.

The boy stepped out from behind the tree. "You should be careful," he said. "You lost a lot of blood last night." Then, without any further explanation, he took off into the woods.

"Hey, wait!" I called. "What happened to me? Who are you? How did I get here?" I stumbled after him but couldn't follow at my usual fast speed. I felt incredibly weak as nausea turned my stomach.

After a few minutes of pointless searching, I gave up. The boy was nowhere to be found.

I gave myself a quick once-over. I was wearing the same disgusting, seafood-drenched jacket I had been last night. I realized the entire left side was soaked in a deep red—my blood. Not caring that it was likely only thirty degrees out and I wore nothing but my bra underneath, I unzipped the jacket to investigate my wound.

I gasped, clutching my side, pulling at the skin. There was nothing there. No wound. No bandages. Not even a scar. Except for the large bloodstain on my clothes, there was no indication that I had ever been shot.

I had been shot, hadn't I?

Nothing about this situation made sense. I'd woken up in the woods fifteen miles from where I'd lost consciousness. A stranger was (rather creepily) watching over me. And I had no bullet wound—or a wound of any kind, for that matter—yet my jacket was clearly soaked in blood. Had that boy saved me? He obviously had something to do with my present condition.

Exasperated, I decided it was best to head inside and confront my dad. He was sure to be furious. It might be early morning, but

I had no doubt he was already awake and had noticed my empty bed. I stomped through the woods, hesitating only slightly before opening the front door.

The TV in the kitchen was on with the local news blaring— they were talking about a bank robbery in downtown Denver. Crap.

Dad sat in his red plaid bathrobe at the far end of the kitchen table, facing the front door, a bowl of untouched cereal in front of him. His head snapped up as I walked in. I watched as a mixture of relief and fury warred on his face. Fortunately, for the time being, relief seemed to be winning out.

"Hey, Dad," I said, walking forward cautiously. He stood from his chair slowly. Then he rushed forward, scooping me up into an enormous bear hug.

"Oh, sugar bean! I am so glad you're safe! I've been so worried."

"Sorry, Dad. I know I should have told you what I was doing."

He released me, grabbing the tops of my shoulders instead. He bent his neck so he could look me in the eye. "Avalon Rosaline Tanner," he began. Uh oh. Full name—never good. "If you ever sneak out of the house again, you will be grounded until the day you move out. No friends, no fun, no social life. Nothing but school and home. Do you understand?"

"I understand, loud and clear," I affirmed.

Dad's face crinkled in disgust as he sniffed in. "You smell, sweetie. Really badly." He stepped back to take a better look at me.

Oh boy. His mouth dropped in horror as he took in the large bloodstain smeared across my gray jacket.

"Oh my heavens, Ava, you're hurt. We need to get you to a hospital! How did this happen?"

"Believe me, Dad, it looks a lot worse than it is. I'm fine, I promise. I just… caught my side on something sharp and got a little cut. No big deal," I lied. He raised his eyebrows skeptically.

The sound of gunshots and screaming emanated from the TV, catching both our attention for a moment. I glanced over to see video of the robbery last night taken with a bystander's phone. A reporter's voice picked up. "There were five burglars total, each of whom have been apprehended and are in police custody. There were six security guards in the bank at the time. One of the six guards on duty was harmed; he received a bullet wound to the upper abdomen. His condition is critical but stable. Doctors estimate he will make a full recovery with time.

"Many questions about the attack remain. To shed some light on the circumstances, we now turn to our team member, Brett, who stands by with Police Chief Rollins."

"Hello, Amanda. I'm here with Chief Rollins who led the law enforcement officers dealing with last night's burglary at 25th Street Bank in downtown Denver. He has agreed to answer a few questions for us this morning, to the best of his knowledge at this time.

"Good morning, Chief Rollins," the reporter said, gesturing

25

for Chief Rollins to take a step closer to the camera.

"You've already said that," the Chief answered grumpily as he reluctantly stepped into better view of the camera. Brett laughed uncomfortably.

"Right. Um, can you provide any additional insight into how your team successfully extracted the hostages from this dangerous situation while also managing to apprehend all five suspects?"

"Well, the credit goes to my team of officers, of course, for their diligence and presence during this crisis situation. Each one of them carried out their duties as assigned and were well equipped to deal with the crisis at hand. We also received help from an unidentified individual inside the bank at the time of the incident."

Uh oh. This wasn't good. I tried to hide the stress from my face as Dad and I continued to listen.

"There are consistent reports from security guards, one of our officers, and some of the thieves that there was a teenage girl, approximately 16 to 18 years of age, who was present in the bank last night. Reports from our witnesses indicate she is likely between five foot four and five foot seven, 115 to 135 pounds with brown hair that is medium length."

I chanced a glance at Dad who stood staring at the TV, dumbfounded, his face turning from red to purple. I swallowed hard.

"It's been difficult to nail down specifics about her description due to the darkness of the bank's interior at the time and because security cameras were rendered useless by the thieves prior to their entrance to the bank.

"We have reason to believe this young lady assisted the injured security guard and provided intel to officers via the injured guard's cell phone. She is, of course, in no danger from us. We simply would like to encourage her to come forward in order that we might thank her and obtain any additional information from her that may be helpful in the prosecution of these criminals."

I pulled the TV remote from the kitchen counter, through the air, and to my hand. I flicked off the power switch. "It's a crazy, sad world out there," I said, shaking my head. "I guess the important thing is that everyone is alright. So, you ready to eat some breakfast?"

"You sneak out past your curfew, interfere in a bank robbery, show up here smelling like death itself, covered in blood, and ask if I want to eat breakfast?" Dad hissed.

Time to drop the act, apparently. I fell heavily into one of the wooden chairs around the kitchen table, slouching and exhausted. "I'm really sorry, Dad. I know it was reckless, and irresponsible, and stupid, and worthy of a serious grounding, but I had to do it. I knew something awful was going to happen at that bank, so I've been watching it for the past four nights from the dumpster at La Sefoya Seafood, which is why I smell like a three-day-old fish stick. Last night, something did happen, and it was a darn good thing I was there because I very likely saved the life of one of the guards and probably more. Those thugs were completely trigger happy."

"Trigger happy?" Dad asked, glancing down at my gory jacket. "Did you get shot?" His eyes widened and his breath came in rugged gasps.

"Okay, calm down, Dad. Deep breaths. I'm fine." I stood up and wrapped my arm around his back, guiding him to one of the table chairs. He sat down, resting his head on his palms as he sucked in large gulps of air.

"Yes, I was shot, but you don't need to worry. Somehow—miraculously—I'm healed. Like 100% better, so it's no big deal," I said.

"Healed? Healed how? Let me see," Dad demanded, yanking up my jacket on the side with the blood. He sucked in a sharp breath. "Are you sure you were shot? There's nothing here."

"I know, crazy, right? I guess I'm not completely sure, but it definitely felt like being shot. Not that I've ever been shot before, but I'd imagine that's what it would feel like. It sucked."

Dad looked at me skeptically for a moment before he pulled me onto his knee. "I'm proud of you for helping save that guard—and probably others, too. But next time you get a feeling like this, please talk to me about it first—"

"Dad," I interrupted, "you don't understand what it's like, knowing things the way I do. I can't imagine getting a feeling like I did about the bank and not doing something about it. It's not who I am, I can't just—"

"Ava, honey," he cut me off, "that's not what I'm asking. I

28

may not perfectly understand, but I get it more than you might think. All I mean is, when you get these kinds of bad feelings, tell me about it and we can work on a plan together. At the very least, I would have liked to be there with you last night. You probably could have used the help, too. We both know your telekinesis leaves a bit to be desired." He winked.

I jabbed him in the ribs playfully. "That was low. If we lived in Cyrus, I'd swim laps around you, old man."

He laughed. "That's probably true. But we don't live in Cyrus, and I will always be the better telekinetic, so deal with it."

"I don't know... maybe someday I'll get good enough to compete. You better watch it."

"In your dreams," he laughed, which turned into a cough. "Ava, darling, you know I love you, but you positively reek. There is no way I'll be able to swallow anything until you've taken at least a half hour shower. Go jump in and I'll start the laundry." He paused, considering. "Better yet, I'll throw away your clothes and take the bin out to the curb. No amount of detergent is going to solve that problem."

I sniffed myself and gagged, then stood from my dad's lap. He shouldn't be subjected to that odor. "Fair enough. You'll write me a slip to excuse me from first period?"

"I shouldn't, considering this is all a result of rebellious sneaking out, but yes, and only because I am the coolest dad ever." He stood from his seat, breaking out in a dance that was a cross between the electric slide, the robot, and a rabid squirrel feasting

29

on peanut butter.

"Uh huh," I agreed, leaving the kitchen as quickly as I could. Best to leave Dad to his dancing at times such as these.

CHAPTER 3

BLUNDERS

Five days after the bank fiasco, I saw the boy again—the one who'd saved me from the dumpster and somehow healed me from my bullet wound.

I was out with the track team running next to my best friend, Lana. We were supposed to do a quick mile jog around the perimeter of the school as a warm up. Nobody was moving all that fast, preferring to stay in small groups and chat as we ran. My precognition had given me a warning that some sort of injury was going to happen at track practice today, so I was on high alert as we jogged.

We had just turned the corner onto Lincoln Avenue when time slowed. About an eighth of a mile down the road, I saw a young boy—maybe four-years-old—out playing on his driveway with a red ball. A large truck was headed north, facing me. The child's ball rolled out onto the street. He chased after it, running directly into the truck's path, not even twenty feet in front of it. His mother's face contorted in horror, her arms stretching out toward the child who was oblivious to the danger.

I stopped running, deliberating.

Option one: run. I could easily reach the boy in time. But there were witnesses—lots of them. And they were all people who knew me personally. If they saw me reach the child who was a fair distance away in a matter of seconds, there would be questions about how I'd done it.

Option two: use telekinesis to move the truck. That option was almost certainly doomed to fail, though. An object that large with telekinesis as erratic as mine was likely not going to end well. Dad might have been able to pull it off, but not me.

Option three: use telekinesis to move the boy. The problem there was similar—I didn't know how well I could control where the boy landed. I didn't want to risk harming him.

Less than half a second passed as I weighed my options. Ultimately, the choice was clear—the only thing I could trust myself to do was use my speed. Granted, that did risk the greatest exposure by far, but I couldn't let the child die to protect myself.

I took off, running as fast as I could push my legs. The truck's wheels screeched. The driver was trying desperately to stop, to swerve, anything before hitting the child.

I reached the boy just in time, scooping him into my arms and diving for the sidewalk. I turned in midair, trying to protect the child, and landed hard on my back on the cement. I could feel my shirt shredding from the impact, scraping my skin raw.

"Ugh," I groaned, slowly sitting up. The child in my arms bawled. I released him. His mother came running over to us, scooping him up in an enormous hug and kissing every inch of his head.

"Thank you," she said, her eyes burning with sincerity. I gave her a weak smile in return.

Pain pulsed through my bleeding back as I looked over at my teammates on the other end of the street. Every one of them stood frozen, their mouths hanging open in shock—all except Lana who stood with her arms crossed, worry creasing her forehead. She didn't know precisely what was different about me, but being my best friend for four years had exposed her to enough odd situations that she knew I wasn't quite like everybody else.

One other face stood out among the hordes of people looking at me—the boy from the night at the bank. He stood on the same side of the street I did, directly across from the rest of my teammates. He stood casually, no worry in his stance or face, unlike every other bystander. Instead, he looked at me with curiosity, a small smile playing at his lips. His eyes met mine briefly before I was distracted by a voice next to me.

"Are you okay?" a balding man asked as he knelt beside me.

I glanced around in alarm. Uh oh. Here come the crowds. That's the worst part about saving someone—the crowds. People just can't seem to leave it alone. They have to rush you, thank you, make sure you're okay, wonder how you did it… I was tempted to run away, then and there, but I knew that would only raise more questions.

"Yes, I'll be fine," I assured the man.

"I've already called an ambulance. It's on its way."

I tried to smile politely in response, though riding away in an ambulance was the last thing I wanted to do.

Out of curiosity, I looked back at the mysterious boy down the road. He wasn't there. I couldn't find him anywhere in the surrounding crowds. How odd. I was disappointed; I wanted to ask him how he had saved me the other night.

I couldn't dwell on him long, though. Others had reached me now, including people from the track team.

"Ava, are you okay?" Selma asked. Teammates followed behind her, asking the same question. I slowly stood up from the ground, trying to hide the amount of pain I was in.

"Yes, I'm going to be fine, everybody," I assured the crowd.

"How did you get over here so fast?" Lance Jacobs asked. I had to work really hard not to glare at him in response. I already didn't like the guy. He was a pompous jerk who thought his speed on the track was something worthy of worship.

"Ava was running ahead of all of us," Lana jumped in. "Didn't you notice? All she had to do was lunge across the street and she was to the kid."

I shot Lana a grateful glance. She gave a half smile in return. She clearly didn't know quite what to think of the situation yet, but had decided to cover for me regardless.

"No she wasn't," Lance insisted. "She was right next to you."

Shut up, Lance, I thought.

"That's crazy. No I wasn't. You must have been looking at someone else," I denied. "I was running ahead of you guys, just like Lana said. No need to get all worked up about it just because you can't keep up with me, Lance."

"Ooooh, dang!" Jared laughed, punching Lance in the arm. Lance glared at Jared with annoyance.

"Whatever, Ava. We both know I'm faster than you," Lance said. He turned brusquely and shoulder checked Jared as he walked away.

"Idiot," Karissa said. "Don't pay attention to him. We're all glad you're okay, Ava. That was really brave of you."

"Umm, thanks," I said awkwardly, avoiding everyone's eyes.

The ambulance pulled up at that moment. I didn't know whether I was mortified by it or grateful for the escape. A couple of first responders looked me over, deciding they better take me to the ER despite my complaints. The ER meant no hiding this from Dad. He would be less than thrilled by the news. Since I was a child, we'd already had to move six different times to various locations surrounding Denver because I'd exposed my abilities. We'd both begun to settle here in Littleton, though.

Trying to play it cool, I hauled myself into the back of the ambulance and settled in for the long ride.

CHAPTER 4

THE SCIENTIST

Dad arrived at the hospital twenty minutes after I did. By that time, I'd already been checked out, bandaged up, and given a prescription for pain meds I had no intention of filling.

I sat relaxing in one of the waiting room chairs as he burst through the ER doors, yelling, "Avalon Tanner, that's my daughter. Where is she? Hello? Anybody? My name is Michael Tanner, I'm here to see my daughter—"

"Dad," I interrupted his embarrassing shouting, "I'm right here." I hobbled toward him, my back becoming more and more stiff with passing time.

"Oh, Ava," he breathed, running toward me. He hugged me tightly. I yelped in pain. "Oh, sorry, honey. That was stupid, I wasn't thinking."

"Yeah, no kidding." I rubbed my back gently where his hands had just grabbed.

"Are you okay? What happened? What did the doctor say?"

I intentionally ignored his second question—that could wait until later. "I'm fine. The doctor bandaged me up, gave me some antibiotics, and said I'm good to go, so let's get out of here already."

"Alright, alright. Let me go check in with reception and make sure we're really okay to leave."

I watched as Dad talked with the nurse behind the desk. She was flustered, of course. Women seemed to have that reaction to my dad. He was one of those guys that always had more than enough women lining up to date him as long as I could remember, but he never seemed all that interested. Though he didn't talk about it much, I got the feeling it was because of my mom.

My knowledge of her was extremely limited. All I could gather is that they were never married and she had broken his heart. A couple years after that, she died in a series of battles in Cyrus. He never seemed angry toward her, just sad. I often got the sense that there was a lot he wanted to tell me about her, but he could never find the right words. More than a few times, I've been tempted to ask, but I know it hurts him when I bring her up, so I stopped trying a long time ago. I've never even seen a picture of her.

I often wondered what she looked like because I couldn't see a trace of myself in Dad. His skin was tan, mine was white. His eyes were brown, mine were green. I had freckles, he had none. His hair was sandy blonde, mine was auburn brown.

Sometimes, I thought I must look a lot like my mom. It seemed that occasionally, Dad would get lost in thought while looking at me. The familiar, sad look would creep into his eyes that I had come to associate with thoughts of Mom. I suppose I'd never be sure.

"Alright, looks like we're home free, kiddo," Dad said,

wrapping his arm around my shoulder gently as he guided me out to the parking lot. He opened the door for me and lowered me into the seat, treating me like a fragile object. It was kind of nice—I really did hurt a lot.

"So, you gonna tell me what happened?" Dad asked as he jumped into the driver's side and started the car.

I sighed. The ride home from the hospital was at least twenty minutes. I may be good at stalling, but I wasn't that good. "Fine, just try not to be mad, okay?"

I explained everything that had happened, scrutinizing my dad's face as I went. It fluctuated between abject horror, intense concern, and... happiness, maybe? I wasn't quite sure.

"You know, if we lived in Cyrus like we should, none of this would have happened. Not only because I wouldn't have been remotely close to the boy, but because I could have used my telekinesis and nobody would even know I was the one that saved the kid," I complained.

Dad's lips twitched in frustration like they always did when I brought up Cyrus. "I know you wish you could experience life in Cyrus, Ava. I know you get frustrated by your limitations in this realm. I understand, I really do. You think I don't miss it too? I do. More than you could possibly imagine. But Cyrus is gone. Destroyed. There's nothing to go back to anymore. We're lucky to even be alive. So many other Cyruns are not. It's important that we focus on the positives."

I didn't respond. I looked out the window instead, watching

the trees pass. I knew he was right. I knew my complaints were pointless. It was frustrating, though, to be stuck here, where I was so different from everyone else. If we lived in Cyrus, I wouldn't have to hide who I am all the time. I could run at full speed. I wondered how fast I would be there. Fast enough that this afternoon wouldn't have been such a close call for the boy, that's for sure.

"I'm proud of you," Dad said unexpectedly, reaching out to grab my hand. "You did a good thing today, Ava."

I looked up at him. "You're not mad that I exposed myself? Especially so soon after the bank incident?"

"Mad? Are you kidding? Of course not. You saved a boy's life today." He reached over and ruffled my hair playfully. I smiled. My dad was the best.

"What if we have to move again?" I asked.

"Well, it sounds like we might not have to. If you and Lana stick with your story, you might be able to convince enough people that nothing extraordinary happened today. Humans have a funny way of wanting to believe things that make sense with what they think is true. It's easier than adjusting their understanding of life, so they'll often believe what they see as logical even if it doesn't line up with what they've seen or experienced."

I fervently hoped he was right. Finding Lana was one of the best things that ever happened to me. She and Dad were the only two people I felt like I could be myself around.

"Thanks, Dad," I said, sinking down into my seat. I wasn't sure what consequences I'd face for today, but I was grateful that occasionally, my abilities allowed me to do something that made a difference.

When we got home, I headed upstairs to take a bath. Normally, I was a shower kind of girl, but I didn't think that would go over well with my new back injury. Dad got busy with dinner in the kitchen, whistling a tune I didn't recognize.

The bath water was soothing. It eased some of the pain shooting through my back, allowing me to relax. Too soon, Dad called out to let me know dinner was ready. I hurried as best as I could to get dressed and headed down to the kitchen.

We sat across from each other at our small table with large plates of baked ziti in front of us. After a few minutes, Dad was first to break the silence.

"You feeling okay? You're uncharacteristically quiet tonight. I'm sure your back is pretty sore. "

"Huh?" I said, distracted. I'd been thinking about the mysterious boy who always seemed to be there when I was using my abilities, wondering what his strange smile meant today. "Oh, yeah, I'm a bit sore. I was just thinking about all the homework I have to finish up before tomorrow. Unless you write me a doctor's note to get out of school, of course." I batted my eyelashes playfully.

"Ha, yeah right. You're going to school tomorrow, Ava."

"Fine," I grumbled, slumping down in my seat as I shoved another forkful in my mouth.

"There's—" Dad paused, shifting uncomfortably in his seat. "There's actually something I wanted to talk to you about." He kept his eyes glued to his plate as he spoke.

"Umm, okay? Did someone die?" I asked, knowing the answer would be no. We didn't have any family and very few friends. This behavior was odd for my dad, though, and it had me worried.

"No, of course not. It's just, well, I was going to ask you what you would think about me leaving for a while again." His eyes flashed up to mine for a moment before dropping to his plate. "My team is doing a research project up in Alaska for a couple weeks, and I'd love to go along and head the study. I mean, I know Shaffer would do a great job—he always does—but I'm really excited about this one, hon. We're going to be taking a few glacier and rock samples to study for carbon dioxide levels, and we're hoping to make a connection between them and the declining reproduction rate of the—"

"Dad," I interrupted, "That's enough." I was relieved. Dad left somewhat often on these types of studies and my precognition had told me one of his excursions was coming soon. Being a professor kept him busy, and field work was his favorite part of the job.

"Right, sorry," Dad said sheepishly. He had a tendency to get carried away in his technical jargon that I knew nothing about.

"That sounds great, Dad. When would you leave? And when would you be back?"

"Well, the team is leaving tomorrow, actually, but I don't have to go that soon, of course. I can head out in a couple days and catch up with them later, especially where you've just been hurt. I don't want to leave when you need me..." Dad's voice drifted off. He looked up at me through his thick lashes, his brown eyes sparkling with anticipation.

I laughed. "Okay, okay. Tomorrow is fine."

"Really? You mean it? Oh, Ava, honey, you're the best daughter any man could ask for. Now I won't be gone too long— three weeks at the most—and you can reach me anytime you want. Well, not any time, I guess, because we'll be out of cell range most days, but you can leave a message for me at the hotel, and I'll call you back as soon as I'm home for the night. And if anything comes up, you just say the word and I'll be back on the next flight out of there, okay?"

"I know the drill, Dad. I'll be fine." I rolled my eyes.

"I know, sugar, but I'll make sure Ms. Jackson checks in with you at least every other day, and I'll leave my credit card behind so you can buy any food you need. You could even take Lana and Jessica or any of the other girls out for girls' night."

This part of the speech was especially typical. Dad always made himself sick with guilt about leaving me, so he'd try to make it up to me with money. Normally, I'd end up spending less than

$50 while he was gone—just what I needed for enough cold cereal, granola bars, and store-bought cookies to make it by until he was home.

"Dad, you're going to give yourself a stroke. Deep breaths, remember? I'll be fine. I'm not a little girl anymore."

"I know, which is the only reason Ms. Jackson isn't going to be staying here, but I'll always worry about you, Ava. You're still *my* little girl." He winked at me, his tan face crinkling.

"Please don't worry, Dad. It's going to be great," I assured him.

"Thanks again, honey." Dad stood to clear our plates from the table. "I guess I better get busy if I'm catching a flight out of here tomorrow. And you better get going on *all* that homework you have," he added slyly, looking at me out of the corner of his eye. Apparently his guilt wasn't enough to get me out of school tomorrow.

With a sigh, I stood up from the table and went straight to my room to get busy.

CHAPTER 5

STALKER

My little accident yesterday must have taken its toll. Normally, I was a light sleeper, but I didn't even stir until my alarm clock woke me up too late the next morning. I had just a half hour until the first bell rang, and Ms. George was not a forgiving woman.

In my rush to get ready, I found a note on the fridge door from Dad that read:

Hope you slept well, sweet pea. I thought about waking you to say goodbye, but frankly, you looked like the walking dead last night. I figured you could use the sleep. And don't think you're too clever—yes, I know you're keeping something from me, and you know it's only a matter of time before I find out.

I'll call as often as I can. Be good and have fun while I'm away!

LOL,

Dad

Dad once saw this internet meme that showed a mom texting her daughter, "Just wanted you to know Grandma died last night.

LOL!" Apparently the mom had thought LOL meant lots of love. So now Dad uses it that way whenever he has a chance. He thinks he's hilarious.

I rolled my eyes and put the note back on the fridge. I grabbed a swig of milk straight from the carton to chase down the granola bar I'd just shoved down my throat.

I hopped in my old, blue, beater Nissan Maxima, throwing my backpack in the passenger seat, then sped off for the next seven hours of purgatory—I mean high school.

Truthfully, I didn't mind school all that much. In fact, I rather enjoyed learning. My only complaint was the social aspect. It was complicated trying to hide so much about myself all the time, and today was bound to be particularly awkward. The news of my heroics was sure to have traveled fast. Nothing remains a secret for long in high school.

In an attempt to avoid as many questions as possible, I stayed in my car in the parking lot once I got to school. My plan was to wait it out until the bell rang. Running late as I was, I didn't have to wait long.

As I entered my English class, I was unsurprised to find Lana—already seated in her desk—bouncing with anticipation, her soft golden waves of hair rippling with the movement. I had a feeling yesterday that something exciting was going to happen to her soon. Before I'd even taken my seat, she was bursting with the news.

"You will never guess who just asked me to the fall formal," she said, her smile so large that it was borderline creepy. She knocked her dolphin folder off her desk as she flailed her arms in excitement.

"Whoever it was, I hope you weren't this enthusiastic in front of him," I joked as I bent to pick up her folder.

"Of course not. I played it cool. But that's beside the point. Go on, guess," she persisted, her blue eyes sparkling.

Lana liked guessing games like this. I did not. "I don't know, Lana. Just tell me."

"Fine, but you're no fun. Jeremy Hastings, that's who!" she gushed.

Lana had had a crush on Jeremy for as long as I could remember, though that wasn't saying much since she usually had a crush on about ten different boys at the same time. Jeremy was simply the most consistent name on her ever-changing list.

"That's amazing, Lana. You're going to have so much fun." Faking enthusiasm didn't make me a bad person, right? I was just being a good friend.

"I know," she squeaked. "So when do you want to go dress shopping?"

I knew that question wouldn't be far behind. Truth was, I never wanted to go dress shopping; I found it a complete bore. But I'd been on more than a few of these trips with Lana and they were unavoidable, which was crazy because she never listened to my opinion anyway.

Fortunately, Ms. George saved me from having to answer, as

she started class at that moment. Also fortunate (for me, at least) was the fact that Lana didn't do so well on her last essay and had to stay after class to talk with Ms. George about her grade. That would delay the dress discussion until lunch, at least.

The rest of the school day was rather uneventful. I did get several comments about the almost-accident, but nobody seemed overly suspicious of how I'd done it. Maybe Dad was right— people would rather believe what made sense over what they'd actually seen. I relaxed more and more as the day went on without being asked any directly suspicious questions.

I did end up having to agree to go shopping with Lana tomorrow, but I'd say my chances of surviving the trip were pretty high. Besides, I totally owed her for covering for me yesterday. She had every reason in the world to wonder what was wrong with me, but, like a true friend, she always let it slide.

All in all, I was in good spirits by the time track practice rolled around after school. When Coach Ramos called for the 400 meter dash, I lined up on the blocks with the other girls. I wasn't feeling very motivated to perform my best today. Honestly, showing up to practice was only necessary to maintain good status on the team, not because I would actually improve any. I basically only did track for Lana's benefit; she really wanted me on the team, so I joined last year. It was more of a pain than anything because I had to let other girls beat me from time to time. That didn't sit well with my competitive side.

My good mood came to an abrupt end as I crouched in my

runner's stance, ready to take off. A nasally voice tickled my ear. "Good luck, *Tanner*," Lance Jacobs sneered my last name. "You need all the practice you can get."

I turned around to say something snarky back at the jerk, but was stopped short. The boy—the one from the bank and the road yesterday—was sitting up at the top of the stadium leaning against the back gate, his arms crossed over his chest. He looked directly at me and smiled.

Lance began to say something else stupid, but I cut him off. "Lance, I really don't care what you have to say. Just shut up already." I pushed past him as I jogged toward the boy in the stadium seating. This was too much of a coincidence. I needed to know who he was and why he was following me.

The mysterious boy—realizing I was coming for him—sat up with a start and hurriedly made his way down the opposite set of stairs toward the gate. I cut across a section of bleachers, following. Once I was out of sight, I could run and catch up to him with ease. No point in trying to hide my powers from him. He obviously knew something was different about me.

Once I made it through the gate, I glanced around, checking for bystanders. I couldn't see anyone, so I took a chance and broke into a run. I caught the boy by his left arm in seconds.

"Who are you and why are you here?" I demanded as I tugged on his arm, forcing him around to face me.

I was slightly taken back by his face—he was handsome, strikingly so. His hair was short and dark brown. His hazel eyes betrayed fear underneath his heavy-set eyebrows. I could feel his strong biceps underneath my palm where my fingernails dug into his green jacket. He was about five inches taller than me— probably 6 feet even, yet he cowered away from my intense stare.

"Look, I'm not going to hurt you. All I want is an answer. Did you follow me here? I know you saved me at the bank last week. And you were on the roadside when the truck almost hit that boy. It can't be a coincidence you just happened to show up at my track practice today as well," I accused.

The boy relaxed as I talked, gaining back some confidence. "No, it isn't a coincidence I'm here," he agreed. His voice was smooth and deep. "I was trying to find you."

"Is that why you were there yesterday, too?"

"Yes. That was no coincidence either."

"Why would you want to find me? *How* did you find me?" I demanded, trying to sound confident, though I was anything but. This stranger had witnessed two blatant displays of my unusual abilities. I had no clue how to talk myself out of this mess. Plus, I was confused. He was creepy, no doubt, but he didn't seem like the typical stalker type. He'd also saved my life under impossible circumstances, so I kind of owed him big time.

"You know exactly why I wanted to find you." He looked at me with his eyebrows raised.

What did that mean? I panicked.

"As for how I found you, well, I don't think I'd like to reveal that just now," he said, a smirk twisting his features, erasing the

49

last trace of fear that was once there and replacing it with the confidence I sorely lacked.

"Okay then, how about a name? Can you *reveal* that?" I chided.

"My name's Trenton, but I go by Trent. And yours?" He extended his hand out in front of him.

"I'm Avalon, but I go by Ava," I said, mimicking his casual tone. I ignored his extended hand. I wasn't going to shake hands with a creep.

"Well, Ava," Trent said, dropping his hand back to his side. "I believe we both have a few more questions for each other, but I hardly think this is the right place for them. What do you say we go grab an early dinner together and we can discuss things a little more?"

I chewed on the inside of my lip, sure that Dad would flip if he knew I even considered going to eat with a total stranger who knew way too much about me. Somewhere in my head, the stranger danger light was blazing, but truthfully, I was intrigued. So far, Trent had not had the response I had come to expect from people who saw what I could do. The only fear he had betrayed seemed to be a result of being caught stalking, not in response to any manifestations of my abnormal powers. And I had to know how he'd saved me at the bank.

"What sort of place did you have in mind?" I asked tentatively.

"I'm not from around here, actually, so I was hoping you

would have a suggestion?" A half smile exposed his perfectly white, straight teeth. My heart gave an involuntary stutter in response. He was definitely better looking than any of the guys at Littleton High.

"Well, there's a little Italian place called Bertolli's not far from here. It's pretty good." I swallowed loudly. I hoped he didn't notice.

"Sounds great. Did you want a minute to change? I'll wait here," he offered.

I looked down at my spandex shorts, tank top, and tennis shoes, feeling embarrassed. So far, this guy had seen me stuck in a trash can covered in seafood, in a shredded t-shirt with blood dripping down my back, and now like this. Plus he'd witnessed two instances of magic. Could I have made myself any more vulnerable?

"Umm, right, I'll go hit the showers. You swear you won't leave?"

He crossed his heart, a playful smile on his lips. "I swear."

"Be back in five," I said, not meeting his eyes as I rushed to the locker room at a normal, human-paced jog.

Trying hard not to overthink what I was about to do, I quickly rinsed off my body in the shower, threw on the jeans, maroon sweater, and rose necklace I'd been wearing earlier, then yanked a brush through my tangled hair. Deciding that was a lost cause, I pulled it back into a high ponytail and rushed outside, hoping Trent hadn't disappeared without any explanations.

Thankfully, he hadn't ditched me. His tall frame leaned against the fence of the baseball diamond, the picture of ease. Shouldn't he look at least slightly more uncomfortable? He was the one who had admitted to following me, after all.

"Hey," I said awkwardly as I approached him. Was that an appropriate greeting for a guy I simultaneously feared, disliked, and was slightly attracted to? I was overthinking things.

"That was fast," he commented lightly. "I thought ladies were supposed to take hours to get ready."

"Well, we usually do when we're trying to impress somebody. I'm not too concerned with that right now."

"Ouch," Trent laughed, shaking his head.

"You are an admitted stalker," I reminded him.

"Fair enough. Where to, boss?" he asked, uncrossing his arms and rubbing his palms together in anticipation.

Instead of answering, I began walking out to the parking lot. Trent followed in silence.

As I got to my car door, I asked, "Where's your car? I could drive you over there."

"I actually don't have one," Trent said, looking down at his feet.

"Then how did you get here?"

"It's not important. Can I just ride with you?"

"I guess," I said, not quite sure what to make of that. If he wasn't from around here, how did he get all the way out to my high school without a car? This guy was fishy. What was I doing going somewhere alone with him? It was a good thing Dad was out of town. I could avoid having that conversation for at least three weeks.

Trying to be discreet, I unhooked the clip-on pepper spray I had on my keychain as I unlocked the door. I kept it in my left hand as I got in the car. I reached over and unlocked Trent's door.

Trent climbed in beside me. "Ava, I know I'm a stranger, and you have good reason to be a little freaked out, but I'm not going to hurt you," he said, smiling at my closed left fist. "You can put the pepper spray away."

Abandoning all pretenses, I replied, "I think I'll keep it handy, just to be safe."

He chuckled. "Suit yourself."

CHAPTER 6

THE TRAVELER

We arrived at Bertolli's in under five minutes. I jumped out of the car before Trent could get any ideas about opening my door for me. I also hurried ahead of him, reaching the restaurant door before he could. I walked in without waiting, the door catching him off guard. I heard a small grunt as he caught it in the gut.

"Table for two?" the thin, blonde hostess with fake eyelashes smiled at us. I folded my arms and looked away.

"Yes, please, for the two of us," Trent said, wrapping his arm around my waist and pulling me close in jest. I shrugged away from him, looking at him with disdain as I followed Malibu Barbie. He laughed and followed after me.

"Is there something wrong with you?" I insisted as soon as the hostess handed us our menus and left. "Mentally, I mean?"

"No, and I'm sorry about that. I simply find your discomfort at the situation a bit comical," he said, coughing to hide another laugh.

"My discomfort? Oh yes, quite hilarious. Why should I be uncomfortable being forced to eat with a stalker who's been following me around for reasons he has yet to explain? Naturally, I'm overreacting," I hissed.

"I don't believe I've *forced* you to do anything, but when you put it that way, I suppose I can see why you might be a little… on edge," he conceded.

"How very empathetic of you." I rolled my eyes, picking up a menu to scour the options.

A minute later, a stocky brunette showed up to take our order. "Hi, I'm Aislee, I'll be your waitress this evening. Are you ready to order or do you need another minute?" she trilled, overly friendly as most servers are.

"I'm ready. I'll have the meatball sandwich with a lemonade, please," I said, handing the menu back to her.

The waitress turned to Trent who looked taken aback. He obviously wasn't ready. "I'll have the same," he stammered.

"Excellent, I'll be back with your food in two shakes," Aislee said, sweeping Trent's menu off the table as she turned to head back to the kitchen.

I glanced around the restaurant, avoiding Trent's eyes. There was only one other couple here and they sat on the other end of the large, dimly lit room. I suppose that would be best if we were going to be talking about my abilities. My palms started to sweat at the thought.

"So, you can run pretty fast," Trent began casually, as if he were talking about the weather. "A lot faster than I'd assume was normal around here."

"What do you mean 'around here'?" I pressed, not missing the slip.

"Nothing. I just meant, you reached that boy a lot faster than

55

anyone else could have." He stared at his hands as he spoke.

"No, that's not what you meant," I said, scrutinizing him.

A lot of puzzle pieces fell into place all at once. He didn't seem surprised at what I could do. He said he wasn't from around here. He had come to my school without a car. He had somehow miraculously saved my life. Was it possible he was like me? Like Dad? I'd never met another Cyrun before.

Just then, the server appeared with our food, sliding our plates in front of us. "Anything else you two kids need?" she asked, chomping on a piece of gum in her mouth.

I ignored the slight—we were hardly kids. "No, we're fine, thanks," I answered, looking back at Trent, suddenly very excited.

"Tell me again who you are, Trenton—who you really are," I demanded, ignoring the plate of food in front of me.

"I already told you. My name is Trenton Cavanaugh. There's nothing more to tell."

"I don't think you lied about that. But I think we have a few things in common, don't we? You seem to be very unsurprised at the things I can do. In my experience, most people don't take seeing my abilities quite so easily."

"And what exactly is it that you can do," Trent asked, leaning closer to me over the table.

I lowered my voice and leaned into Trent so as not to be overheard. "I have abilities, magic, power—whatever you want to call it. But that's nothing new to you."

Trent lowered his tone to match my own. "Yeah, I already

56

knew that. In fact, I knew it before you entered the bank or ran out in front of that truck to save the kid. I knew it before I saw you do anything noteworthy. I could feel you, Ava. That's what drew me to the alleyway that night to save you from the dumpster. That's how I came to that street precisely when you were going to be there and how I found you at school today. You see, we're all connected. Anyone from Cyrus has the same magic running through them. We call it Cyril. Each of us is basically just a part of it. That's why you feel so much more comfortable around your dad than anyone else. Being with him is familiar because you're part of the same energy. It's likely why you trusted me today though you had no reason to. It felt right."

Interesting. I'd never thought of my discomfort around human beings a result of some sort of "Cyrun energy" running through me. It all sounded a little too mumbo-jumbo-VooDoo to me. But then again, with magical abilities like I possessed, I suppose nothing about the supernatural should be all that surprising. I knew the world—or worlds, rather—were not always what they seemed.

For now, I decided to let that issue rest and ask a more important question. "You know about Cyrus?" I asked. "How? Are your parents from there, too?"

"Of course they are. All of our parents are from Cyrus," Trent rolled his eyes.

"How did your family escape before it was destroyed?"

Trent raised one eyebrow. "What are you talking about, Ava? I told you I'm not from here, remember? I came here *from* Cyrus."

He said it matter-of-factly, no hint of humor in his eyes. But that couldn't be possible. Cyrus was gone. Long gone. Dad told me it was.

"You don't mean you came here from Cyrus recently, do you? That's not even possible."

Trent shifted in his seat uncomfortably. "What do you mean it's not possible, Ava? Of course it is. I mean, you and your Dad got here somehow, didn't you? Haven't you heard of Travelers?"

"Dad said they're people who have the ability to teleport anywhere, including between the realms. He says that ability is rare though. But that's not what I mean. Cyrus is gone. Destroyed. It was by its own rulers at the time of the Schism. Dad and I were lucky enough to escape, but most didn't," I stated sadly, thinking of my mother. "I'm happy to know at least one other Cyrun did too."

Trent stared at me intensely for a long moment, a strange look in his eyes.

"What?" I asked. This Trent guy was freaky.

"Ava, Cyrus wasn't destroyed. I don't even know what you mean by 'the Schism'. I'm not sure what you've been told or by whom, but it doesn't seem like you know very much about Cyrus. It still very much exists. In fact, I can take you there right now. You see, I'm a Traveler," Trent whispered, glancing over his shoulder as he said it, "though I'd appreciate it if you wouldn't tell anyone that. I'm not supposed to be here right now, which is why I've avoided you every time you've noticed me."

I stared at Trent open-mouthed as I let what he said sink in. Then I stood up from the table, threw down the 20 dollar bill I had in my wallet, and stormed out of the restaurant. I could hear Trent running behind me, but I was faster. I jumped in my car and threw it in reverse as he pounded on the passenger side window.

"Ava, don't leave! Please! I'm sorry, I should have been more careful. I didn't know you didn't know!"

Lies. Everything he said was a lie. It had to be because Dad was not a liar. He had no reason to lie to me about any of this. Angrily, I sped home. I'm sure I broke the speed limit more than a couple times, but I was too distracted to care.

I ran into our little, yellow house, went straight up the stairs, and sunk into my mattress, throwing the covers over my head. I shouldn't have let Trent get to me. I shouldn't have agreed to go with him in the first place. He was clearly a crazy person.

My phone buzzed in my pocket. Someone was calling me, but I ignored it.

My phone buzzed again. And again. And again.

Finally, I wrenched it from my jean pocket and looked at the screen. I had 7 missed calls from Lana and several texts. I decided to tackle the texts first.

Where are you?

What happened at track practice?

What did Lance say that made you leave?

Answer the phone or I'll call your dad and tell him you're missing!

Okay, no I won't, but you better pick up your phone!

I mean it, Ava!

I probably should have been more concerned about Lana. She did have a tendency to overreact even when there was nothing wrong—and this time there was. I simply had no desire to ever tell anyone about Trent. Anyway, there's no way I'd be able to make her understand.

There was a knock on the front door. "Ava, it's me, Trent! Open the door, please!"

"You have got to be kidding me," I grumbled as I buried my head under my pillow, clenching it tight around my ears.

"I will come into your house if you don't come to the door," he threatened.

I locked it behind me, so he could just go ahead and try.

"I'm serious, Ava. I'll do it!"

I don't care if the guy was from Cyrus or Mars, he should be able to take a hint. I did not want to talk to him.

"We need to talk," a voice said from the foot of my bed. I screamed and threw the blankets off me in surprise as I sat up. There Trent stood, not five feet from me, his hands up in surrender.

"How did you get in here? Get out or I'll call the police!" I shouted, chucking my purple pillow at his face.

He casually knocked it to the side before it hit him and explained, "I'm a Traveler, Ava. I can go anywhere I want. I usually don't abuse my abilities like this, but you made it sort of

60

necessary."

I fished my phone out of the mess of blankets, preparing to call the police.

Trent's hand shot out, covering the screen. "That's not going to do any good. I'll disappear before they're anywhere near this place."

"What part of 'go away' am I not making clear here, Trent? Just go back to wherever you came from and leave me alone," I said through gritted teeth. I picked up the next pillow and prepared to throw it at him.

"If you still want me to, I promise I'll leave after we talk. I want to clear a few things up, that's all. Then I'll go. Can you just calm down and let me explain?" he asked, a sincerity in his face that softened me a bit. To be honest, it probably wasn't the sincerity. He was simply insanely handsome, especially when his eyes got all big like that.

"Fine, I'll give you two minutes," I grumbled, crushing the pillow into my stomach instead of throwing it at his head. I brought my knees up to my chest.

Cautiously, Trent moved to sit on the end of my bed. He looked at me with hesitation, as if dealing with a deranged animal. I suppose I had freaked out. But what did he expect when he dropped a massive lie like he did?

"Actually, I was hoping you'd explain a few things first. Will you tell me how long you've lived in the human realm?"

"I'm not in the mood to answer your questions," I grumbled.

61

"Please, just humor me for a second. I think it will help me explain everything to you."

I hesitated but decided it was best to get this over with. He promised to leave after we talked. The sooner, the better. "I've lived here as long as I can remember. Dad says we came here when I was only a few months old."

"Did he ever give a reason for why he chose to take you here?"

"Yes, he said Cyrus was at war. The king and his brother were battling for control and using the people as pawns. Cyruns were dying. He wanted us both to be safe. A Traveler was offering to take people to the human realm if they chose to do so. My Dad and Mom both agreed I should come here with him. The Traveler came back a few days later to let Dad know Cyrus was gone. Any survivors now live here, in the human realm. Everyone else was killed." My voice shook as, again, I thought about my mother.

"How old are you, Ava?" Trent asked.

"I'm seventeen. Why?"

"Ava, please listen to me. I hope you can trust what I'm telling you. For whatever reason, your father and the Traveler who took you here have not told you the truth. Cyrus was not at war seventeen years ago. In fact, Cyrus and its people haven't been in any serious danger for nearly a thousand years. Overall, it has been a relatively peaceful place."

I examined Trent's face, looking for any sign of a lie. I did not want to believe him. Not because it wouldn't be fantastic news. In reality, I'd longed to visit my home for as long as I'd known about it. No, I didn't want it to be true because it would mean my father had lied to me. I couldn't fathom any reason he would keep something like this from me. If what Trent said was true, not only did Dad keep the truth from me, he fabricated some story to keep me from thinking visiting Cyrus was even remotely a possibility.

Bottom line, I didn't trust Trent, but I could think of only one way to put the matter to rest for sure—I would have to let him try to take me there. When he was unable to, I could prove he was a liar, demand he leave me alone, and that would be the end of it.

"Fine, you say you can take me to Cyrus? Prove it." I challenged.

Chapter 7

Cyrus

I ran through my mental checklist one last time. I had called my dad's hotel to check in with him, hopefully buying me a day or two before he'd feel the need to contact me. I called Lana and did my best to smooth things over with her, cancelling our dress shopping plans on the off chance that Trent wasn't a lunatic. I was tempted to tell her about him but decided I was in enough trouble with her for the time being. Finally, I'd called Ms. Jackson to let her know I was fine as well. All in all, nobody should be looking for me anytime soon.

I slung my backpack—which carried a change of clothes, my toothbrush, and some deodorant—over my shoulder and jogged down the stairs. Trent sat on the couch in the living room, arms folded in his lap, apparently having not moved a muscle since I left him there about a half hour ago. He followed orders well, at least.

"Ready to prove you're insane?" I chirped.

"I'm ready to show you the truth, yes," Trent corrected with a smile. His sense of humor had returned since I'd calmed down some.

We stepped outside to a brisk fall evening. The wind whipped my unzipped jacket around me. I quickly did it up and crossed my arms over my chest.

"Where to?" I asked.

"Let's go back there a ways. We can use the trees for coverage in case anyone is watching." Trent motioned to the small grove to the east of my house. We walked toward it hurriedly.

"Okay, Ava, Traveling is going to be a bit of a new sensation for you," Trent said, stopping just inside the cover of the trees. "You don't need to worry about it, everything will be fine, just remember to hold onto my hands tightly so we don't get separated. You ready?"

"Let's do this," I said, hiding the terror rising in my chest. What if he was right? I wasn't ready to face a whole new realm I'd been convinced was destroyed my entire life. I took a deep, steadying breath, trying not overthink this.

Trent reached out and took both my hands in his. I met his eyes, and he smiled at me reassuringly. Butterflies rose in my stomach at his casual touch. I pushed away those feelings—now was not the time. Then, before I had time to mentally prepare, we were being yanked off the ground and shoved into what felt like an incredibly bright and stuffy tunnel. Light danced around us as we twisted and turned in the air. I lost all sense of which way was up. I felt Trent's hands squeeze more tightly around mine, holding me firmly to him.

Then, as suddenly as it had started, we were slammed into solid ground, the bright light disappearing. I fell flat on my back from the jarring impact. I gasped for air as the wind was knocked out of me.

"Ava, are you okay?" Trent asked urgently.

It took a moment, but my eyes adjusted, and I saw Trent's face hovering above mine. My heart gave an involuntary leap in my chest.

"I'm fine. Just... wasn't expecting that," I gasped.

"Sorry, I should have held on more tightly."

I ignored him, looking around me instead. The light from the sun was fading, coating everything in deep purples and blues, but there was still enough light to make out my surroundings. I sat in a lush, green patch of grass. Immediately to my left, there was a beautiful garden that seemed to stretch on endlessly. Behind us, a thick forest of trees created a foreboding wall. Directly in front of us was the backside of a small, brown cottage. It reminded me strongly of a house from a storybook Dad read me as a kid. It was the only home within sight. There was a hushed silence that hung in the air.

"Where are we?" I asked.

"We're in Cyrus. This is my home," Trent said, nodding toward the cottage in front of us, its windows glowing a soft, flickering yellow.

He straightened out of his concerned crouch and offered his hand to me, pulling me to my feet. I blushed in the darkness.

"It's charming," I said, flashing a genuine smile. "But it doesn't prove we're in Cyrus. You could have taken me anywhere in the human realm."

Trent rolled his eyes. "You are completely and totally ridiculous, you know, but fair enough. Give me a few minutes to check in with my parents, and I'll be back to *prove* it to you." His fingers drew quotation marks around the word. "There's a garden bench over there. You can sit while you wait." He motioned to a spot next to a very tall vine a couple of feet from where we stood.

I walked around the vine and took a seat on a small, wrought-iron bench which looked out over the rows and rows of plants. Some I recognized, like the tall stalks of corn about seven rows down, but others were not easily identifiable.

I shifted my feet underneath me, trying to get comfortable when a soft, but angry, "Hey! Watch it!" echoed from somewhere nearby. I looked around, trying to find its source.

"You stink, you know. You reek of humans and fast food."

I jumped in alarm as a tiny man sprung up from the ground to stand on the bench next to where I sat. In all, he was no taller than my forearm. He was round in the middle, his face was deeply wrinkled, and his graying hair curled around his tiny face in sporadic wisps.

"You should be more careful where you step around here. There are plenty of us out in the gardens. You could have killed me!" the little man said, obviously insulted.

"I'm sorry. I didn't realize there was anyone around." I hesitated. "Please don't think me rude, but what exactly *are* you?"

"I knew I smelled human on you. You smell like Master Trent every time he comes back from that disgusting realm. Not familiar with the place, are you? I am a garden gnome. Name's Archie," he said, extending his tiny hand out to me.

"Nice to meet you, Archie." I grabbed his hand between my forefinger and thumb and gave it a gentle tug.

"You said there are many of you out here?" I asked, looking around under my bench for any more miniature visitors.

"Oh yes. We're one of the largest clans in all of Cyrus, my family. In sum, there's about two thousand of us. So like I said, watch your step, will ya?"

I felt distinctly uncomfortable at the thought of two thousand invisible sets of eyes out there watching me.

"Of course I will. Sorry about earlier."

"I won't hold it against you this time," Archie growled. "Well, best be off. This garden doesn't tend itself!" And he was gone with a quick dive off the bench. I lost sight of him as soon as he reached the dirt, his brown clothes making a perfect camouflage.

"He's a bit eccentric, Archie," Trent said, making me jump as he appeared out of the growing darkness. "But he's an excellent gnome. The perfect condition of this garden is, in large part, thanks to him."

"It's beautiful," I agreed, not sure what else to say.

"Do I still need to prove myself to you? Or did Archie convince you?" Trent asked, nudging my shoulder playfully.

"Oh, Archie was rather convincing. Now you just need to convince me I'm actually awake and not dreaming," I laughed.

Trent chuckled. "Come on inside, my parents want to meet

you."

My heartbeat accelerated. I hadn't anticipated Cyrus still existing, so I hadn't thought much about what would happen if we actually showed up here. I wasn't ready to meet a real Cyrun! Let alone two of them.

"You're not scared, are you?" Trent teased.

"Of course I'm not scared," I lied. "Lead the way."

I watched my step carefully as I followed Trent along the winding garden path. We walked through the backdoor into a small, cozy kitchen. The walls were planks of wood, causing the cheerful yellow cabinets to stand out. The room was lit only by lanterns but was still plenty bright. There was a sink, but no stove. Instead, a fireplace occupied the length of the far wall where a large, black pot sat, the top sizzling as the contents boiled.

"Mom, soups ready!" Trent called, hurrying over to remove the pot from the fire.

"Go ahead and have a seat, Ava." Trent nodded toward a small brown table set for four along the opposite wall of the fireplace as he lugged the large pot away from the flames.

I took a seat as two people rounded the corner from what I assumed was a front sitting room.

Trent's parents were as attractive as he was. His mom was curvy with tight, natural, caramel-colored curls that framed her kind face. His dad looked a lot like him with the same angular face and strong eyebrows. His hair was graying, but seemed like it was once the same shade as Trent's.

"Ava, this is my mom and dad, Emeritus and Samson Cavanaugh." Trent motioned to each of them in turn.

"Hello, Ava. It's nice to have you with us tonight. You can call me Em," his mother said, taking my hand in both of hers. Her caramel eyes matched the color of her hair.

"And you can call me Sam. It's a pleasure to see you conscious this time," Trent's dad winked at me.

"What do you mean conscious?" I asked.

Sam looked over at Trent who was busying himself filling bowls of soup from the black pot. "You haven't told her?"

"Told me what?" I asked, alarmed now.

"Nothing you didn't already know, at least generally speaking," Trent said, walking over with surprising agility as he juggled four bowls of soup. He set them down and the three of them joined me at the table. Whatever it was didn't look familiar, but it smelled delicious.

"Are you going to explain what you mean?" I asked impatiently.

"That night at the bank, after you were shot, I grabbed you and Traveled here. My father," Trent indicated Sam, "has healing abilities. That's why you had no trace of the bullet wound when you woke up in the forest."

I looked at Sam with wide eyes, surprised. In the craziness of Trent telling me Cyrus existed, I completely forgot to ask for an explanation of the events that night.

"Thank you," I managed to squeak out. "I've been meaning to

70

ask Trent how he pulled that off."

"It's my pleasure," Sam smiled. "So, Trent tells us you left Cyrus with your father when you were just a baby, is that right?" he asked, clearly changing the subject. He was obviously a humble man who didn't like to be given much credit.

I looked over at Trent, surprised he'd told them that. I suppose they needed some explanation as to why I didn't know anything about the world in which they lived.

"Umm, yes, that's right."

"What is your father's name?"

"His full name is Carmichael Ross Tanner, but he mostly goes by Mike or Michael. His last name used to be Longfellow in this realm, though."

"That doesn't sound familiar to me. Does it to you, honey?" Sam asked his wife.

"No, he must have grown up in a different province," Em agreed. "What abilities does he have?"

"He can control animal life and is telekinetic," I explained, swallowing my bite of soup too soon and scorching my throat in the process. It was very hot. I grabbed my glass of water and gulped some down.

"Impressive," Sam nodded, eyebrows raised. "And do you have any abilities, Ava?"

"Yes," I answered, gasping slightly after chugging my water. I heard a small chuckle from Trent. I ignored him. "I am telekinetic like my dad, I can run quickly, I have some vague precognition abilities, and I can sometimes move through solid objects." I looked at Trent who smirked knowingly. If I'd been able to move through objects with any sort of consistency, he wouldn't have had to save me from that atrocious dumpster.

"Four abilities is quite a lot! And to have discovered all of them in the human realm is very impressive," Em said, looking at me strangely.

"Yes, quite unusual," Sam concurred, looking thoughtful.

I wasn't sure what to make of their strange reaction, but all this talk about Cyrus versus the human realm had me itching to try out my abilities here, where I was meant to be, though I didn't want to immediately. One, because I figured that would be rude at the dinner table. And two, because I wasn't sure I was actually good at anything I could do. I'd always felt so limited in my powers, but maybe that had nothing to do with being in the wrong realm. Maybe I was simply weak.

"Well, I think we've bombarded you with enough questions for now, Ava. You're welcome to stay here for the night if you wish. I can make up the couch with some sheets," Em offered.

I thought about it for a moment. I really did want to stay for just a while. Maybe tomorrow Trent could show me around a little more. And tomorrow was Saturday, so nobody would be missing me back home.

"I would like that, if it's okay with you both."

"Of course," Em smiled kindly.

We ate in silence for a few minutes, enjoying the soup. When

72

we'd finished, Em stood from the table. "I'll let you know when the couch is ready." She gathered our bowls in a precarious pile.

Trent stood from the table as well. "Do you mind if we go on a short walk, Mom? We'll be back in half an hour."

"That's fine, just make sure you don't stay out any longer than that. You'll both end up cleaning trash in the city square if you break curfew."

Trent looked at me with excitement. "You want to go?" he asked.

"Definitely," I answered, thinking that I could try out my powers. Running, at the very least.

"What did your mom mean about a curfew?" I asked as we stepped out the door.

"It's a general curfew for all of Cyrus. Everyone has to be indoors from 10pm to 5am unless on duty for your civil service," Trent explained.

"Civil service?"

"Your job, basically."

"Interesting word for it," I laughed.

The night air was cool but not uncomfortable as it had been at home. It felt like a nice late-summer's evening. We walked along the cobblestone street, occasionally passing small houses similar to Trent's. There were no sidewalks. It seemed to me that we were in an area remote enough that they wouldn't be necessary.

"Ava, I don't know what your plans are from this point forward, but if you intend to have any kind of association with this

73

realm, there are a few things you need to know," Trent began, his chin tucked, looking up at me through his eyelashes. It gave him a boyish charm that made me smile.

"Well, I'm not sure how much I'll be able to come around. I have quite a few questions for my dad. I'll have to work things out with him for sure, but I'd like to stay for as much of the next three weeks as you'll let me."

"That would be great. I think it's really important that you get to know what life is like here and explore your abilities more fully. But Cyrus isn't exactly a perfect place, Avalon. There are very rigid rules and expectations that you have to follow. If you don't, you put your own life—as well as the lives of those you care about—in danger."

Thinking he was pulling one over on me, I laughed. "I think I can handle myself."

Trent grabbed my forearm and pulled, spinning me to face him. If the anger on his face hadn't been so blatant, I may have thought he was making some romantic gesture. His face was only inches from mine as he spoke through his teeth.

"If you can't take this seriously, I'll take you back to the human realm this very minute and never come for you again. You will be stuck there, never getting any of the answers you want, always wondering what life is like as a Cyrun. I cannot impress the seriousness of the situation on you enough."

I studied his furious expression, taking a step back out of fear. I had only known Trent for a few hours, but he seemed like the positive, happy-go-lucky type. This sudden mood swing frightened me.

"Sorry, I thought you were teasing me. I can be serious, I promise." I looked him in the eye steadily to try and convey that I meant it.

Trent sighed, dropping my arm. "Sorry," he said. "I just know you can be a bit... unpredictable, and I can't risk my family's safety for your sake. We lead a quiet, safe life around here. We fly under the radar and we want to keep it that way."

His words offended me slightly, but in all fairness, I suppose they were deserved. Besides, what did I expect? He barely knew me. Of course he cared more about his family.

"I understand. I promise I will never intentionally put your family in any danger. Go ahead and tell me what I need to know," I instructed.

"Let's sit down," Trent suggested, pulling me down to sit on the small, grassy hill we'd been walking toward.

"Okay, where to begin," he mused. "Cyrus is ruled, as you seem to already know, by a king. Our current king is King Tenebris. He took over his brother's rule about twelve years ago when King Trinnen was killed. A group of rebels attacked the palace, aiming to kill the royal family. They were successful in killing the king, the young prince, and the queen. Prince Kevin was only five years old at the time."

"The rebels killed a five year old?" I interrupted, incredulous. "What kind of twisted—"

"I know, Ava, believe me. The entire kingdom was sick over it. Rebel attacks are not very common, so to have one that was so devastating was difficult. I was only six at the time, yet I remember it clearly." Trent hung his head at the memory.

"Right, sorry, go on." I apologized.

"King Tenebris was brought out of exile—"

"Exile? Why had he been exiled?" I blurted.

Trent gave an annoyed laugh. "Are you going to keep interrupting?"

"Sorry. Remember that this whole story is new to me. Can you blame me for being curious?"

"We can come back to that question later. Suffice it to say the two brothers didn't get along. King Trinnen sent Tenebris away.

"Anyway, Tenebris was brought out of exile to take over as king. He has been our ruler ever since. Overall, he isn't the worst king Cyrus has ever had, but he's close," Trent said, his voice dropping to a whisper as he checked over his shoulder. "We're not supposed to speak ill of the royal family, but he has imposed a rigid social structure that is completely ludicrous.

"Every Cyrun is ranked based on the number of magical abilities they have. If you have no abilities—as is the case for some Cyruns—you are without rank, essentially homeless, left without any meaningful way to provide for yourself. If you have one magical ability, you are a One, if you have two, you're a Two, so on until Four. Any person who has more than four abilities is an Elite—basically royalty. They are very rare. There are maybe

76

fifty of them in all of Cyrus.

"That is why my parents were so surprised you have four talents. With that status, you'd be very much upper class. Threes and Fours are highly respected, invited to fancy dinner parties and guaranteed the best civil service positions, if they even want them. Most Fours don't have to work at all. They live off the service of everyone beneath them and the taxes paid by the rest of us."

I raised my hand, patiently waiting to be called on. Trent, humor in his face, asked, "Do you have a question, Ms. Tanner?"

"A comment, rather. Permission to speak?"

"Permission granted." Trent smirked.

"This system seems arbitrary and unfair. Perhaps a person does have only one magical ability. That does not mean they are useless. Sounds to me like those at the bottom contribute much more to society than those at the top."

"That's definitely true. More true than you know," Trent agreed.

"So why don't you do something about it? If life is so unfair, why don't the people come together and demand change?"

"It's not that simple, Ava. There is a reason one family has ruled Cyrus for a thousand years. Remember when I told you all Cyruns are connected by a shared energy called Cyril?"

"I remember," I nodded.

"Cyril is pivotal to Cyrun life. It covers this realm and each of us is a part of it. Cyril chooses which gifts it gives each person, and our powers work through its energy. That's why it's so much harder to use your talents in the human realm. The only part of Cyril that's there is you.

"Nearly a thousand years ago, a man named Ganton was gifted the power to control the will of any Cyrun. Whenever he gave a direct order, the person would have to obey—they had no choice. His ability essentially gave him control of Cyril itself, and since Cyruns are just a part of Cyril, he could manipulate anybody. He used those abilities to become the first king Cyrus ever had. Before that, we were a realm of many small countries that were almost constantly at war.

"There's lots of debate about whether or not Ganton's actions were good or bad. Some are grateful he used his powers to end the continual fighting, but most of us are tired of his family abusing his power. You see, the power didn't die with him. He violated the laws of Cyril and used blood magic to preserve his powers. Blood magic is a form of dark magic, and I don't really understand how it all works because we're not supposed to talk about. It's rarely used because it always comes with a heavy price. The blood magic allowed Ganton to encase his abilities in a ruby necklace, which is known as Praesidium. Whoever wears the necklace has Ganton's power to force obedience. The blood magic restriction means the power can only be used by a direct, blood relative of Ganton. Whoever Praesidium chooses as its owner is the king or queen of Cyrus.

"As if forced obedience through direct commands isn't bad enough, Praesidium also manipulates Cyril so that even when not directly ordered, all of us feel this strange desire to follow our king's wishes at all times and even when we don't want to. It's not impossible to break through that enchantment, but it is difficult. It just feels... wrong to disobey. Like it goes against your core. But it is impossible to ignore a direct order when given by the king or queen wearing Praesidium," Trent finished.

"So what you're saying is that a lot of people want to revolt, but it's basically useless to try because Cryus' ruler can squash any rebellion with a simple command," I inferred.

"I think so, but it's hard to be sure how people really feel. Most of us are too afraid to talk about what we honestly think in any public space. The king has guards everywhere. They're always listening. To speak badly of the royal family is considered treason. You will definitely be put in prison and can sometimes even be killed, depending on how the king feels that day. It's barbaric," Trent said as he threw the chunk of grass in his hand.

"Sounds awful," I agreed.

An uncomfortable silence hung in the air. Trent seemed to be brooding over circumstances in Cyrus, not really in a chatty mood. I desperately wanted to try out my abilities, but didn't feel like this was an appropriate time.

I was also distracted, thinking about what Trent had said and what it would mean for me. It was hard for me to fully comprehend the level of control Tenebris had over his kingdom. I'd always lived in freedom. I knew essentially nothing of tyranny. Did I really want to be a part of a world controlled by such a heavy hand? Was it better to stay in the human world, with only partial abilities but personal freedom?

The dilemma was beginning to hurt my head, so as usual, I ignored the problem and focused on something easier.

"So what are your parents according to the social system?" I asked.

"They're Twos. A married couple always takes the social standing of the man of the house. I know, the patriarchy, right?" Trent rolled his eyes. "The kids also take the social status of their parents until they turn eighteen. At that age, they are reevaluated based on their own abilities.

"My dad has the ability to heal broken bones, flesh wounds, and most internal infections, so he's a healer, or doctor, as you know them. My mom can shapeshift to a swan and has the ability to control plant life, hence the enormous garden in our backyard."

"But families are organized according to the father's abilities? Didn't you say your dad has only one power? How are you all Twos?" I asked, confused.

"Yes, that's true. Sometimes, you can move up in rank if your ability is seen as particularly useful. Healing is almost always a step up. So is Traveling," Trent said.

"Hey, well, that's cool for you," I said, leaning sideways and bumping his shoulder. "How many powers do you have total? Anything besides the Traveling?"

"No, that's all I can do," Trent said, ducking his head as if embarrassed.

"What's the matter with that? That makes you a Two at least. That's not so bad. Plus, it's a stupid system anyway. It doesn't actually reflect your worth," I said, trying to get him to look me in the eye.

It took him a moment before he finally looked up. "Ava, there is one more thing you need to know. Tenebris has ordered all Travelers to be in his direct service. They live near the palace or serve in the different provinces as a glamorized taxi system. In return, they're all given a status of Three."

"So you're a Three then?"

"No. According to government records, I have no magical abilities."

"What? Why not?" I asked, stunned.

"Because I refuse to be a prisoner of Tenebris in any more ways than I already am. Travelers aren't even raised by their families. As soon as their ability is discovered, they're forced to leave and serve the king."

"Why does Tenebris want to control the Travelers so badly?" I asked.

Trent looked around warily, as if checking for eavesdroppers. He dropped his voice to a low whisper. "Not many people know this. The only reason I do is because my grandpa was a guard in the palace and overheard an important conversation about it. Tenebris wants to control Travelers because they can weaken Praesidium's abilities in a way. You see, a person who spends a lot of time in the human realm becomes disconnected from Cyril, and therefore, they are influenced less by Praesidium. You, for example, probably feel no inward loyalty to King Tenebris or even Cyrus in general, right? You don't feel any different here than you did in the human realm?" he asked.

"Well, no, I can't say I feel any pull that way," I answered. "Do you feel it?"

"Yes, but not as much as most because I do Travel to the human realm frequently. But there's definitely this constant gnawing inside, telling me to abide by the law, do my duty, yadda, yadda, yadda."

"So Tenebris wants to control the Travelers so that none of them become too immune to Praesidium's influence?" I clarified.

"Exactly. It didn't used to be like that. But the group of rebels that killed Trinnen and his family were a group of Travelers. Because of that, Tenebris changed the law to keep a closer eye on Travelers. Now the thing is, Ava, my parents are not fans of Tenebris. When he became king and demanded a census to record every person's abilities in order to organize us into social classes, my parents reported that I had not yet manifested any powers. At the time, it wasn't unusual. I was only six and many young kids don't have any abilities until they're older. When I was old enough to understand, they gave me the choice about whether or not I wanted to report my Traveling talents. I decided not to," Trent finished lamely, pulling at more grass.

"So what happens when you turn 18 and you're not a Two anymore?"

Trent sighed. "I lose my rank. I become a Zero, homeless. Those without powers are not given any civil service position. They have no way of providing for themselves and it's illegal for them to beg for food or money. It's basically a sentence to living alone and hungry for the rest of your life." His face crumpled.

"How much longer do you have?" I asked, tears threatening my eyes.

"A little less than two months 'til my birthday."

"Trent, you've got to report your abilities. You can't be a Zero. You're not a Zero!" I exclaimed, pulling at the hand he'd put over his eyes.

He looked up at me suddenly. "It's not that simple, Ava. I won't do it. Tenebris uses the Travelers to do horrible things— carry out his dirty business and enforce his baseless laws. Besides, it's too late. Any Cyrun who is going to develop abilities should have by age 12. If I reported now, my entire family would be killed for keeping a secret from the government."

My heart swelled with pity for Trent while simultaneously pounding with anger at this coward Tenebris who was too afraid to find out how loyal his subjects could be willingly. Instead, he forced their loyalty through corrupt laws, evidently aware of his own shortcomings to be a worthwhile leader.

"Why don't you come back to the human realm with me? You could still use your abilities to visit your parents when you wanted. You'd be free of this silly social system and free to do as you please," I suggested.

"I've thought about it. Perhaps that is what I'll end up doing. But the thought of leaving my parents is difficult. Plus, there's always the possibility that one of the surveyors will come along asking questions, wondering where their useless son disappeared to. Seems unlikely, but maybe they could make the leap, figure out I'd skipped realms. The consequences would not be pretty for my parents." Trent grimaced at the thought. "So I guess I'll be staying here."

"That just plain sucks, Trent. There has to be something that can be done."

"Not likely. And definitely not tonight. We'd better get back home. We're past curfew. Here," Trent said, holding out his hand to me. "I'll get us home."

I could have just run to his house and been there in a couple of seconds, but I didn't want to upset Trent any more than I already had tonight. The exploration of my powers would have to wait for another time. Though I didn't want to, I took his hand and braced myself for the discomfort of Traveling.

CHAPTER 8

CURIOSITY (NEARLY) KILLED THE WOLF

The following morning was awkward. It took me a minute to remember where I was when I woke up. Then the memory of the previous night hit me. I sat up suddenly, which caused blood to rush to my head, making me feel dizzy.

The Cavanaugh's couch was comfy enough, but their living room was a bit overwhelming. There was red everywhere—red carpet, red couches, red lamp shades, red pillows. It all looked kind of gory.

I ducked into the small guest washroom I had been shown last night. Though Trent's family didn't have electricity, they did have running water, so there was a small, metal sink to wash my face in and brush my teeth. I'd forgotten a brush, so I yanked my fingers through my hair, trying to tame the wild waves. I'd never been much of one for makeup, but the red spots that danced across my face made me slightly jealous of those girls who had perfect skin.

Speaking of perfect skin, when I walked out the back door of the Cavanaugh's house—not wanting to wake anyone in case they weren't up yet—I was met by a beautiful, tall, slender girl with thick, brunette hair that reached her waist. She had brown eyes and thick eyelashes. Her heart shaped face turned up into a smile as she met my eyes. She had enough beauty to make any girl envious.

A little too late, I returned her smile. She had already gone back to picking peas in the garden, filling a wooden barrel she carried on her hip.

I sat down on the porch steps to put on my sneakers as the door opened up behind me. Trent came running down the steps shouting, "Meraki! I didn't know you were coming today!"

The girl dropped the barrel and opened her arms just as Trent scooped her up and spun her around. She kissed him swiftly on the cheek as he set her back on the ground. He shot a furtive glance in my direction, though I pointedly looked the other way.

The scene was perfect enough to make anyone puke. A surge of jealousy ran through me. Stupid not to realize he must have some girl in his life. A guy as good looking as Trent was likely to have a following bigger than I wanted to think about. I hadn't realized I'd been letting myself develop feelings for him. I had to put a stop to that immediately.

Without a word or any further introductions, I headed into the woods in the opposite direction of Trent and Meraki. It was time to discover my limits.

Once I felt sufficiently hidden amongst the trees, I stopped, looked around at my surroundings, breathed in deeply, and then took off as fast as my legs could carry me.

Instantly, a smile broke across my face. This was pure joy. The trees moved so quickly passed me they were barely recognizable. The forest turned into solid walls of green that twisted and turned exactly when my body did. I didn't have to think about missing trees or dodging roots on the ground. It was like a sixth sense was keeping track of all of that for me, telling my body exactly where and how to move.

Apparently, my sixth sense needed some work.

Without warning, my body was totally emerged in cool water. I splashed to the surface, sputtering for air, shocked by the chill of the water which permeated every inch of skin. The air had been relatively warm—how could the water be this cold?

Glancing back, I realized I'd unknowingly plunged off the edge of a mossy cliff into a large lake below. The water stretched on for quite a ways in front of me before narrowing into a rift between two tall cliff sides.

"Who are you?" a high, clear voice rang out over the water. I looked around frantically, trying to identify its origins to no avail.

"Excuse me?" I asked. "Is someone out there?"

There was a slight rippling in the glassy water in front of me. Whatever was causing the disturbance was headed in my direction, and my sense of self-preservation told me I really didn't want to meet whatever it was. Treading water as quickly as I could, I began to retreat to the cliff where I'd fallen.

"I asked you who you are." A cold, silvery hand shot out of the water and grabbed my forearm. The sound of the voice sent shivers up my spine. My progress toward the cliffs was immediately halted. Whatever had hold of me was strong—

extremely so.

The rippling water wound around me as I continued to tread water with my feet. Then a beautiful female face with yellow irises and brown hair that was nearly purple emerged from the water. Her eyes were frightening yet enchanting. The hand belonged to her and matched the silvery tone of skin that wrapped around her exposed neck and collarbone.

"It's dangerous for strangers to enter these waters, darling," the creature hissed, her voice sounding less human and more snake-like. "There are many hidden creatures lurking beneath the glassy surface."

"Right, I wasn't aware of that, so I'll just be going then. Sorry to disturb you," I answered breathlessly as I tried to pull my hand away and continue toward the cliff.

"I'm afraid not," the creature said, pulling me closer to her frighteningly beautiful face. "You see, your King Tenebris may be king of the lands of Cyrus, but he has no say over what happens in the waters. We serve a different master. Any creature who enters our waters is subject to our laws, our rules. And Master doesn't take kindly to intruders." The creature's eyes grew hungry as she pulled me closer.

I jerked my arm up and, to my surprise, it slipped right through her grasp, as if she were nothing more than a ghost. Thank heavens my abilities worked better here! The creature let out a shrill shriek of exasperation at my small escape.

As soon as I was free, I swam, frantically. I knew I couldn't out swim her, but any time she tried to grab me—around the stomach, around my legs, by the arm—I simply slipped through her grasp as effortlessly as wind whips through the air. The creature let out shrill gasps of anger at my continual escape but never gave up pursuit.

Finally, I reached the cliff side. It was about a twelve foot stretch to the top with very few footholds. I'd never been much of a rock climber, but I had no choice other than to try. The creature continued to grab at me as I scrambled up the slippery slide, but her hold found no purchase. I could feel my entire body being positively filleted as I moved clumsily over sharp edges of rock that protruded at every angle.

Another sharp screech rang through the air as the creature finally stopped clawing at me. A glance below showed a flick of a scaly tail as the monster emerged itself back in the depths of the water. I figured I must have climbed too high for her to follow— she likely couldn't leave the water entirely and had been forced to give up.

Gasping for air, I flopped face down on the top of the black cliff, feeling the intense pains from my frantic climb. I gave myself only a few seconds to catch my breath before dragging myself into a sitting position to assess the damage. There were several scrapes and cuts that covered my body. My clothes had been torn in several places, exposing bloodied skin underneath. The two deepest wounds appeared to be on my right thigh and just below my collarbone. The one at my chest tugged painfully with every breath I sucked in.

I peeled myself off the side of the cliff, knowing I needed to get back to Trent's house so Sam could heal me—again. I owed the man big time.

Then, to my utter horror, a sharp, yellow talon swiped at my shoulder. I thought for certain the sea creature had found a way to follow me, but as I looked up, I saw that it belonged instead to an enormous, bird-like creature quite different from the one I'd just encountered, yet every bit as terrifying.

The fiend bared its sharp, gruesome teeth at me, snapping at my face. I was barely able to dodge unscathed. Its body was covered in scales rather than feathers, and it beat its leathery wings into my sides over and over. Each blow stung, allowing no time to recover before the next blow would hit.

Desperately, I tried to break into a run, but the creature moved as fast as I did, swooping in front of me and berating me with its wings and talons.

I stopped attempting to run, calling out for help instead.

"Help! Anybody!" I screamed.

The bird snapped at my face again, its teeth grazing my cheek. I could feel the blood trickle down my face. As if I needed any more of that leaving my body. Sheesh!

I began to tremble, convulsing and moving in strange ways. My mind couldn't make sense of what was happening. A frustrating fact, considering I really needed my mind to focus at the moment.

A warmth spread throughout my body as my own shape began to blur, fading in and out of focus. The warmth grew stronger until a rush of heat tore through my body. It was so intense I thought I was burning from the inside out. What was this creature and what was it doing to me?

Then, inexplicably, I was on four furry legs. I looked down at where my hands should be and found paws instead, with sharp, dangerous claws. My teeth also felt dangerous.

A ferocious snarl ripped through the morning air. I looked around with exhaustion, trying to locate what new vicious creature was coming for me. There was nothing else in sight. With a start, I realized the sound had come from me—I had growled.

The bird's sharp claws grazed my furry neck where I felt more blood trickle. Instinct took over, and I snapped at the bird, my jaws locking around its ugly talon. I yanked forcefully and the talon ripped from its body, dropping to the ground with a sickening thud. The bird cried out in fury and swung for my eyes with its talon that was still intact. I lunged again, narrowly missing.

Another guttural snarl ripped from my chest. The bleeding bird snapped its wings at me, hovering over me in the air, trying to decide how next to attack. I released another ferocious snarl, warning the creature to leave. It debated for a moment, then took off into the air, disappearing after a few flaps of its leathery wings.

I breathed deeply in and out, trying to calm myself down. I realized my breaths sounded like a dog panting.

Though afraid of what I was going to find, I dared to look

myself over more carefully. One thing was for sure—I was completely and totally covered in a thick, silvery-white fur. I had four legs, sharp teeth, and could growl. Did this mean I was a dog? No, I felt too large for a dog. A wolf maybe? That felt more accurate.

Curious, I ran to the lake's edge. Hesitantly, I looked out over the edge at my own reflection. To my horror and amazement, a silver-white wolf stared back at me. An enormous, beautiful, frightening looking wolf with large patches of blood in all the same places I was bleeding.

Okay, so I was a shapeshifter. No need to freak out. I'm sure a lot of Cyruns could do this. Trent's mom could turn into a swan. No big deal, right?

Except it was a huge deal! I just morphed into a wolf! How could I turn into an entirely new creature and not even know I had that ability? This place was mega-scary.

I took one last look at my reflection, shuddered, and decided I'd rather be myself again. As soon as I thought it, the same warmth I'd felt earlier filled my body. It grew weaker, receding back into my chest. I felt myself moving, changing.

Within seconds, I was back on two feet, fur gone, and clothes fully intact—well, at least to their pre-shapeshifting state. I looked down at my Cyrun body and smiled. That was scary. Beyond scary. But also super cool. I had no clue I was a shapeshifter! Not to mention, I turned into something pretty awesome, if I do say so myself. The discovery of that ability at that particular time

92

definitely saved my life.

At that thought, I realized it was probably best not to hang around in the same area where I'd been attacked by two vicious creatures. Who knew what else was hiding out here, waiting to finish the job?

Though I was slower now that I was wounded, I ran as fast as I could back to Trent's house, hoping Sam would be there to heal me.

CHAPTER 9

AWKWARD

Meraki and Trent were sitting on the garden bench, talking and laughing as I approached. Meraki reached up and stroked her hair, batting her eyelashes. Trent's smile widened. The whole scene sickened me, but I had bigger worries at the moment.

Trent jumped to his feet at the sound of my approach, his expression changing in an instant as he took in my haggard condition.

"What happened? Ava, are you okay?" he gasped.

Meraki's face peered over his shoulder, her expression twisted with a mixture of concern and disgust. Even still, she was beautiful.

"It's a long story. For now, could you please track down your dad?" I asked through clenched teeth. The pain was becoming excruciating.

"Sure, sure," Trent said. "He went to the clinic earlier, but I'll Travel over there and bring him right back, okay? Mer, will you stay with her please?"

"Of course," Meraki responded, though it sounded almost like singing. Dang it. Even her voice was perfect. And apparently she knew Trent's big secret—another indication they were close.

I stumbled over to the garden bench that Meraki and Trent had vacated moments earlier. I slumped down and leaned my head against the back, hardly comfortable, but it would do for now.

"Can I get anything for you?" Meraki asked. I peeked through my eyelashes at her gorgeous face. Why did she have to be polite when I was intent on hating her?

"Nah, I'm good. Sam will be able to take care of me. Thanks," I added at the end, begrudgingly.

Thankfully, it didn't take Trent long to reappear, his father at his side.

Sam rushed to where I sat. Without saying a word, he passed his palm over me from the top of my head, down my torso, and then over both thighs. For the first time, I noticed he was missing his thumb on his right hand. His palm glowed with a faint bluish color, and wherever he passed, my skin seemed to stitch itself back together, though without any needle or thread. There was a strange prickling sensation, as if I could feel my flesh moving and expanding to reseal itself. It was incredible.

"There," Sam sighed contentedly. "Good as new as soon as you wash up and we get you a change of clothes."

"Thank you," I said, looking up to meet his eyes. "That was amazing."

"I'm glad I could help," Sam said. "Now, do you care to tell us what happened?"

"Well, I'm still not completely sure myself," I began. I proceeded to tell them all about the sea creature and the bird-reptile thing, though I left out the shapeshifting details for the time being. Sam's face remained the calm, collected look of a professional doctor as I spoke. Trent's expression grew more and more anxious. And Meraki looked... bored, but insanely beautiful.

"What were those creatures? Are the forests always that dangerous?" I asked as I finished my tale.

"The sea creature was likely a mermaid. They're not exactly the peaceful creatures many of your human fairytales make them out to be. They typically drown their victims and then eat their flesh," Sam explained matter-of-factly. My stomach churned.

"Hmm," I said. "I haven't been much of a fan of seafood since my dumpster diving days, but that definitely puts an end to it. I'll never eat it again." Sam and Meraki looked confused, but Trent smiled knowingly.

"The other creature," Sam continued on, "was a vulonine. They are attracted to the smell of blood, like sharks. I'm sure your injuries from the cliff are what drew it to you."

"Wonderful. Large, vicious, flying sharks. Any other magical creatures in Cyrus I should know about?"

"Plenty," Sam chuckled. "But I'll let Trent tell you about those later. I need to get back to the clinic." He turned to his son.

"Right, of course," Trent said, hurrying to his dad's side.

Meraki cleared her throat daintily. "I'm really glad you're okay. Ava, isn't it?" Meraki asked, extending her hand to me.

"Yes. And you are?" I pretended not to already know.

"Meraki. I'm Trent's girlfriend." She emphasized the last

word and gave me a falsely sweet smile. "You should really get a change of clothes." She looked pointedly at the gaping holes in my clothing that revealed large patches of skin. I blushed and shot a quick glance at Trent. He looked uncomfortable at our exchange.

"Nice to meet you, Meraki," I lied, taking her hand and giving it a half-hearted shake.

"You as well." Meraki took a step closer to Trent. "I better get back to the shop. My parents needed me there almost an hour ago. I was just having too much fun with you this morning." She squeezed Trent's bicep and gave a flirtatious laugh as she flipped her long hair over one shoulder. He gave a low, uncomfortable chuckle in return.

I fought the urge to roll my eyes. Looking at Sam, it seemed he shared similar thoughts.

"See you later," she whispered in Trent's ear before she walked toward the cobblestone street, her curvy hips undulating.

"I'll be back in just a minute, Ava," Trent said. He seemed unable to fully meet my eyes as he grabbed Sam's arm, and the two of them disappeared.

I knew my hatred for Meraki was unjust—she was here long before me. There's just something about perfect girls like her that have a way of getting under the skin for no reason besides their own perfection.

I sat back again, crossing my ankles in front of me, and closed my eyes for a few minutes, trying to process the new discoveries about myself. It was a lot to take in—the ease of using magic, the unknown power of turning into a large wolf. I was still trying to work through it all when I heard a quiet chuckle next to me.

"You're kind of cute when you're deep in thought," Trent laughed as my eyes flew open. He stood leaning against the post of the garden gate, his arms crossed casually in front of him.

"You scared me! Don't you know it's common courtesy to announce yourself with a cough or something?" I exclaimed, disregarding the minor compliment. He certainly didn't mean anything by it. Not with a girl like Meraki in his life.

"True. Sorry. So how did it feel to do magic here in Cyrus?" Trent asked, walking forward to take a seat next to me.

"It was amazing. I had no idea how... natural it would feel. It's like I barely even have to think about it."

Trent laughed at my amazement. "I'll bet you're very good. You'd have to be, doing as well as you did back in the human realm."

"Trent," I began, hesitating.

"What is it?" Trent asked, his face suddenly serious. "You know you can tell me, whatever it is."

"Okay." I exhaled the breath I'd been holding. "I think I discovered a new ability today. Well, I don't *think*, I know. It just freaked me out."

"Awesome! What is it?"

"I'm a shapeshifter. I can turn into some sort of silvery-white wolf," I explained. "It sort of just happened when that nasty bird was attacking me."

"The vulonine, you mean," Trent laughed.

"Whatever you call it," I rolled my eyes.

"You don't seem very excited. Most people are thrilled when they discover a new gift! You seem, well, ticked off."

"I'm not. I realize it's pretty cool. But didn't you say Cyruns can't develop powers after age 12?"

"Yeah, but you were raised in the human realm. That means Cyril hasn't had a chance to develop your powers, so the same restriction wouldn't apply to you. It's not all that surprising that you're seeing changes."

"But that means I have five powers, which puts me in the highest classification. I don't want to be an Elite. I don't want anyone thinking I'm some stupid, high-class snob. I'm not. I don't care how many powers I have or anyone else. I refuse to be forced into an incorrect, pompous social system based on arbitrary numbers." I looked up at Trent. His expression had changed to one of sadness. His lips were drawn in tight, as if he had something to say but couldn't find the words.

"Go on, spit it out," I said.

"What?" he denied, looking too innocent.

"You have something to tell me, so go on, just say it."

"Alright, alright. You're going to have to know soon anyway. The thing is, Ava, you're not going to be an Elite. Truthfully, you can't be anything. I don't think you're going to be able to stay in Cyrus, whether or not you want to. And I know you probably haven't even thought about if you want to stay, but the government doesn't accept outsiders. Tenebris knows that people who come from the human realm can resist his power. He sees anyone like you as a threat. If he found out who you are or where you come from, you'd probably be killed. He does not want a repeat of what happened to his brother."

"I see," I mused.

I wasn't quite sure how I felt about the situation. I don't know that I really wanted to stay in Cyrus anyway. First of all, the social system obviously sucked. Second, I don't think my dad would come back here with me. Whatever reasons he had for leaving and lying to me, I doubt they'd disappear simply because I discovered the truth. Though I was mad at him for that, I don't think I wanted to leave him on any permanent basis. And thirdly, I'd discovered today just how dangerous Cyrus could be—not that that seemed like a very valid reason to avoid the place entirely.

On the other hand, being here felt so right. From the moment I entered this realm, it felt like home. I could feel Cyril pulsing through me, welcoming me back. My abilities were tangible here, ready to obey me at the slightest indication. It was a lot to give up for what was, comparatively, a very bland realm.

I grew self-conscious as I realized Trent was staring at me. Glancing down, I realized how indecent I was—several patches of skin were exposed in places I wasn't exactly used to showing off. Perhaps Meraki had good reason to be looking at me like she did. "Maybe I should go inside and clean up. I brought a spare change of clothes in my bag."

My words snapped Trent from his thoughts. "Umm, right, sorry, I didn't mean to stare." His cheeks grew warm. A shy smile crept to his lips as he redirected his gaze to the dirt at his feet. "I'll give you a minute. Maybe when you're done we could head out into the woods and you can show me what you've been practicing?"

"Are you crazy?" I laughed once as I stood from the bench. "I nearly died twice out there. I'm not going back in that soon."

"It's not nearly as dangerous if you don't go so far in. Sounds to me like you reached Meshon Lake which is several miles into the forest."

Really? Several miles? I'd only been running for a few minutes. How fast could I go here?

"Oh, okay then. That sounds great. I'll be back in a sec." I walked stiffly into the house to change my clothes, suddenly very glad Meraki had to work today.

CHAPTER 10

CLUELESS

By the time Trent and I decided to head back to his house, night was beginning to fall. I had such a good time out in the woods practicing my magic, becoming more familiar with who I am. It was empowering. And thankfully, we'd avoided any more run-ins with dangerous magical creatures.

Trent had also been too adorable for my own good. He'd laughed, joked, teased, and complimented my abilities on many occasions. I continually had to remind myself not to get my hopes up. Sure, I liked him. But he already had a perfect girlfriend here, and by all accounts, I wasn't going to be staying in Cyrus.

Trent walked close to me through the thick forest, the night beginning to cool around us. His arm would occasionally brush mine, and though it was an insignificant touch, my heart would skip a beat every time, then increase in speed for a moment. I smiled at my silly reaction. Trent caught that.

"What's so funny?" he asked.

"Nothing," I lied. "So, Meraki seems like a nice girl," I mentioned casually, though I felt anything but casual about the topic.

"Yeah, she's the best. I've known her practically my whole life," Trent said.

A childhood best friend turned lover. How typical.

"She's extremely beautiful," I said, trying to keep any trace of jealousy out of my voice.

"She is definitely something else in the looks department. That's actually her magical ability. She has a certain degree of magnetism over people using her physical appearance," Trent chuckled, shaking his head as if he couldn't believe how lucky he was to be with her. "She can turn practically any guy into a drooling fool if she wants to."

Great. I shouldn't have asked. My envy just increased tenfold in an instant. Looking at Trent's incredulous face over his own luck was too much. I decided to change the topic.

"Well, I guess I better head back home tonight. Hopefully no one has tried to check on me today."

"Really? You have to go so soon?" Trent's face fell. My heart skipped a beat in response.

Stupid, I thought. *He's clearly in love with Meraki.*

"Yeah, it will be best not to push my luck," I said. "But I can come back, right?"

"You just tell me when, and I'll come get you," Trent smiled.

"Do you think you could come back for me tomorrow afternoon?"

"Sure thing," Trent gushed enthusiastically, as if eager to have me back so soon. I told my heart to shut up again.

"Thanks. You ready to take me home then?"

"If you're sure you have to go, then yes."

103

We had just reached the edge of the woods. His house was visible a ways in the distance, the smoke pouring from the quaint chimney perched on the roof.

"I'm sure," I said, extending my hands out for him to grab.

He held my hands in his. It took a tremendous effort not to smile, though I knew this was nothing more than a necessity. I looked up from our hands to Trent's face, and noticed a strange expression there. He looked... happy? I wasn't sure.

Then, suddenly, we were being squeezed into the bright tunnel of Travel I had experienced only twice before. I knew I would have to get used to it, but that was going to take some time.

The air around us returned to normal as we were spit out of the imaginary tube. Trent's arms grabbed my sides, holding me steady. We'd landed exactly on my front porch. He was good.

"Thanks," I sputtered, trying to deal with the heaving in my stomach.

"No problem," Trent chuckled. "I gotta say, it's kinda funny watching your reaction to Travel."

I threw my elbow into his side, but he dodged out of the way. I was too tired to try again, so I let it be. He laughed again.

After a few deep breaths, I was beginning to feel normal. Trent still had one hand wrapped around my back, making sure I wouldn't lose my balance. I debated playing up the dizziness just to keep him there, but decided he'd probably notice. That would just be embarrassing, so I straightened up.

"I think I'm feeling okay. Thanks again."

To my surprise, Trent's arm didn't drop as I expected it to. Instead, he slid his arm around to my side, placing his other hand on my hip. He gently turned me so I was facing him.

I met his eyes, startled, but pleased, my heart pounding in my chest. He looked at me for a moment as I stared back at him, unsure what to do. No boy had ever tried to make a move on me, so I wasn't sure what it was like. This seemed sort of like what I saw in movies all the time though. But it couldn't be.

Trent smiled faintly as he moved his face closer to mine, his eyes closing.

I panicked.

"Umm... thanks for the fun day, Trent. I'll see you tomorrow," I stammered, twisting out of his arms as I hurriedly shoved my key in the front door and turned the lock.

"Uh, yeah, see you tomorrow," he responded as he straightened up.

I slammed the door without looking at his face. I stood on the other side of the door breathing deeply.

I was such an idiot! I couldn't believe myself. Trent was most likely about to kiss me, and I'd run away like a scared little girl. I guess I was a scared little girl. How awkward could I be? I bet Meraki never did anything stupid like that. What was Trent doing anyway? He had a girlfriend, for heaven's sake!

Inwardly cursing myself as well as Trent, I stomped up the stairs to my room, throwing my bag in the corner. I kicked off my shoes before flopping into bed, facedown. I endured a fifteen minute mental beating before I decided to hit the shower.

Once clean, I gave my dad a call, getting his hotel room's answering machine again, thank goodness. I had no desire to talk to him directly. Honestly, what would I say? *Hey, Dad, mind explaining to me why you've lied to me about everything for the past 17 years?* Yeah, that was a conversation that could wait until we were face to face. Instead, I left a message, lying about my busy Saturday of homework and laundry and wishing him well on his trip.

I had no desire to cook any real food for dinner, so I drummed up a bowl of cold cereal and then dropped into bed, exhausted.

CHAPTER 11

HEARTBREAKER

The next morning was a drag. I busied myself with the things I'd lied to my dad about last night—homework and laundry—and tried not to think about what a fool I'd made of myself in front of Trent.

My mind wandered idly, thinking about Cyrus, Trent, Sam and Em, Meraki, my abilities. I pushed open Dad's bedroom door and walked inside, picking up clothes he'd left strewn on the floor and dumping them in the laundry basket on my hip. I reached for a pair of dress pants, which were mostly shoved under his bed, shaking my head at his slavish ways.

As I bent over to grab the pants, I noticed a small, blue box decorated with yellow moons and stars tucked under the edge of his mattress. Interesting. I'd never seen it before. I yanked it free, falling on my butt with a thud. I set the laundry basket down at my side.

The box was small—no bigger than the ballerina jewelry box I'd had as a child. I held it in my hand, debating whether or not I should open it. Obviously, Dad had hidden it away for a reason. It wasn't really my place to pry. But at the same time, I was tired of Dad's secrets. Perhaps whatever was in the box would shed some light on his reasons for hiding the truth for so long.

In the end, my curiosity won out. I undid the golden clasp and opened the box.

The contents were disappointing. As far as I could tell, it was full of a bunch of junk. I rifled through the random objects, stopping when I came to a beautiful gold ring. I pulled it out of the box by the necklace chain on which it hung. Dangling the ring in front of my face, I examined the intricate rose design that was etched into the golden band. It looked like an engagement ring. I dropped the ring into my palm.

As soon as it touched my skin, my vision went black. I panicked, thinking the ring must have been cursed with some sort of dark magic that caused me to go blind.

An audible scream escaped my lips as the darkness was replaced by a vision. It felt like I'd entered a dream, though I knew I was fully conscious.

In front of me, a young boy—maybe twelve years old—sat in an animal pen, surrounded by sheep. One lamb sat in his lap as he stroked its wool and quietly hummed to it. The other sheep all stood around the boy, fixated on him as if he were some fascinating creature. It was odd behavior.

I stepped closer to the boy. As I did, I recognized his brown eyes and tan skin. His sandy blonde hair was familiar as well. I was looking at the child version of my father. A short laugh bubbled up in my chest. He was kind of funny looking as a kid— lanky and awkward, unlike the strong man I'd come to expect. The sheep's behavior made sense now—Dad could control animal life.

Animals always loved him wherever he went.

Realizing what this must mean, I looked around myself. Out in the distance, I could see a cobblestone street, just like the one in front of Trent's house. Between the boy and the road, a small, brown cottage stood, similar to Trent's as well, though not precisely the same. The clear blue sky and thick forest to the east also reminded me of Cyrus, which is exactly where we must be if I was looking at the 12 year old version of my dad.

A voice interrupted my reverie. "Hey, Carmichael!" a young girl called, as she ran from the direction of the road to where my dad sat in the pen. It was odd to hear him called by his full name. I was used to people calling him Mike or Michael.

"Hey, Rosaline," the boy responded, his face lighting at the appearance of the young girl.

Rosaline was my middle name, I realized with a jolt. Could I be looking at my mother for the first time? Intrigued, I moved closer to the kids, examining the girl in particular.

The resemblance between us was unmistakable. She had long, auburn hair, freckles that danced across her nose, and green eyes, just like me. There was even a similarity in the wideness of her forehead and the shape of her lips. If I had pulled out a picture of me at 12, I would have looked just like this girl.

In the same instant, my heart threatened to explode with delight and shrivel up in fear. I had always wondered what my mother was like, but I'd never expected to meet her, and certainly not like this, whatever *this* was.

"Are you going to come to the clearing today? The kids from school are going to play Catch the Fiddler," the girl asked, looking eager.

Carmichael's face fell. "I can't. My dad has a lot of chores for me to do around here, and he would not be happy if he came home to find them undone." Something gleamed in the sunlight as the boy shifted in his seat. I realized he was wearing the ring I had just found on a chain around his neck.

"Okay, maybe next time," Rosaline said, obviously disappointed.

Suddenly, the scene before me started to ripple and fade until it was no longer visible. In its place, a new scene began to take shape.

I was standing outside at twilight in an open, grassy field. I spun around and saw a large, white tent with lanterns strung about, lighting the inside brilliantly. Music was playing from a live band that sat on a small stage on the opposite side of the tent from where I stood. A table of food lined one tent wall. In the middle of the tent, several teenagers wearing dresses and suits were dancing. A banner above the band read, "Fifth District of Cyrus Spring Formal: Welcome, Students!"

Interesting. So they must have some sort of schooling in Cyrus where they also had dances, just like in the human realm. I'd have to ask Trent more about this sometime.

I scanned the faces of the pimply teens until I found two faces that were familiar. Carmichael and Rosaline spun around in the middle of the dance floor, looking awkward but happy.

The song that was playing ended. Rosaline—in a silky purple dress that draped around her lean frame and fell to the floor—grabbed Carmichael by the hand and pulled him over to the food table. I quickly made my way over as well, accidentally stepping on one girl's foot, though she didn't react in the slightest. Apparently, I couldn't be seen or felt in these visions.

Carmichael scooped some red punch into a glass and handed it to Rosaline. "Thanks," she said shyly, sipping from her glass.

Though the similarities between Rosaline and me were still apparent, she was older than she had been in the last vision, closer to my age. The differences between us were more pronounced than I'd noticed before—primarily the fact that she was a hundred times more beautiful than I was.

I scanned the crowd again, looking for a face that could compare. There wasn't one. Rosaline was, by far, the most beautiful girl at the dance. Carmichael stared at her, as if realizing the same thing I was at that moment.

"What?" Rosaline asked shyly, her long eyelashes flashing as she looked from the floor to Carmichael's eyes.

"Nothing," Carmichael answered, looking quite good himself. He'd thickened up since the last vision and had grown several inches. "You're just... beautiful, you know." His eyes dropped to his shoes as he finished his compliment.

Rosaline's face lit up. "Thanks, Mike," she said, blushing.

"Want to go for a walk?" Mike asked.

111

"Sure," Rosaline answered. Mike took her hand and they left the dance, wandering out into the open fields.

The scene faded once more as a new image appeared.

This time, I stood on top of a hillside that overlooked a beautiful, crystal clear lake. I looked around, trying to find Mike or Rosaline. I spotted them about twenty yards off, just below the crest of the hill.

To my surprise, Mike was on one knee, holding out a ring to Rosaline who stood in front of him, her hands covering her mouth.

I wasn't close enough to hear what was being said, but I saw Rosaline nod as Mike jumped up, grabbing her in an enormous hug. He spun her around and then kissed her jubilantly.

The scene faded and recreated itself once more.

We stood outside a small brown cottage—the same one from the first scene, I realized, as I saw the pen of sheep in the distance.

Carmichael and Rosaline stood on the front porch, bathed in light from a lantern that hung by the door. Both looked older—in their early 20s or so. They were deep in conversation, and it didn't appear to be a pleasant one. Mike's face was contorted in a deep, saddening pain.

I moved closer to hear what was going on.

"I'm so sorry, Mike. I really, truly am. I can't do this," Rosaline said, tears streaming down her face as she shook her head in dismay.

"Please, Rose, we can make it. I'll take you anywhere you want to go. We can get away from all of this. No one will be able to tell you what you can or can't do anymore. It can be just you and me. I promise," Mike's voice broke.

"I wish it were that simple, Mike. I really do. I'm sorry, but I have to go now. Please don't try to follow me." Rosaline ripped the ring off her finger and slammed it in Mike's open palm.

She turned to leave as Mike caught her arm. "Please, Rose, I'll do anything," Mike begged, blatant desperation in his eyes.

"I'm sorry," she sobbed as she ran down the steps into the night.

"I love you, Rosaline!" Mike called after her. "Please, no!" Mike's sobs rent the night air. He turned and punched the lantern behind him, the glass shattering at his feet.

The scene faded once more. This time, the setting that replaced it was my father's bedroom and the gold ring in my hand. I'd returned to reality.

For several minutes, I couldn't move. The sound of my Dad's cries ripped at my heart. Why had she left us? They seemed so in love, even though I'd only seen the briefest glimpses of their life together. If only she had come with us, to the human realm. If she had, she would still be alive.

With a shock, I realized she might not be dead after all. Dad had always claimed she'd died in the wars in Cyrus, but Trent said there were no wars recently. It would be so wonderful to meet her in person.

I ached to pick up the phone and call my Dad for some answers. I also wanted desperately to comfort him. Though I was

113

furious with him, I also loved him and hated seeing the depth of his pain as my mother left him. How could I, though? What would I say? *Sorry, to have snooped through your stuff, but your relationship with my mom really sucked, and I wanted to let you know I'm here for you.* I don't think that would go over very well.

Besides that, I couldn't very well explain what had just happened. Perhaps the ring was magical—it could hold memories connected to it and then share them later on. If that was the case, I'm sure my Dad would know about it. I wonder why it would have chosen those specific memories to hold onto.

If only Trent was here. I could ask him if he'd ever come across any objects like this one.

That thought had me looking at the clock. It was only barely afternoon. Hopefully Trent would be eager to come get me today and show up sooner rather than later. Though after how awkward I was last night, that wasn't likely.

I spent the next few hours trying to be patient. I distracted myself with more mundane household chores, which wasn't helping. I checked the clock every few minutes, wondering why he hadn't shown up yet.

When two o'clock rolled around, I began to really worry. He probably wasn't going to come at all. I'd totally blown everything with my awkwardness.

A horrific thought hit me. Maybe he hadn't meant to do anything at all last night. Maybe he wasn't leaning in for a kiss, and I'd just embarrassed both of us for no reason. Of course that was it. He wouldn't want to kiss me when he had a perfect girlfriend like Meraki.

The next hour was consumed with another mental beating. I was such an idiot. Trent was not interested in me.

Finally, I heard a knock at the front door. I checked the peephole first and saw Trent standing on the steps, hands in his jean pockets. The slightly tattered green t-shirt he wore hugged his chest muscles nicely, not that I should be thinking anything like that. I was determined not to make a fool of myself today.

With a steadying breath, I opened the front door.

Trent smiled widely. "Hi, Ava. Sorry it took me awhile to get here. My mom needed a lot of help in the gardens. She's running a produce stand out in the city center today and tomorrow."

"You kidding? I didn't even notice the time," I lied. Trent didn't look convinced.

"Of course not," he winked with an easy smile. My stomach fluttered. "Ready to go then?"

"Just one second," I said. I took off up the stairs to grab my backpack, which had the ring shoved into the front pocket. I ran back down the stairs, tripping on the last step. Fortunately, Trent was waiting at the bottom and caught me.

"Sorry," I blushed, standing up quickly and straightening my shirt.

"You're sort of clumsy for someone who has the gift of speed," Trent chuckled.

I ignored the jab, holding my hands out for Trent to take so we could Travel.

CHAPTER 12

THE COTTAGE

We landed in the middle of Trent's red living room. I kept my balance fairly well this time. Trent hardly had to hold on to me before the dizziness faded and I felt normal.

"You good?" Trent asked, ducking down to meet my eyes. Even that small amount of eye contact had me blushing again.

"I'm fine."

"Cool," Trent said, pulling me by the hand to sit on the red sofa with him. "So what do you want to do today? More practicing?"

"That would be great!" I said. "But first I have a question for you."

I pulled my backpack around until it rested in my lap. I fished out the ring from the front pocket and dropped my bag to the ground. I looked at the ring with trepidation, not quite sure how to proceed.

Trent laughed. "What's up, Ava? Just tell me."

Before I said anything, I decided I wanted to see if the same thing would happen to Trent when he touched the ring.

"Give me your hand," I said. He gave it to me, and I opened his fingers, turning his palm so that it faced upward.

"Are you a fortune teller too? You gonna read my palm?"

Trent teased.

I rolled my eyes, dropping the ring into his hand. I waited with bated breath.

Nothing happened.

Trent stared at me, his left eyebrow raised. "You gonna explain why you gave me this ring?" he asked.

I frowned. "Nothing unusual is happening? You can still see me here in front of you?"

"Yes?" Trent questioned. "Shouldn't I be able to? You're kinda scaring me, Ava."

"Dang it. You were supposed to see a vision," I explained.

"Ha, I'm not a seer, Ava. You know I'm just a Traveler."

"A seer?" I asked. "There are Cyruns who can see the future?"

"Of course. Or the past. They're pretty rare though. Even more rare than Travelers are."

I took the ring back from Trent's hand and examined it closely.

"Is there any possibility that an object can be enchanted to retain memories?" I asked.

Trent thought for a second. "I've never heard of anything like that, but maybe. Why do you ask?"

I sighed. "I found this ring today in a box of random things my dad had hidden under his mattress. When I picked it up, I saw pieces of memories from the past."

I explained every detail I could remember about what I'd seen that afternoon. Trent's expression increased my anxiety as he

118

became more and more engrossed as I went on.

"—and then I saw her run off into the night. My dad called after her, crying, but she didn't come back. How could she just leave him like that?" I finished.

Trent stared at me, the wrinkle between his eyebrows growing more pronounced as he thought.

"Say something!" I said, exasperated. "You're driving me crazy!"

"Sorry," he said. "It's just strange. I've never heard of a seer receiving a vision like that."

"I'm not a seer," I denied.

Trent gave me a skeptical look.

"I'm not!" I insisted. "It's just the ring."

"Then why didn't the ring show me the vision?"

"I don't know. Maybe it chooses when it wants to reveal its memories."

"Uh huh," Trent said, not convinced. "You said you have some sort of precognition powers, right? How often do you normally get feelings about the future?"

"Usually small things a couple times a day. Bigger things a couple times a month. Why?"

"How often have you had those types of feelings since you came to Cyrus?"

I paused, thinking. "Honestly, I can't remember having one at all. That's kind of weird for me. And it's weird I haven't noticed. I guess I've just been distracted by everything that's been going on."

Trent stayed silent, thinking.

"What is it?" I asked him.

"Well, it could be that your precognition was sort of a stirring of you full seer abilities, which aren't actually about the future at all, but about the past. Maybe that's why you never got any clear pictures of the future in the human realm. This could be further development of your abilities now that you're finally connected to Cyril again."

I considered. "That would sort of make sense. But I'm not convinced yet. One set of strange visions doesn't prove anything. It is definitely odd I haven't been sensing more about the future though."

Trent looked at me incredulously. I punched him in the arm. "Can we just... go do something else? Please?" I begged.

"Sure. What do you want to do?" Trent asked.

"Umm... can you take me to the city center? Where your mom's stand is? I'd love to see what a Cyrun city looks like."

"Sounds great," Trent said, though his tone implied otherwise.

"What's wrong?"

"It's just... the city can be dangerous. There are a lot more of Tenebris' guards around and you're going to be an unfamiliar face."

"We'll keep a low profile, I promise." Trent looked like he needed a bit of convincing, so I batted my eyelashes playfully.

His face broke into a smile. He rolled his eyes and laughed.

"Fine, but you have to promise you'll do exactly what I say."

"Scouts honor," I swore.

"What?" Trent asked, confused.

"Right, uh, it just means I will." I laughed.

"We're going to need to change your shirt," Trent commented, looking me over in a way that made me self-conscious.

"What's wrong with my shirt?" I asked, looking down at my Kate Bossner concert t-shirt.

"Well, nobody is going to have any idea why you're obsessed enough with a girl named Kate so as to wear her face on your shirt, nor will they recognize any of the city names across your back."

"Oh, right," I said stupidly.

"It's fine, come with me." Trent pulled me up from the couch. He led us up the small staircase that separated the kitchen from the front room.

The upstairs of the cottage was exceptionally small, with just two bedrooms on either side of the stairs and a bathroom in between. The angled roof was obvious as we entered his parents' bedroom. The ceiling slanted down until it touched the floor on one end. A bed with a pink quilt on top was shoved against that wall. A small chest stood at the foot of the bed. At the far end of the room, there was a petite wardrobe that would hold only a modest amount of clothes. Trent walked up to it, pulling open the doors to reveal the few articles that hung inside. He grabbed a plain white t-shirt and handed it to me. "Will this work?"

121

"Yeah, that's fine," I said, taking the shirt from him.

I waited for him to leave so I could change. He stared at me expectantly in return. It took him a moment to realize why I hadn't started. We stood in an uncomfortable silence until he said, "Oh, right, sorry, I'll uh, just step out while you, ya know—"

He tripped over the chest at the edge of the bed in his hurry to cross the room. I chuckled once. He glanced over his shoulder self-consciously before he exited, pulling the door closed behind him.

I shook my head, not knowing it was possible for someone to be so adorable and awkward at the same time. I swiftly exchanged my shirt for his mother's. It was slightly too big for me but not terrible.

Trent wasn't outside the door when I left the room but was waiting for me in the living room instead. His expression showed he hadn't quite recovered from his embarrassment upstairs. At least I wasn't the only one who felt a little uncomfortable sometimes.

"You ready then?" he asked, looking down at a spot on the carpet instead of at me.

"Yeah, I just need to put this in my bag," I said, holding up my concert t-shirt.

Trent shuffled to the side, giving me a wide berth to get to my bag. I shoved the shirt inside.

"Ready."

"Cool. So I think it will be best if we Travel to a spot in the forest that's a little closer to the city center and then walk from there. It's about four miles away, so it would be a long walk otherwise."

"Sounds good to me." Not that four miles would be difficult for me to run, but it would take Trent some time to go on foot.

He took my hands in his, avoiding my eyes this time, and we disappeared from his living room. We reappeared in a thick part of forest. I didn't need any help keeping my balance after landing, a fact I was proud of.

"Hey, that was pretty good, eh?" I laughed.

Trent laughed too. "Definitely an improvement," he agreed. "Look, Ava, I'm sorry about up in my parents' bedroom. I didn't mean to—"

I cut him off. "Seriously, Trent, no big deal." I held up my hand to stop him from saying anything more. He smiled and seemed to relax into his usual self.

Our conversation was casual as we walked the half mile remaining to the city center. I asked Trent about his schooling—the vision I'd seen made me curious. He explained that school attendance was mandatory until age 12. After that, parents had to pay to keep their kids in school, so only those who were well off were able to continue.

Once you were finished with school—whether at age 12, 18, or somewhere in between—you were required to take what they called your Power Final. This was used to place you in your civil service position where you'd serve for the rest of your life. You were also given your own social rank at that time. Everyone had to take their Power Final by age 18 at the latest. That meant less than two months for Trent.

"That doesn't seem very fair," I pointed out. "A student at the age of 12 wouldn't have much opportunity to develop their talents, I would assume. So they likely wouldn't receive a very good placement."

"Exactly. It's a system designed to keep those in poverty without any way to break the cycle. To make matters worse, once you take your Power Final, you are not allowed to live in your parents' home, which means there are plenty of young kids out there trying to make it on their own." Trent kicked a rock in his frustration. It sailed through the air and hit a nearby tree trunk with a thud.

"How does Tenebris enforce that law? It seems like it would be very difficult to check up on every household all the time."

"Have you noticed my father is missing his right thumb?" Trent asked.

I was confused by his question, but answered anyway. "Yes, of course. I didn't want to be rude by asking, but I've wondered why."

"Once, when he was helping my mother get her cart into town, he gave a beggar on the street an orange. One of Tenebris' guards was watching. It is illegal to give any aid to a member of a lower social ranking than you are. The punishment for such a crime is not set in stone—essentially the guard can do whatever he pleases.

124

In this case, he felt like chopping off my dad's thumb."

"Ugh... that's barbaric," I said, my stomach heaving at the thought.

"It is indeed, but in some ways, my dad got off easy. I've seen plenty of people whipped mercilessly in the city square and some even put to death for a 'crime' that simple. Tenebris wants to keep us in submission. Giving us any idea that we might get away with helping someone—banding together—he views as a threat. He knows the best way to maintain control is to keep us divided and in fear."

"Why didn't your dad heal himself?" I asked, still sick at the thought of someone as gentle as Sam facing that kind of consequence for an act of mercy.

"My dad can heal nearly any physical injury, but he cannot return a severed limb. His abilities don't stretch that far. I'd guess that's why the guard chose that particular punishment for him."

I paused, debating whether or not I should ask my next question. I was fairly certain I knew the answer and it wasn't a happy one. I decided to ask it anyway. "What's going to happen to you? In two months?"

Trent stopped walking, and I followed suit. He hung his head for a moment before meeting my eyes with a sad smile on his face. "I have no choice. I will be a Zero, forced to leave my parents' home, and left without any way to provide for myself. It's the reason my parents have sacrificed so much to keep me in school for as long as they have. We are not a wealthy family, and it has

125

been difficult to pay for the schooling, but they have wanted to delay the inevitable as much as possible. One way or the other, though, my time is up in two months."

I was stunned. I had no idea what I could do or say to comfort Trent. A renewed hatred for Tenebris rose inside me. This ridiculous system served no purpose but to keep him in power and the people afraid. "There has to be something that can be done," I whispered.

Trent looked at me sadly. "There isn't, Ava. As long as Praesidium exists, we are nothing more than captives in Cyrus. It's no wonder your dad left and never wanted you to know about this place."

Though I wish Dad had been truthful with me, I suppose I could see Trent's point—Cyrus wasn't the place I had always dreamed. My father must have realized this and wanted us to escape before I became attached to the realm. Was it better to live in a world without magic but a place where I could be free? Or dwell in a land where societal limitations mocked the undeniable power that ran through my veins—through every Cyrun's veins? I wasn't sure.

CHAPTER 13

MAGIA

The city center was amazing. In my brief exposure to Cyrus thus far, I'd gotten the feeling that the way of life here was very old fashioned. The city said otherwise; it was a bustling metropolis, as busy as any major city in the human world, yet sustained by infrastructure that seemed a logical impossibility. For example, the bridge we crossed that connected the countryside to the city appeared to be suspended in midair. No supports of any kind were visible below or above it.

The architecture, too, was beautiful but didn't make sense according to any physics I'd learned in school. The building that seemed to stand tallest—though it was a close competition with several others—twisted and curved around itself in a beautiful, spiraling pattern. Its glassy surfaces reflected rainbows in different directions like the minute facets of a diamond.

"Welcome to Magia," Trent said as we stood at the base of the bridge, an enormous smile on his face—a stark contrast with his mood in the forest.

"It's incredible!" I gushed. "How does it all work? It doesn't make sense."

"Magic, of course," Trent laughed.

Oh. Right. I guess I'd never met or heard about anyone with

abilities that could create structures like the ones before me, but I suppose they must exist.

"And King Tenebris? He lives here?" I asked, tense at the thought.

"Yes, but the palace isn't visible from this spot. It's actually on the other side of the city. It's magnificent as well."

"Best to keep our heads down then, eh?"

"Definitely," Trent agreed.

We walked the remainder of the short path ahead, entering a cast-iron gate that read, "Welcome to Magia: Capital city of Cyrus," above our heads.

The storefronts we passed were a mixture of the unknown and familiar. Some seemed absolutely normal, like the bookshops and produce stands. Others were foreign, with advertisements that boasted of products that would "turn an enemy to stone" or "rid your home of gargoyles".

"Trolls?" I asked Trent, reading the headline of a newspaper a man carried tucked under his arm. "Are all mythical creatures real in Cyrus?"

"Depends on what you mean. 'All' is probably too generous. I've never met anything that would be called a Boogy Man, though I'd imagine whatever he looks like, even his mother has a hard time giving him good night kisses," Trent joked. "But as far as most of your standard 'fairytale' creatures, yes. There are trolls, dragons, pegasi, goblins, unicorns—you get the idea."

I thought about my previous encounters with the garden

gnome, mermaid, and vulonine. I wasn't sure I was too keen on the idea of meeting the other creatures around here. Though the gnome did have its charms.

Despite the exciting displays in shop windows and the smiles on many faces, there was a sad side to Magia, hidden in the shadows. Several people with nothing more than rags for clothes lurked in the darkness, their faces gaunt with hunger, their eyes silently pleading the words they could not speak.

"Get on with your day, vermin!" a crass voice shouted. A glance behind told me it belonged to a man in a red uniform—law enforcement. He shouted at a haggard looking woman with a young boy by her side. "You know better than to put your indecency on display in Magia's royal city!" The man waved his arms wildly, urging the two to move. "Go on, get out of the street before I whip you both in the square!" The boy gave a small whimper that broke my heart.

I started toward the woman and child, not sure what I could do, but feeling the urge to offer help anyway. A hand grabbed my arm. "Ava, don't," Trent warned. "I know it's hard, but you'll only make things worse for them and for you if you intervene. Trust me."

I looked in Trent's eyes, seeing the pain there that matched my own—the pain of helplessness. An ache grew in my chest, becoming sharper as I remembered this was his fate in two short months.

"A low profile, remember? You promised. Come on, my

mom's stand should be just up this road," Trent said, indicating a turn to the right at the next intersection. Reluctantly, I followed.

We passed a dress shop with fancy evening gowns in its display windows and a candy shop that had some delicious looking sweets. Finally, we reached Em's produce stand, which was parked in the middle of the street.

"Hey, Mom," Trent said. "How's business?"

"Oh, kind of slow, I'm afraid. There are a lot of stands out today, it being the weekend and all."

"True. But everyone knows Emeritus Cavanaugh has the best produce." Trent embraced his mom and kissed her cheek. She smiled in return.

"Would you like anything, Ava?" Em asked, gesturing at the delicious fruits and vegetables in front of her. I was actually very hungry but couldn't bring myself to even think about eating. I kept picturing the frail woman and her child.

"No thanks, I'm fine," I responded.

"Come on, it's on the house, of course," Trent said, picking up an apple and tossing it at me. I caught it lithely as an idea hit me.

"Do you think I could take just a few more?" I asked timidly.

"Sure," Trent said, tossing three more at me.

"Thanks. I'll be back in just a second."

"Wait, Ava, I know what you're thinking. Please don't!" Trent called.

"I'll be too fast for anyone to catch me. Don't worry," I said.

And then I took off at my fastest speed, the buildings becoming blurs around me as I headed in the direction of the mother and son.

After a few seconds, I caught sight of them as they headed up the street that led to the bridge out of the city. They both wore tattered cloaks with hoods that hung below their necks. Perfect. I sprinted up behind them, dropped two apples a piece in their hoods, and then ran back to the produce stand. A few quick glances around told me I was safe. Nobody had spotted me come or go.

Then I caught the look on Trent's face. He was furious. "I told you not to do that," he said darkly.

"Do what?" Em asked.

"Ava just gave two beggars some of your produce," Trent whispered to his mother.

Em's face was surprised. "Really? I didn't even see you go. How generous of you, Ava. Thank you." She smiled and reached out to squeeze my hand.

"What do you mean, 'thank you'?" Trent stuttered. "She could have gotten herself into serious trouble!"

"Son, we cannot allow tyranny to make us cowards. If there's a way Ava can help without putting herself in danger, I'm happy she took the chance."

"Thank you, Em," I said, feeling awkward. I wasn't looking for praise for my actions, though I was grateful she took some heat off me.

Trent gave a sigh that let me know he was still frustrated. He busied himself, straightening produce and restocking the bins with fruit that was stashed underneath the baskets on the cart.

We spent the next short while helping Em at the stand. I mostly felt useless as things weren't busy enough for three workers, but I handled a few transactions here and there and replaced produce as I'd seen Trent do. Over time, he seemed to soften until he no longer held the tightness in his shoulders that told me he was annoyed.

Just as I handed a stout woman her bag of produce, a loud voice echoed around us, halting my outstretched hand. The woman, too, froze. The voice didn't sound like it came from a speaker like the annoying intercom system at school, yet it still surrounded us. Rather, it sounded like a person was standing in front of us, talking in a slightly louder than normal voice. I glanced around, confused, as the voice proclaimed, "Citizens and guests of Magia, his Royal Highness, King Tenebris, has requested a gathering at Tuttenham Square to begin in fifteen minutes. Please make your way to the square as quickly as possible. His Highness will be addressing the public in person. All individuals who can hear this message are invited to attend. Thank you."

"Invited," Trent scoffed. "More like commanded."

I wasn't sure what he meant by that, but it didn't sound good. Em looked concerned. "We better get going," she breathed.

I handed the woman her bag. She took it swiftly and then rushed to the other side of the street to join her husband. They hurried down the street together, arm in arm.

Trent and Em walked around the sides of her stand, unrolling long pieces of fabric that provided a cover. Catching on, I went to the third side and unrolled my piece. We fastened the pieces together, securing the cover in place.

"Thank you," Em said breathlessly. "Come on now, quickly."

We shuffled off down the road, headed in the direction of the crowd. As we walked farther and farther into the city, the crowds became thicker, causing our pace to slow dramatically. A hushed whisper hung over the throng as the gatherers speculated about what might be happening.

"How much farther is it?" I asked Trent.

"Just a few more streets. We should make it in time without a problem," he whispered back.

After another minute, the street where we walked opened up to a very large square with a tall fountain in the center. People crammed in around each other, all sense of personal space forgotten. Beyond the fountain, there was a large building that reminded me of a courthouse back home. It had a wide staircase that led up to the doors of a white brick building with white columns spaced out across its face. A large balcony jutted out of the second story. With a jolt, I recognized the beggar boy from the street. He stood on the balcony, facing the crowd, with his hands and feet tied together, looking frightened. He couldn't be more than eleven years old. His mother sat bound on a chair on one side of the balcony, her mouth covered with a rag. The panic in her eyes was evident, even from this distance. The tension in the atmosphere was palpable.

"What is the boy doing up there?" I asked Trent frantically. "What are they going to do to him?"

Trent didn't answer. His expression remained stony.

I turned to Em and opened my mouth to ask her the same question, but she squeezed my hand and whispered, "It would be best to stay quiet for now, Ava."

A man wearing a navy blue uniform and white gloves stepped out onto the balcony. "His Royal Highness, King Tenebris, king of the people of Cyrus," he barked, turning sharply to the side to make way for the next figure to step through the door.

The king emerged onto the balcony, his hair jet black and smoothed behind his ears. His face and posture were austere, his eyes cold. He wore a black uniform with a red and gold cape draped around his shoulders. It dragged on the ground as he stepped forward to place his gloved hands on the railing. A simple gold crown glinted on his head. Around his neck hung a prominent ruby encased in an elaborate gold chain—Praesidium, the object giving him his powers. It shimmered in the sunlight.

"Citizens of Cyrus," the king spoke, his voice as emotionless as his face. It carried easily over the crowd, just as the announcement on the street had before. "Bow to your king."

I watched as Praesidium glowed a vibrant red at the direct command, exerting its powers over the people who were compelled to comply. I was fascinated by it—so fascinated that I forgot to obey the command. Trent tugged on my hand, pulling me down with him, his eyes glued to the ground.

I quickly obeyed Trent and bowed as well, though I did not keep my eyes on the ground as he did. I looked around the gathering, noticing that everyone was in the exact same position as Trent—knees and waist bent, eyes on the ground—except one dark haired boy who looked to be about the same age as Trent and me. He stood roughly 20 yards from where we were. He, too, was bent in a bow, but his eyes were searching the crowd, just like mine. He seemed to notice me at the same moment I noticed him. We made eye contact. A look of confusion crossed his features followed by a radiant smile.

I broke eye contact with him, looking down at the ground like everyone else. I wasn't sure what to make of it. Why didn't that boy look like everyone else? Why hadn't I? Was it like Trent said? I came from the human realm, so Praesidium had less power over me? If so, was that boy like me?

"Thank you, citizens. You may now stand. You are to stay as you are and silently listen to your king," Tenebris called over the crowd, Praesidium glowing red at his neck once more. I saw Trent's posture stiffen with the weight of the command. I paid more attention to my own feelings and realized the command seemed to tug slightly at something inside me, but held no bearing. I could ignore it as easily as I could ignore my dad's request to clean my room.

"There are two reasons you have been called to gather here this day. First and foremost, it has come to my attention that another census is required. It would seem that some among us are willfully disobeying the law, intentionally hiding their powers from the government and using them in unauthorized ways," the king called.

I shot a glance at Trent out of the corner of my eye; he was one of those people. He swallowed deeply but did not look at me. He stared at the king, his back rigid, just like everyone else. I tried to push my worries away and focus on the king as well, but it was hard. I glanced around the crowd nervously. The dark haired boy who'd noticed me before was staring directly at me, an eager look on his face. I pretended not to notice.

"All households will be visited by a surveyor who will record the number of individuals in each household, the social status of all family members, and all known magical abilities obtained by such individuals. Any who have been concealing known abilities from the government will face punishment accordingly," the king threatened. "The census will be completed over the course of the next two months. A notice will be sent to your home for your scheduled appointment with the surveyor. All individuals in your household must be present for the appointment, no exceptions. Any who are absent will be dealt with in a manner consistent with the seriousness of their crime.

"Second, it would appear that the people of Magia have forgotten our land's important laws regarding social status." King Tenebris stepped back to stand next to the small beggar boy who stood frozen, his eyes wide and frightened. "This young boy and his filthy mother," Tenebris sneered at the woman bound in the chair, "were spotted by one of my noble guards in the streets of Magia with fresh produce. Now, either these two vile beggars stole the produce from a stand, or someone gave it to them. Either way, their actions are illegal and are an abomination in the eyes of the laws of Cyrus. As such, they must face the consequences. Let this serve as a reminder to each of you of the seriousness of transgressing against your king.

"The boy is hereby sentenced to 15 lashes. His mother shall follow with 20 of her own. The whipping shall be carried out by Officer Sandberg of the First Division." Tenebris motioned to a guard who stepped through the door wearing black slacks and a black, long-sleeve shirt. He carried a lethal whip in his right hand.

My stomach dropped. This was entirely my fault. If I had only listened to Trent, this wouldn't be happening. Tears sprung up in my eyes. Glancing around, I saw that many people in the crowd also had tears running down their faces, though their eyes remained glued to the balcony, their footsteps frozen in place by the wicked king's commands.

Everyone was frozen, helpless—except me.

I didn't even have to think about it. Without another glance at Trent or Em, I dropped to my knees and scrambled through the crowd, heading toward a large, red brick building to the east. My hope was that the crowd would have thinned there. It seemed to be the perimeter of the large square where the people were gathered. From there, I could use my speed and sneak behind buildings to the place where the king planned to hold his public display of torture.

I could not let this go on. I would not let this go on.

My hands and knees were scraped and bleeding by the time I finally reached the side of the brick building. Much to my relief, it was, as I hoped, empty on every side. I broke into a run, circling behind the building and darting between alleyways to the next building.

Finally, I reached the side of the white stone building. I circled to its backside, finding a door at the rear. Just as I reached the door, I heard the first crack of the whip and a horrible yelp from the boy.

I had to stop this!

Using my abilities, I slipped through the locked door with ease and found a staircase to my right. I sprinted up it, not stopping at the second level, but climbing one more to a small storage level above. I scanned the ceiling frantically, finding what I was looking for—a ladder that led to a hatch, which should give me access to the roof.

I scrambled up the ladder as another crack rent the air. I cringed.

Hurriedly, I undid the hatch and then dove onto the flat roof. Crouched low, I rushed over to the edge. The decorative railing surrounding the perimeter provided some cover for me, though not much. The guard cracked the whip again and the poor boy cried, his shirt ripped and his back bleeding. The sight was too terrible to behold.

An overwhelming need to protect the child grew in me until it was nearly a tangible force radiating from my being, thrusting toward the small boy. Thinking desperately, yet unable to come up with a plan, I watched as the wicked guard raised his arm again. I outwardly cringed as his arm came down sharply, the whip connecting with the poor child's back.

The boy flinched, yet no cry escaped his lips. His face was filled with relief and confusion. He glanced behind himself, looking at the guard in wonder, as if he wasn't sure he'd actually struck.

The guard seemed frustrated by the obvious lack of response from his latest blow. He wound his arm behind him, putting more effort into it this time. The boy quickly turned away, fear in his face once more as the whip came down again. Like last time, the boy flinched at the crack of the whip, but there seemed to be no pain. How odd. How amazing!

Determined to watch more closely this time, I noticed a blue, shimmering ripple surrounded the boy's back mere inches from it, as if hugging the boy. As the guard brought the whip down with more fury than ever, I saw that it did not connect with the child— it hit the ripple of shimmering blue instead and stopped there. Again, there was no sound of pain from the boy. His mother's face was filled with ardent relief.

What was happening? Did the boy have previously unknown abilities that manifested themselves here, in his time of need, as

139

mine so often did? Did those abilities afford him some sort of protection? The blue shimmer was indeed faint; nobody seemed to notice it. At least nothing was said by Tenebris or the guard.

Whatever was saving the boy, I was grateful, though Tenebris and the guard certainly were not. After a few more strikes that also heeded no response, King Tenebris cried out in frustration, "Forget the child. Bring his mother forward."

The guard roughly slashed the ropes that bound the child to the thick log by his wrists. The boy stumbled to his feet and hurried to his mother, panic in his eyes. The guard followed. He roughly removed the cloth that gagged the woman and yanked her to her feet. He dragged her to the post and tied her to it, as he had the boy. The crowd watched in horror, frozen in their command to stand silently.

Again, my mind was working wildly, trying to come up with a way to stop the horror. Whatever had protected the boy likely wouldn't protect his sweet mother. The terror in her eyes was obvious, though I noticed she was trying to be strong for her son.

The guard stepped back, readying himself for the first strike. The same overwhelming need to protect this innocent woman welled up inside me, filling every inch of my body until it spilled out of me. At that exact moment, I noticed the same faint, rippling blue shimmer that had protected the boy extend around the woman's back.

The whip came down with a sharp crack. Simultaneously, I felt a faint tug in my head. It wasn't painful, simply noticeable.

140

Like the child, the woman flinched at the sound, but did not scream or cry. She, too, looked confused.

With obvious frustration, the guard brought the whip down once more. Again, a flinch and no pain. And again, I felt a mental tug at the same time the whip connected with the rippling blue.

With a jolt of realization, I understood what was happening— I was protecting the woman. I had protected the child. The thin blue ripple belonged to me. It was a shield of some sort, an extension of my dire need to protect the innocent. That is why I could feel something in my head every time the whip connected with the blue ripple. Even as I thought it, I felt another mental tug as the whip connected with my shield once more.

Life in Cyrus continued to baffle me. My abilities manifested themselves so easily here. I was overwhelmingly grateful for the timely discovery of this new gift. I had felt entirely responsible for putting the woman and child in this horrible position. At the same time, I was also frightened by the discovery of a sixth ability. I didn't want to be seen as special, even if it was only by Trent and his family.

Finally, realizing that they were having absolutely no impact on the woman, Tenebris cried out, "Stop!" to the guard, who halted immediately.

Tenebris paced back and forth on the small balcony for a moment before he turned to face the crowd.

"To show that your king is indeed merciful," Tenebris called over the people, "I hereby pardon this woman and her son from

141

their crimes. Let this day stand as a reminder that the laws of Cyrus are to be obeyed by all. I would not expect such acts of mercy from your king in the future. That will be all. You are dismissed." With a swish of the king's cape, he turned and headed back through the doors, annoyance blatant on his face.

The crowd immediately broke free of their rigid stance and began milling about, heading out of the square. It seemed most were in a hurry to leave Magia and get home.

I continued to watch as the woman was cut free from the post. She hurried to her son, embracing him. The boy smiled at his mother with relief. Two guards shoved them back through the balcony doors. I hoped fervently that this would truly be the end of it for the pair of them.

I scrambled down the ladder to the storage space, then down to the first floor, knowing I needed to hurry back to the place where I'd left Trent and his mother before they began to worry. I slipped through the locked back door and into the crowd, breaking into a sprint.

"Ava, what were you thinking?" Trent asked as I reappeared at his side. "I saw you up there on the roof. I'm sure everyone did!" His expression was livid.

"Oh, come now," Em said. "She was very discreet. Most were too concerned with the horrible display of cruelty to examine the roof. Did you have something to do with protecting the child, dear? I noticed the whip seemed to lose its effect as soon as you appeared on the roof."

"I'm not certain, but I think so," I said, unsure how to explain what had happened.

"Well, I'm very glad you did. It was indeed risky. But you helped stop a terrible injustice today." Em smiled kindly. "We should leave the city quickly. We need to speak with your father about the census," Em said, turning to head back up the road as she spoke.

Trent and I followed. I watched him from the corner of my eye. His expression was angry but there was a trace of relief in his eyes.

I tried to contain myself, but my heart was so heavy with worry for how he was feeling that I ended up reaching out and grabbing his hand. He told me he didn't want me to do anything that would endanger him or his family. I had done exactly that today. And on top of that, they now had this census to worry about. If it was discovered they'd hidden an ability as prominent as Traveling from the king, I knew the consequences would be severe. Trent seemed shocked by the unexpected touch, but glanced over at me and smiled. I smiled back, relieved that he seemed to be forgiving me.

We reached Em's stand in minutes. We hurried to uncover the stand and pack everything away in the baskets she'd stashed beneath the shelves of fruit. The stand itself was collapsible. I watched as Trent folded it in on itself, stuffed it in a canvas bag, and zipped it up. He slung it over his shoulder, reaching for the baskets of fruit I held in my hands.

"I'm fine," I insisted. "Take some of your mom's instead." He took his mom's four baskets and we briskly walked out of the city. It seemed like a lot of people were in a hurry to leave. We headed for the bridge Trent and I had crossed earlier that day amidst a throng of people.

"Why do you think Tenebris let the beggars go like he did?" I asked Trent in a hushed whisper.

"He was humiliated and trying to save face. Obviously, what he meant to be a harsh example of what happens to people who are flagrantly disobedient turned into a show of defiance, though I don't think he could figure out how they were resisting the blows. Therefore, his only option was to turn it into a good PR moment," Trent breathed. "I don't think many fell for it. They knew it was a cover up."

Interesting. That would explain Tenebris' annoyed expression as he'd left the balcony. I was relieved he'd decided to let the two go rather than make a further example of them by some other means. Who knew what my shield could withstand?

We walked a short distance into the woods before Trent set down the baskets he was carrying. His mom picked them up as he extended a hand out to each of us on either side of him.

"You're going to have to hold on extra tight this time, Ava, since I only have one hand to hold on to you with. Can you do that?" Trent asked.

"Maybe it would be best if I just ran back to your house. I could be there in just a few minutes," I offered, nervous about

Traveling without his strong hands holding me.

"No," Em intervened. "It's too dangerous to have you using your powers just now. Remember, you're not even known by the government. We need to keep a low profile for the time being. Besides, I prefer we stick together."

"Okay," I agreed reluctantly.

I extended my right hand out to Trent and we took off. At first, nothing seemed out of the ordinary. But just a few moments into our Travel, I felt a tugging on my left leg. We were spinning so quickly through the white tube that I couldn't get my bearings enough to look down and see what caused it, but the tugs became more and more persistent. I felt Trent's hand tighten around mine, trying to hold me to him, but I kept slipping. With a final, strong pull, my hand slid out of his entirely.

CHAPTER 14

ABDUCTED

I felt myself falling a long distance before I hit the ground with a sickening thud. I'd landed face first and had the wind knocked out of me. As soon as I could manage, I turned onto my back, spitting dirt out of my mouth and gasping for air. A cool trickle ran down my face—blood from my nose, I was sure.

Nervously, I looked around, trying to find the cause of the crash. It didn't take long before I figured it out. About ten feet away, a boy lay face first in the dirt, unmoving.

I tried to get a better idea of where we were, but there wasn't much to go on. We were in a very thick part of the forest with nothing but trees around to give any indication of how close to Trent's home we might be.

Hesitantly, I got to my feet. My entire body ached from the impact and my nose was indeed bleeding. I had nothing but Em's white shirt sleeve to wipe it on. I hoped she'd forgive me for ruining one of her few items of clothing.

Cautiously, I approached the boy and nudged him with my toe. "Hello? You okay?"

Nothing.

"Hello?" I called louder with a harder push. Still no response.

I got down on my hands and knees, kneeling next to him. With an enormous shove, I rolled the boy onto his back. He was heavy, not because he was fat, but because he was extremely tall and somewhat muscular. I was shocked to recognize the face from the crowd at Tuttenham Square—the boy who had smiled at me when we were supposed to be bowing. He had black, straight hair that hung past his ears. His eyebrows were thick and his skin pale. His face was handsome, though it was covered in dirt at the moment.

He started to stir as I glanced over his body, looking for any obvious injuries. He didn't seem to be bleeding anywhere, and there were no broken bones. His eyelids fluttered, revealing shockingly blue eyes underneath. His eyes met mine, a look of comprehension coming over him. He jumped to his feet with a start. I did as well.

"What are you doing here?" I demanded, my hands raised defensively. "Who are you?"

"My name is Warren. And I'm here because I wanted to talk to you," he explained, putting his hands up in surrender. "I mean you no harm."

"You followed me? How did you break me off from Trent while we were Traveling?"

As soon as I said it, I regretted it. I shouldn't have revealed Trent's name or ability to a total stranger. I tried to hide my huge mistake, but Warren seemed to catch on. A sly look crossed his features. "Trent, huh? A Traveler?" Warren lowered his hands and slunk casually against the trunk of the tree next to him.

"Yeah, so what?" I asked flippantly, crossing my arms.

147

"So Travelers can cross realms, a fact I'm sure you're aware of. You're not from around here, are you?" Warren took a step closer, a devious look in his eye. I stepped back at the same time. What an odd question to ask. I thought he'd certainly be more interested in the fact that Trent was acting of his own accord, transporting random citizens rather than carrying out Tenebris' every wish and whim.

"Of course I'm from around here. Traveling between realms is illegal without permission from King Tenebris directly," I lied, swallowing hard.

"You're an appalling liar," Warren laughed. "I saw the way you resisted Tenebris' command. You ran up to the roof and somehow helped that boy and his mother. Only someone from outside this realm could have done that."

"How do you know that?" I asked. "Never mind, it doesn't matter. You could also resist Tenebris' commands. I saw you looking around when we were supposed to be bowing. Does that mean you're from the human realm?"

"Actually, yes, that's exactly what it means," Warren flashed a smile, exposing his perfect teeth. His smile made him handsome in a dangerous way. Something about this kid screamed trouble.

"Wait, what?" I was caught off guard. I thought for sure he'd deny it.

"I am from the human realm," he repeated slowly, as if I was stupid. "Just like you."

"I never said I was," I denied again.

"Of course you are. There's no other way. Not even your friend Trent was able to resist, did you notice? Even though I'd be willing to bet he Travels more than he should." Warren looked smug.

"You know what? I don't have to stick around for this," I said, turning away from Warren. I was about to take off at a dead sprint when I felt his hand wrap around my upper arm.

"Wait," he called, all traces of teasing erased from his voice. "I have a lot to tell you. I think you can help me."

"Who says I want to?" I said, using my abilities to slip through his hold, though he was too quick to grab my other arm.

"Because I believe we have common goals," Warren said in a rush. "Look, you obviously are hiding things, as am I. I don't need to know all your secrets—or all your friend's secrets. But I think the both of you hate Tenebris just as much as I do. You hate his laws, you hate his unjust social system, and you absolutely HATE that he can completely control people's will. Seriously, just think about that ghastly scene in the square today. Nobody should be able to abuse their power like that."

I looked back at Warren briefly, betraying my interest at what he was saying. "And if you're right?"

"There's something we can do about it. You and I, we're different, but not entirely unique. There are some out there who are able to fight. It's what I do. I search all of Cyrus and the human realm for people like you. I recruit fighters. We're a small group, but a powerful one. You and your friend would be a magnificent addition to our cause."

"I don't believe you," I said through gritted teeth, trying again to pull away.

"Why wouldn't you? I have nothing to gain from lying to you. You saw with your own eyes that I'm as free from Tenebris as you are. Together, we can do this," Warren said confidently.

"How old are you? 18? You really think a couple of kids like you and I can make a difference against someone as powerful as King Tenebris?" I scoffed.

"Absolutely. Besides, you're not actually concerned about that. Otherwise, you wouldn't have rushed to save those beggars today. That was a huge risk, yet you took it anyway."

"You don't know anything about me," I countered.

"True. But I'd like to change that."

I gave Warren a look of loathing. He smiled more broadly. I rolled my eyes.

"Here's the deal," Warren said, brushing residual dirt from his black sleeve. "You take me to meet your friend Trent, I'll explain more about myself and my team, and the two of you can decide if you want to join us. No pressure, no further questions." I looked at Warren with disbelief. "Okay, well, maybe a bit of pressure, but what can you expect? I'm trying to recruit." He smirked.

"And if I don't agree?"

"Then I'll report Trent for concealing his abilities. Enforcement will be swarming his house before either of you can Travel back to the human realm."

"You don't fight fair," I spat.

"Never claimed I did."

I deliberated. My gut told me there was a lot more to Warren's motives than he was revealing. But at the same time, if what he said was true, I'd love to try and stop Tenebris. Today's incident was enough motivation on its own, but thinking about Trent's future here was an even more compelling reason to take some action. One way or the other, Trent and his parents were in grave danger. It was only a matter of time before the census would catch up to them. Their big secret would be discovered, and after watching what happened when two beggars came upon fresh fruit, I could only imagine how unfair the punishment for concealing a Traveler would be.

"Fine," I agreed reluctantly. "I'll allow you to meet Trent under a few conditions. First, we set up a neutral meeting point. I run ahead and bring Trent to the meeting point on my own. You cannot follow me to his house. Second, you must promise that if we choose not to join you after our meeting, you will leave both of us in peace, never reporting us, and never trying to make contact again." I measured Warren's reaction to my terms. His face didn't betray much emotion—he had a good poker face. Then, suddenly, he broke out into a smile so broad it was creepy.

"We have a deal," he said, extending his hand toward me.

I reached out my hand to meet his. As we shook, my fingertips brushed the leather band he was wearing on his wrist. Immediately, Warren's face faded from view, my vision turning black. Then, a new vision took its place.

I stood in a dark, cold room, lit only by a small torch that hung on a bracket on the wall. The room smelled musty. Straw was scattered across a stone floor. A small cot stood a few yards from where I was. A woman lay on the cot, breathing heavily, her golden hair pulled back into a braid, her stomach bulging; she was pregnant and currently giving birth. A man stood at her feet, helping deliver the baby. I noticed the same leather band on her wrist that Warren now wore. The woman, covered in sweat, screamed in agony as the man tried to talk her through the pain.

The scene faded and then took shape again. The same blonde woman—looking much cleaner now—stood outside a jail cell, a tiny baby wrapped in her arms. With a shock, I recognized the prisoner—it was a younger King Tenebris. This must have been during the time his brother had imprisoned him. How fitting to see him behind bars. If only it had lasted.

He looked at the woman with pure hatred as she said, "You don't care to see your own child?" She extended her reach, pushing the babe toward him, though the bars stood as a barrier between them.

"You take that thing away from here now," Tenebris sneered. "That is no child of mine. If you ever try to convince anyone it is mine, I will have you killed." He turned his back on the woman, marching over to the barred window on the other side of his small cell. The woman wept behind him.

The scene changed again. I crouched in a small, canvas tent,

152

which was lit by a small lantern on the ground. A boy—maybe six or seven years old—sat in one corner, playing with a wooden knight and horse. I recognized him immediately as a young Warren. The blonde woman sat on a few blankets on the ground, sewing a pair of pants. The leather band bobbed up and down on her thin wrist as she sewed.

There was a disturbance at the tent door. The woman jumped to her feet in alarm as the cloth door swung to the side, revealing King Tenebris.

"What are you doing here?" the woman gasped, her hand clutching her chest.

Tenebris shot a glance at the boy in the corner who looked to be on the verge of tears at the sudden appearance of a stranger. "Come outside," Tenebris' cold voice commanded. Praesidium— which now hung around his neck—glowed a fervent red at the order. "We need to talk."

The woman looked at her son worriedly. "Stay here," she said quietly. Then she ducked out of the tent to meet Tenebris.

I, too, scrambled out of the tent, finding myself in a dark patch of thick forest. The woman stood nervously, her fists clenched at her sides. Tenebris appeared to be alone, a fact that surprised me. He wore Praesidium now, which meant he was king. I thought he'd come better protected. He also came without any cape or crown like he'd worn at the square when I'd seen him. Instead, he wore simple black pants with a black long sleeve shirt.

"I warned you never to claim that child was mine," Tenebris

153

hissed. "I told you what would happen if you did."

"I didn't. I haven't," the woman gasped with desperation.

"Silence!" Tenebris commanded, Praesidium glowing red. "You liar. There have been rumors—dangerous ones—floating around these parts. Yes, people are talking. 'King Tenebris has a son,' they say. Of course I didn't have to think long before knowing the source of such rubbish. You disgusting beggar. Any child of yours would never be worthy of a crown. You're a Zero, and so is he."

The woman stood in stunned silence, tears streaming down her face.

The next few events unfolded very quickly. Tenebris withdrew a sharp dagger from a sheath at his waist. The woman's eyes grew wide. Then, the young Warren tore through the tent door and placed himself in front of his mother, his arms outstretched protectively, though his head barely reached her waistline.

Tenebris smirked at the small boy as he plunged the dagger directly into the woman's chest. It happened so quickly she didn't even have time to try and defend herself. Blood poured through the wound at an alarming rate. Her breathing became uneven as she staggered backward. Warren turned, horror on his face, to see his mother fall to the ground. Tears sprung from his eyes, spilling down his cheeks. "No, Mama! No!" he cried, tugging on her body uselessly.

"No!" I called as I watched Tenebris lunge for the boy with

his dagger. Warren dove out of reach, the blade slashing at the air violently. Warren stared at Tenebris with a look of complete loathing before he sprinted off into the forest, tears still streaming down his face.

Tenebris yelled, "I command you to stop!" at the boy's retreating figure. Praesidium glowed red, but the boy didn't hesitate in the least—the object appeared to have no influence over him. He continued on into the forest without looking back again, though his sobs could still be heard as he ran.

The scene faded. As it solidified again, I was brought back to the present, staring at the matured Warren, unsure how to process the horrible scenes I had just witnessed.

"Hello?" Warren looked at me with concern. "Are you okay?"

I wasn't sure what to think, but I was certain I did not want to reveal what I had just seen nor what I thought it all meant. "Yeah, I'm fine. Sorry," I apologized. "I just... got distracted."

"You were completely zoned out for a couple seconds there," Warren said, his eyebrows raised.

"A couple seconds?" I asked. It felt like it had been a lot longer than that. A lifetime, really.

"Yes. Are you much of a daydreamer?" Warren teased, his usual conceited expression returning to his face.

"Guess so," I laughed shakily. "I better get going and grab Trent. Where did you want to meet up?"

"Tell Trent I'll meet you both at Centaur's Gully. He'll know the spot," Warren said. "Oh, and I feel like I should probably know your name."

"Right, I'm Ava," I said. "I'll see you within a half hour at the gully." I turned and sprinted off to find Trent, trying to wrap my head around all the new information I'd been given over the course of the past ten minutes.

First, there was the fact that I'd had another vision. Trent's theory that I was a seer was seeming more likely. I suppose it did make sense with my precognition powers, though I wasn't sure why those abilities seemed to have vanished.

Second, the idea that any group of people was crazy enough to try and defeat Tenebris was overwhelming. I don't know how anyone could even hope to get close to him with the number of guards he has. Then there was the small problem of Praesidium to consider—any person who attacked him could be stopped with nothing more than words.

But what if there was someone who could resist—or even two people? How long would my immunity to Praesidium's powers last? I didn't know, though I'd assume it wouldn't be forever. The more time I spent in Cyrus, the more susceptible to Praesidium I would become as I reconnected with Cyril.

Finally, Warren himself was quite the mystery. I didn't know how much of my vision could be trusted; perhaps I wasn't seeing actual events from the past at all. Yet something about them felt truthful, and if I had seen the truth, Warren very well could be the son of Tenebris. From what I had just seen, Praesidium held no influence over him, which would make him the best person to try and fight against Tenebris.

Was I willing to put my life on the line and join him, knowing he was the best chance Cyrus had of breaking free from a tyrannous king? I already knew that answer—absolutely. For Trent alone, I had to try.

CHAPTER 15

DEADLINE

When I arrived at Trent's house, Em answered the door. "Thank goodness you're alright!" she sighed, stumbling onto the porch and wrapping me in a hug. "We were so worried about you."

"I'm fine. Completely fine. I must not have been holding on tight enough. Sorry, still learning," I grimaced with pretend embarrassment. I decided now wasn't the best time to tell Em about Warren. I'd rather tell Trent first and get his take on him. "Where's Trent?"

"He and Meraki are out looking for you. They were going to search the west forest first since that's between home and Magia."

"Oh... any idea how I can find them to tell them I'm okay?" I bit my lip.

"No need. They were going to Travel back every fifteen minutes to check in with me in case you showed up here. They should only be a couple more minutes. Come in and sit. I was just getting started on dinner." Em smiled as she gestured for me to follow.

I sat on the red couch watching the clock above the fireplace tick slowly. Two minutes passed. No movement outside the window. Five minutes. Ten minutes. Twelve minutes. Are you kidding me? I thought Em said he'd only be a few minutes. Fifteen minutes passed and he still hadn't showed up. I hoped Warren wouldn't do anything rash thinking we were going to stand him up.

Finally, after seventeen minutes, I saw Trent and Meraki walking hand-in-hand up the path to the front door, both with worried expressions. I ignored the pang of jealousy and jumped up to meet them on the front porch, slamming the door a little too loudly in my nervousness.

"Ava!" Trent called in relief. "You're okay!"

"Yeah, I'm fine," I half smiled. "Listen, Trent, something happened on the way back that I really need to talk to you about. Alone." I glanced pointedly at Meraki, trying to be polite yet firm. After all, she had just spent who knows how long looking for me, but my half hour was nearly up.

"Oh, umm, yeah, that's fine," Meraki sang, her perfect voice sounding like wind chimes, even with a broken sentence.

"No, no. You don't have to go, Mer," Trent said, looking confused. "Meraki's trustworthy, Ava. She won't say anything if she shouldn't."

I looked back and forth between the two, little stabs of jealousy poking me every time I took in Meraki's perfect face. I wasn't personally opposed to having her along. Seemed to me like the two of them were sort of a packaged deal—which made no sense if Trent had tried to kiss me last night. Anyway, I was much more concerned with Warren's reaction if an uninvited guest showed up to our little rendezvous.

"I'm sure you are, Meraki. It's nothing personal against you. It's just that this particular situation is something I really need to talk to Trent about alone. We might be able to fill you in later," I said somewhat rudely, hoping to end this conversation. We desperately needed to get going.

"Not a problem," Meraki said, her eyes tightening. She obviously wasn't happy with me excluding her. "I'll just wait inside," she said to Trent. She brushed his hand as she kissed his cheek lightly, then stomped up the front porch steps.

Trent's face was bright red. He opened his mouth to say something, but I really didn't have time for a lecture on being nice to his girlfriend. I cut him off, explaining what caused me to slip as we were Traveling. His expression changed immediately to one of concern as I told him all about Warren and the vision I'd had.

"—and he's given us half an hour to meet him at Centaur's Gully or he's threatened to report both of us. That was about 25 minutes ago, so we should really get going," I finished, bouncing up and down in my urge to get moving.

"Wow," Trent breathed. "That's a lot to take in. So you really are a seer. Super cool. And there's someone out there who is actually capable of defeating Tenebris. Also cool. And he wants our help. Not so cool. But maybe cool? I don't really know," Trent said, mostly talking to himself, trying to sort out all that had been said. He paced up and down the path in front of the house as dusk began to settle in.

"Shouldn't we get going?" I asked anxiously.

160

"Yes, definitely," Trent said, his head whipping up. He walked over to me and grabbed both my hands. We left the ground in the same instant, reappearing moments later in a rocky part of the forest. I could hear water running nearby; it laughed as it tumbled over the rocks, though it wasn't readily visible.

"Is this Centaur's Gully?" I asked, searching for Warren. I panicked. Maybe he'd gotten impatient and had already given up.

"Yeah, it is," Trent said.

"You're sure?"

"Positive."

"You're in the right place," a voice called. A kid who looked to be roughly 16 years old emerged over the top of a large boulder about 15 yards from where we stood. His skin was dark, his brown hair cut short. He wore jeans, a red t-shirt, and a gray jacket, which was pushed up to his elbows. Though the jacket distorted his figure somewhat, it was obvious he was extremely muscular. He had the body of serious weight-lifter. He smiled arrogantly as he jumped down from the boulder, landing lithely in a crouch. He stood up and walked slowly toward us.

"Who are you?" I asked.

"You mean that isn't Warren?" Trent breathed next to me.

"No," I whispered back.

"No need to panic," the boy said, raising his hands in a gesture of surrender. "Warren's around here somewhere. Name's Jameson, by the way. I'm Warren's right hand man," the boy nodded. "You must be Ava and Trent."

161

"Ava," a new voice called. Warren appeared on top of the same boulder Jameson had just been standing on. He, too, jumped down, coming toward us. "I was beginning to worry you wouldn't show. Glad you decided to after all."

"Hi, I'm Trent." Trent extended his hand out to Warren in greeting. "We're super pumped you've asked us to join you. When do we begin?"

A look of shock crossed Warren's face, though I'm sure it was nothing compared to the surprise on my own. How could Trent agree without any real discussion?

Warren's face lit up, a huge smile stretching his cheeks. "Excellent. We start now, I suppose."

"Uh, hold on a minute," I interrupted. "Shouldn't we give this some thought?" This seemed very unlike Trent, who was uptight every time I crossed a line. He'd made it clear he intended to keep a low profile in his life here. Joining a rebel group intent on taking down the king hardly fit that category.

"What's there to think about, Ava? It's sort of do or die for me right now. If there's a chance we can make a difference—a real difference—I think we should take it," Trent said, his gorgeous eyes boring into mine.

"Um, well, okay then." I turned to Warren, slightly dazed. I'd already made my decision, I simply never dreamed Trent would agree so easily. "I guess we're in."

CHAPTER 16
THE MINERS

We trudged through the forest for what felt like an hour. In reality, it was probably about a half hour, but I tended to get impatient with a normal pace these days. Between Traveling with Trent and my ability to run at high speeds, moving at a walk was positively mundane. The hike had been almost entirely uphill and quite strenuous. I may be able to run without getting tired, but when I wasn't using my abilities, it was clear I was out of shape.

Before we started this endless trek, Trent had Traveled back home to let Meraki and his mother know we would be gone for a while, though he kept the fact that we were going to a secret hideout for a rebel group to himself. When he'd returned to the gully, it was clear the conversation hadn't gone over well with Meraki. I probably should feel bad about causing discord in their relationship, but it actually brought a sense of satisfaction. I was a horrible friend.

"Are we there yet?" I asked, feeling like a five year old child on her first road trip.

"Just a few more minutes," Jameson answered in his relaxed tone. I got the feeling there wasn't much that would bother Jameson. He was very go-with-the-flow.

"You said that a few minutes ago," I grumbled.

"If you'd stop concentrating on it, the time would probably go faster." Trent laughed at my impatience.

The further we walked, the thinner the trees became and the more rocky the path. We approached a very large boulder on the trail, which was pressed up against the side of the mountain. Warren and Jameson stopped at the boulder's front.

"Home again, home again, jiggity-jig!" Jameson exclaimed.

"This is it? Your headquarters are out here? Seems a little exposed, don't you think?" I asked incredulously.

Warren rolled his eyes. "Of course not *right* here. This is just the entrance." He stated it as if that fact should be obvious. I was confused. There was nothing here but the large boulder. How could this be an entrance to anything? I'd been expecting an abandoned cabin or a discreet cave or something of that sort.

Jameson ducked down, wedging himself in the small space between the side of the mountain and the boulder, his broad shoulders filling the space entirely. He crept forward until I lost sight of him. Warren followed closely behind until he, too, fell out of sight.

"Uh, are you as confused as I am?" I asked Trent.

"Yep, pretty much. You think this is some sort of trap?" he asked, taking a step closer to the narrow opening where Jameson and Warren had just disappeared.

"It could be."

Trent stood, deliberating for a moment. "Well, only one way to find out. Stay close to me and if something goes wrong, we'll

Travel back home, okay?"

"Got it," I agreed.

I followed directly behind Trent as he crawled into the crack. I scrunched myself between the rocks, immediately feeling claustrophobic. After a few paces on our hands and knees, the direction of the crevice began to curve to the left as the last bit of light was extinguished. Odd, I expected our path to go straight through to the other side of the massive boulder. It was as if we were crawling into the side of the mountain itself.

Gradually, the crevice began to widen and lengthen until we could crouch and then fully stand. Shortly after, a faint glow became visible ahead. We followed it forward until we found ourselves in a large space entirely surrounded by rock, yet well lit by several lights which hung on the rock walls. There, Warren, Jameson, and two teenage girls waited for us.

"So, that was... unexpected," I began. "What is this place?"

"Awesome, isn't it?" the petite girl with blonde hair gushed, bouncing on her toes. "You guys are really brave. It took a solid ten minutes before Warren could convince me to squeeze through that pathetic crack. I thought it was some lame prank on the new kid. I'm Elsie, by the way."

I had to fight to keep a smile off my face. Was this girl for real? She was unusually bubbly considering the dank surroundings. "Nice to meet you, Elsie. I'm Ava and this is Trent."

"And I'm Katherine," the brunette standing next to Elsie said. She was taller than Elsie, but still had a very petite frame. Her brown hair was board straight compared to Elsie's wavy curls.

"So, is this everybody? You're a group of four?" Trent asked.

"There are eight of us, actually," Warren said, evidently proud of his numbers. "Trevor and Damion are out on a watch in Magia, and Amos and Teresa aren't thrilled with newcomers. It will likely take a bit before they warm up to you. Try not to take it personally."

"Eight, wow, that's impressive. But still not enough to take on an entire government on your own. You do realize that, right?" I asked critically.

Warren smirked. "You're absolutely right. Fortunately, that's not precisely our plan. What do you say we give you the grand tour?"

"So there's more to this place?" I asked, surprised. Elsie giggled and Katherine shook her head, smiling.

"A bit more, yeah," Jameson laughed, clapping Trent on the shoulder as he passed into a tunnel on the opposite side of the crevice from where we stood.

"Alright then, lead the way," Trent said.

"This room we're in is the main entrance," Warren explained before heading down the tunnel Jameson had ducked under. We followed, walking for a short distance before the rock opened up into another large area that contained a long wooden table. On the adjacent wall, a stove sat next to a small table with a sink on the other side. It was a kitchen. A simple one but functioning nonetheless. "And this is the kitchen, obviously."

My mouth hung open wide. "What in the world? This doesn't make any sense. We are *inside* a mountain, are we not?"

Elsie giggled and Warren shrugged nonchalantly. "Yes, we are inside a mountain. Trevor—one of the guys out in Magia—is an earthshifter. He created these tunnels for us. Damion, who is out with him, can manipulate energy. He's the reason we have light fixtures and a stove in here without any power source. And yours truly," Warren gestured to himself, "can control water sources. I re-routed a nearby stream to run a small branch this direction, which fills two wells underneath us. You'll notice any sinks around here are pump-only. At least for all of you."

"That's incredible," Trent breathed next to me.

"Glad you're impressed," Warren said dryly. "Let's carry on. I don't have all the time in the world."

Warren walked toward another small tunnel to the right. The tunnel was very short and branched off into a spacious room with several couches, sitting chairs, and barstools. There was a card table against one wall and a pool table on the other. Light fixtures hung low from the ceiling, creating a cozy feel to the room.

"Pool exists in Cyrus?" I asked, surprised.

"There are a lot of similar games across the realms. This one happens to be a Cyrus original, though," Trent explained.

"Just don't challenge Warren to a game," Jameson bent sideways to whisper in my ear. "He's a pool shark." He straightened up and winked at me.

"This is the game room. We use it for pretty much all

167

gatherings. You're welcome to use anything you'd like for your entertainment when you are not on assignment," Warren explained.

"How did you get a pool table into these caves?" I asked.

"In addition to being able to control water, I have the ability to shrink and enlarge inanimate objects. I simply shrunk down all the furnishings you see in here and carried them in," Warren said.

"You can *only* affect inanimate objects, right? Not people?" Trent asked nervously.

"Almost right. I can shrink or enlarge myself, but nobody else."

"That's awesome," I said.

Warren ignored the compliment and ducked out into the hall. We crossed back through the kitchen to another tunnel on the opposite side. This tunnel was long and large with a few smaller tunnels that stemmed off of it. Warren ignored the branches, continuing straight forward to a large arch which stood at the end of the path. We passed underneath the arch, then the tunnel curved immediately to the left.

Again, my mouth hung open in shock at the sight before me. We entered the largest room yet, by far. It was also the brightest and tallest room we'd seen. It reminded me somewhat of the gym at my high school, though it was drastically different in many ways. For one, the walls and floors were made of rock. The far end of the room had full length mirrors that stretched across its face. In front of the mirrors were several mats. A punching bag

168

and boxing gloves sat nearby. There were a few weight lifting machines along the right wall and a basketball hoop was attached to the left wall.

"There's basketball in Cyrus too?" I asked.

"Actually, no. Jameson was a big fan back in the human realm and insisted on bringing a hoop back here to play," Warren explained.

"You're from the human realm too?" I turned to Jameson, surprised.

This time Katherine was the one to laugh. "You haven't told her?" She looked at Warren who simply shrugged. "We're all from the human realm."

"How did you get here?" Trent asked, his tone as surprised as I felt. "When did you get here? Is one of you a Traveler?"

Everyone looked uncomfortable at the question. Warren let out a long breath before he answered. "It is true. We are all from the human realm. Most of the group are orphans, like me. The best we can figure, we were left there by our parents because they didn't want us growing up here, with a tyrannous government. Some of the group's parents came with them to the human realm. They chose to leave their parents behind and return here to fight.

"When I was fifteen, I was found by a Traveler named Fox Springs. He was a rogue Traveler, much like you, Trent," Warren nodded in Trent's direction. "He spent a lot of time in the human realm, trying to maintain his resistance to Praesidium. After we found each other, we made it our mission to find others like us and

169

form a group. Over the course of three years, I managed to put together this motley bunch," Warren chuckled, "knowing that those who were raised in the human realm have the best chance of resisting Praesidium's powers."

I kept quiet, not sure what to make of Warren's story. The vision I'd seen—if it was real—contradicted his account. He wasn't born or raised as an orphan in the human realm. He was from here—he was Tenebris' own flesh and blood. I flashed a glance at Trent who also seemed skeptical of Warren's words.

"What happened to your friend Fox Springs then?" Trent asked.

Warren sighed. "About a year ago, he was caught by one of Tenebris' guards on his return from the human realm. They killed him." He hung his head low.

My breath caught in my chest. What if that happened to Trent?

"He was a good man, Fox," Jameson said. "It's a shame you'll never know him."

"I'm sorry," I whispered.

"It's a risk we all take as a part of the Miners," Jameson explained.

"The Miners?" Trent asked.

Warren rolled his eyes. "We are not the Miners, Jameson, for the thousandth time! We don't have a name. We're not anything."

"'Course we are!" Jameson slugged Warren's shoulder playfully. "We live in tunnels in the mountain and our life's purpose is to harvest a jewel—a ruby, to be exact. What better

170

name is there?"

"I like it!" Elsie chimed in. "I always have. The Miners—it sounds kind of dangerous." She swung her arms in mock karate moves until she knocked a ball off a nearby rack. The ball flung forward, clipping Warren on the side of the head. "Oops, my bad," Elsie danced forward, picking up the ball at Warren's feet.

"O-o-o-kay, that's enough of the tour for me," Warren said, rubbing the spot on his head where he was hit. "Elsie and Katherine can show you to your room, Ava, and Jameson will take you to yours, Trent. We'll convene at 7:00 tomorrow morning in the game room for a debriefing with the whole group. Make sure you let the others know."

Chapter 17

Rebels

My room at headquarters was extremely simple, but still amazing considering that I was living inside a mountain. It contained a mattress with no bed frame and a miniscule set of plastic drawers; I kept the few clothes I'd brought along in there. A wooden chair sat in one corner, and the place was lit by a light on the wall that turned on whenever I entered and off when I left. I wasn't sure how Damion's powers worked, exactly, but they seemed pretty awesome.

I wondered how many homes actually had electricity in Cyrus—Trent's sure didn't. But all the shops in Magia appeared to be well lit by the types of light fixtures I was used to in the human realm. Tenebris must have people like Damion in his control who help light the major city areas.

I learned that Elsie and Katherine are sisters. Both seemed like they would be good friends to me. I liked Elsie, but Katherine was probably my favorite of the two—she was reserved yet bold when she needed to be. Elsie, on the other hand, was a ball of enthusiastic energy but reluctant to engage in conflict.

I'd spent the remainder of my first night as a Miner with the two of them. They'd showed me to the small yet intriguing collection of books they had at headquarters, and after a few card games and an abysmal game of pool, I had retreated to my room to read. I was eager to learn as much as I could about Cyrus' history.

I trudged onward in the dull book I held in my hands. Though I enjoyed learning, history had never been my strong point, and that was especially true when it came to war. As far as I could tell, the first several thousand years of recorded Cyrun history was nothing but conflict after conflict. Small kingdoms battled for control of each other's lands, using their most powerful people's abilities as weapons.

My mind continually wandered to a place I wished it wouldn't—Trent and Meraki. During our game of pool, Jameson had informed me that Trent left the caves shortly after he'd been shown to his room. Apparently, after a long debate, Trent had convinced Warren to let him bring Meraki into the group. Trent had stopped by to tell me he was going back home to spend the night there. He hadn't made any mention of Meraki, but Jameson insisted that he'd practically begged Warren to allow him to bring her back with him tomorrow. My stomach twisted with jealousy. The last thing I wanted was to have Meraki around this place all the time.

After another fifteen minutes of morbid warmongering, I decided to call the studying quits for the night and rolled over in bed, pulling the thin blanket Elsie had given me over my head.

The next morning came early. I'd set an alarm on my watch to make sure I wouldn't miss the meeting. As soon as it beeped, I jumped out of bed, hurriedly changed my clothes to a simple t-shirt and jeans, and made my way down the unfamiliar corridors to the game room.

As I entered the room, I was met by the sight of Trent and Meraki cuddled up in one of the small loveseats, kissing. Mortified, I turned to leave the room unnoticed. In my haste, I caught the lamp by the door with my toe and sent it clattering to the ground.

"Ava, I uh, didn't see you there," Trent said, standing up quickly, his face slightly red, though not possibly as red as mine. It felt like my face would melt with the heat of my embarrassment. I prayed a hole in the floor would open up and swallow me.

Awkwardly, I scrambled for the lamp on the ground and stood it back up, avoiding both Trent's and Meraki's eyes. "I forgot to… grab some breakfast. Better go—" I didn't bother to finish the thought and dove into the hallway, out of sight. I rushed into the kitchen, trying to dispel the awful image of Meraki wrapped around Trent from my mind. What were those two idiots thinking anyway? Making out in a room where a meeting is about to happen?

I shuddered as I entered the kitchen and was greeted by a chipper laugh. "Cave life not all you imagined?" Elsie's bubbly voice asked.

"Um, no, it's not that," I said, catching sight of her next to the

174

stove. Whatever she was making smelled delicious. I walked over to her side. She examined my face more closely.

"Oh, I see. It's Trent—you like him, don't you?" She smiled, wiggling her eyebrows suggestively.

"No, definitely not," I said, my mouth turning down at the memory of the scene I'd just witnessed.

"He is very good looking, isn't he?" Elsie said dreamily. "I guess you saw him and Meraki sucking face in the other room? Yeah, I saw it too. Decided it was best to get a head start on breakfast and wait for that to calm down." She rolled her eyes.

"No kidding," I snorted. "So what are you making?" I asked, obviously changing the subject.

"Oatmeal—nothing fancy. Just wait for dinner though. That's going to be delish!"

"Do we eat together around here?"

"Yes and no. I'm sure Warren will cover all of that in the meeting today. For now, dish yourself up a bowl. I made enough for you, guessing you're not much of a cook." Elsie looked at me through narrowed eyes, as if this fact personally offended her.

I laughed. "You got that right." I reached for the spoon and filled the paper bowl Elsie handed to me.

Either my dad was really bad at making oatmeal or Elsie had some powers related to cooking because this was twenty times better than any oatmeal I'd ever had. "This is amazing, Elsie."

She shrugged. "Like I said, nothing special. But thanks. Eat fast, the meeting is going to be starting. Hopefully somebody else has interrupted the make out sesh by now."

Someone did—me—knocking over a dang lamp. I wasn't about to admit that to Elsie though. I gave a breathy laugh, "Yeah, hopefully," and then followed her back into the game room.

The room was a mixture of familiar and unfamiliar faces. Trent and Meraki sat together on the short couch. I tried not to gag and avoided their eyes. Warren leaned casually against a stool at what I assumed was the front of the room since everyone seemed to be facing him. Jameson sat to his right in an armchair. Katherine sat on the long couch next to a red haired girl whose build was sturdy. It was obvious she was well muscled and had a face I didn't want to cross. On her other side sat a scrawny boy with mousy black hair. On the blue couch pushed up against the wall, a friendly looking boy with brown, short hair sat with his arms crossed. He gave a brief smile as I glanced his way. On the opposite side of the couch from him was a blonde haired, blue eyed boy who looked pleasant but bored by the fact that he had to be here.

"Hurry, let's grab a seat," Elsie whispered, cowering slightly at the glare Warren gave. She pulled me over to the blue couch with the two boys and plopped us down between them. Both scooted to the edges to try and make room for us, but it was still a tight fit.

"I thought I said 7:00 sharp," Warren said, looking at me intently.

I glanced down at my wristwatch. It was 7:02. "Sheesh,

176

lighten up. We're only two minutes late," I replied. There were a few uncomfortable chuckles around the room. From the look on Warren's face, I gathered he wasn't accustomed to being talked to that way. Jameson gave me a thumbs up behind Warren's back.

Apparently, Warren thought better of replying and began speaking to the group.

"Hi, I'm Trevor," the brown-haired boy sitting next to me whispered. He extended a hand to me.

"I'm Ava." I took his hand. "Why are we whispering?"

"Warren doesn't do too well with interruptions. Better listen now, but we should introduce ourselves better later," Trevor winked at me. My face grew hot. I chanced a glance at Trent who was watching us. His lips tightened into a straight line. I snapped my eyes back to Warren, giving him my attention.

"—had three new recruits added to our ranks yesterday," Warren stated authoritatively. I sensed he very much enjoyed his leadership position. "They are Ava, Trent, and Meraki," Warren motioned to the three of us in turn. "Each is a great asset to our team, and I expect you to show them the same respect you give all of us." Warren seemed to look at the red haired girl in particular.

"As such, I have needed to make adjustments to our training, eating, and reconnaissance schedules. Those schedules will be posted after this meeting is adjourned. For our new recruits, you are expected to be wherever the schedule dictates on time each and every day. If you are assigned to train, you meet in the practice room. If you're sent on a recon mission, you'll meet your partner or group at the main entrance before you depart. And if you are on kitchen duty, you are responsible for making dinner as well as kitchen clean-up for the day. Breakfast and lunch are on your own. Dinner is to be ready at 7:00 pm, but you can come eat whenever you'd like.

"Also, for those who haven't already heard, Trent here is a Traveler. Each person is to arrange a time with him to Travel to the human realm at least once a week to maintain your resistance to Praesidium. Trent, because this will likely keep you rather busy, you have slightly fewer reconnaissance assignments than the rest of us. Any questions?" Warren looked at us with an expression that made it obvious he didn't actually want us to ask questions. I raised my hand anyway.

"Yes, Ava," Warren exhaled with frustration.

"I still have places I need to be in the human realm. Like school. Otherwise, they're going to call my dad and he's going to completely flip out. Have you left time in the schedule for that?"

"Yes, your schedule is clear every weekday for you to maintain your presence there," Warren breathed as he pinched the bridge of his nose.

"I also have to help my parents in their shop every day," Meraki's perfect voice chimed in. "Will that be an issue?"

"Oh, uh, I didn't realize that was the case." Warren's face was suddenly the warmest I'd seen it yet. He looked at Meraki with total fascination, his mouth gaping open. I glanced around the room. All of the guys were watching her with dazed expressions.

She must be using her abilities. I rolled my eyes.

"I'll rework the schedule if you can give me the times you need to be available to help your parents," Warren said.

Meraki flashed her eyes flirtatiously at him. "Thanks. That is very kind of you."

"No problem," Warren chuckled, straightening his shirt nervously.

I caught Elsie's eye. She looked at me with raised eyebrows. I nodded knowingly then cleared my throat loudly, hoping to break the spell every male in the room seemed to be under.

Warren jumped slightly. "Right, well, umm, next item of business then." He paced at the front of the room for a moment. "I suppose we should explain to our newbies exactly what we're after. As the best fighter in the group, Jameson takes point on training schedules and our planned attacks. Fill them in, Jameson?"

"Sure thing," Jameson said energetically as he stood from his chair and joined Warren up front. "As Ava pointed out yesterday, we'd be crazy to think we'd be able to successfully take on Tenebris and his guys. I mean seriously, nobody wants a repeat of the French Revolution, right? Didn't end so well for anybody."

"Jameson's sort of a history nerd. Human history, I mean," Trevor whispered through the side of his mouth. "Though I think he makes a lot of it up. He once told me about a German brigade that won a war armed with nothing but blow horns."

"I think he stole that one from the bible," I whispered. Trevor

179

and I laughed quietly together. Trent looked over at the two of us again, his eyes narrowing slightly.

"So our plan," Jameson continued at the front of the room, "is not to attack the palace or the guards surrounding it—that would be a suicide mission. Instead, we need to find a way to draw the king to us at which point we go for Praesidium. As soon as we steal the necklace, Tenebris will no longer have control over the people of Cyrus and bada-bing! We let the chips fall where they may once the people have their own say."

I raised my hand.

"Ava, m'lady?" Jameson bowed.

"Umm... I know I'm the new kid and all, but that plan sounded just a smidge too simplistic. I mean, if it was really that easy, wouldn't someone have done this already? Wouldn't *you all* have done this already?" I gestured to the room.

"Ten points for Gryffin-puff!" Jameson shouted.

"What?" Meraki asked.

"It's a human thing," Trent answered.

"You're absolutely right, dear Ava, for two reasons," Jameson explained, plopping down on Warren's stool. Warren glared at him and Jameson jumped to his feet again. "First, the king very, very rarely leaves his palace. The little display you saw in Magia yesterday was unique, to say the least. That has been one of our biggest challenges. We need to find something to draw him out, or at least a better way to guess where he'll be and when. Second, Praesidium appears to be enchanted. No power—magic or otherwise—can remove the object from Tenebris' neck. Not telekinesis, not the ability to make objects disappear, and you certainly couldn't physically remove it from him. We've actually tried a couple of times with our various abilities and nobody has been able to come close to removing Praesidium."

"So isn't this whole Miners group rather pointless?" Trent asked the obvious. "If Praesidium can't be removed, why are we trying? What is it you're all doing here every day? Seems like a massive waste of time."

"There are exceptions to every magical law and weaknesses in every magical defense," Warren said, straightening up from his casual stance and walking forward. "We observe to track movement of the guards as well as the king. We also observe to find the weakness; there is something out there that will allow us to seize Praesidium. We just don't know what that is yet. We train so that we're ready for when that day comes. Though we intend to draw the king away from the palace when we attack, we know he will not be alone. He is never left alone. We must be prepared to fight. This is the work of the Miners. You're either in or you're out."

"Hold up, hold up, hold up," Jameson said, cocking his head to the side and raising his right hand. "Did you just call us 'the Miners'?" An enormous smile spread across his face.

Warren's face darkened with embarrassment at the slip. "Okay, fine, yeah, your stupid nickname slipped out. It doesn't mean anything."

Jameson punched Warren's bicep. "You just called us the Miners! It's official, y'all. From this day forward, we are," he hopped onto the barstool and placed his hands on his hips majestically, "the Miners!"

The room erupted in laughs. "It's true, man," the blonde boy next to Elsie smiled at Warren. "You called us the Miners. There's no way you'll reign in Jameson now. Might as well embrace it."

"Okay, okay, can everyone please calm down and be serious for a minute? Geez, you have the attention span of five year olds," Warren shook his head. "This is serious. Trent, Ava, and Meraki, if you don't agree with our methods and what we do here, now is the time to walk. There's no going back later."

For the first time today, I looked directly at Trent who met my eyes. I'd shared my vision with him. We both knew there was more to the story than Warren was sharing. We also now knew that targeting Praesidium was going to be a lot harder than we envisioned. Regardless, would I be able to walk away from all of this? It would mean Trent was doomed to life as a Zero—homeless and hungry. Even if the way ahead wasn't clear, I wanted to stay and work it out. There had to be a way to bring down Tenebris.

"I'm in," I said, standing up.

Trent also stood. "Same here. I think you're all crazy, but I guess I am too."

Meraki didn't stand, but said, "I'm with Trent."

Yeah. Way to state the obvious.

Warren took our answers as good enough. "Excellent. The

182

new schedule is already out on the kitchen table. Look it over and get to work!"

CHAPTER 18

NERVOUS WOULD BE AN UNDERSTATEMENT

There was something different about a Cyrun sunrise. I couldn't quite put my finger on it, but the colors seemed even more vibrant than they had in the human realm, as if they glimmered with the magic of this world. The sight was breathtaking, though I didn't need any help in that department today. It seemed like no matter what I did to try and calm myself, my breaths came in hurried gasps, my heart thumping.

"I thought I might find you out here," Trent laughed as he emerged from behind a tree trunk in the thick woods. "What's with you and this tree?" He skipped over to where I sat on one of the lower branches and looked up at me with those hypnotic eyes.

I was surprised he'd noticed. I'd run to this tree in the forest near the top of our mountain anytime I needed a break from the bustle of the caves. Over the past three weeks of being a Miner, I'd come here maybe five or six times, but I didn't think anybody knew where I was going.

"What do you mean? Have you been following me again? I thought your stalker days were behind you."

Trent shrugged. "I saw you head out of the caves a couple weeks ago and was worried about you. I followed you the best that I could until I found you up here. You're sure fast, though—it took a while before I found you. You looked deep in thought, so I decided not to bother you."

"And why's today any different?" I asked, a touch of annoyance in my voice. I knew it wasn't deserved—I was testy today and it had nothing to do with Trent.

Trent ignored my bothered tone and jumped for the branch I sat on. He hauled himself up in one easy pull. I tried to hide the fact that I was staring at his biceps, but I think I lingered a second too long. He smirked knowingly as he sat next to me on the thick branch. I averted my eyes.

"Today's different because I know what's bothering you, and I want to try and help. Everything is going to be fine, you know. I think you'll be relieved to finally have these secrets out in the open between you and your dad. The conversation might be a bit rocky, but it'll work out, you'll see," he said, leaning in to nudge my shoulder. I pushed back the butterflies that accompanied his casual touch.

"Easy for you to say," I mumbled. Today was going to be Dad's first day back from his trip. I was terrified to tell him that I not only knew the truth about Cyrus, but that I'd been practically living here for the past three weeks, with the exception of the seven hours a day that were necessary for attending school. I'd likely caused irreparable damage to my friendship with Lana by always being gone, and I'd quit the track team. But most of all, I was worried about his reaction as I accused him of lying to me for all these years. And I was scared to hear his reasoning for it. No

185

matter how I spun it, today was bound to be awkward and life-altering. I enjoyed my relationship with my dad. I didn't want it to change.

"Well, you still have a little time before your dad gets back," Trent said. "And you are due for a training session in about fifteen minutes. Warren will freak out if you miss another one."

That was true—Warren was a bit anal about everyone keeping to the schedule. I'd already missed a session last Thursday because I'd had to stay after school to redo a calculus assignment.

"Here, I brought you a sticky bun," Trent said, fishing in his pocket as he pulled out a roll inside a plastic baggy. "Elsie made them this morning."

"You brought me a sticky bun in your pocket?" I laughed, shaking my head.

Trent laughed too, his hazel eyes crinkling with his handsome smile. "What's wrong with that?"

"I dunno. Just a little weird." I took the pastry from Trent gratefully. Elsie's cooking was the best. Warren didn't consider her magical ability to speak with animals or her telekinesis to be all that useful to our cause, but she was definitely worth keeping around for none other reason than her phenomenal cooking skills. "Thanks for this."

"You're welcome," Trent said, settling in so that his arm touched mine. My heart pounded in my chest. Unfortunately, my attraction to Trent had only grown stronger over the past three weeks, though he hadn't made any indication he felt the same since the day he tried to kiss me.

We sat in silence as I ate and watched the sun continue its rise.

"It's so beautiful out here. I can see why you chose this tree. It gives a good vantage point of the valley."

I simply smiled in response. Trent extended his hand, reaching for the empty plastic bag I held in mine. "Here, I can take that."

The charm on the necklace he wore grazed my bare shoulder as he leaned forward. Suddenly, I was thrown into a vision of Trent's past—a sensation I was beginning to grow accustomed to.

I stood on a cobblestone street where I could see a slightly younger Trent walking toward me in the distance. He was leaving a small town center and heading out into a rural area. He wore tattered jeans, a faded red t-shirt, and held two books in his hands. Behind him, a group of three boys whispered to each other and snickered.

"Hey, Cavanaugh!" a thick boy from the group called out. He wore a tan shirt and black pants. "How's life at the Zero farm?"

Trent's eyes flashed but he otherwise ignored the comment and continued his walk. The group of boys sped up until they were directly behind Trent.

"Cavanaugh," the thick boy growled, grabbing Trent by the shoulder as he spun him around. "I don't like being ignored by a Zero. You should show the proper respect to your superiors." The other two boys who were smaller than their ring leader laughed appreciatively. One had light hair that was almost white, the other a dull brown.

187

"Just shut up, Parker," Trent said as he ripped his shoulder free from Parker's grasp.

"Shut up? Oooo," the boy named Parker taunted. "Mommy didn't teach you to play very nice, did she? Is this a gift from your precious mommy, Cavanaugh?" He ripped the leather string from Trent's neck that contained the small charm which had cued the memory. Trent jerked back, the unexpected pull choking him until the string snapped.

"Give that back!" Trent growled, reaching for the necklace. Parker swiftly moved it out of the way and punched Trent in the gut. Stupidly, I lunged for the thick boy, eager to take down the bully, but I passed right through him as if I were a ghost. Meanwhile, Trent stood hunched over, catching his breath. The three cronies laughed at his pain.

"That'll teach you to mess with Twos. You're nothing, Cavanaugh—a Zero. I don't know why your parents keep throwing away good money on your education when you're completely worthless. It's obvious they don't have the money to spare. Just look at those rags you're wearing."

Trent's eyes flickered with anger as he lunged for the necklace again. This time, the white haired boy punched Trent in the face as he moved forward. The impact sent Trent backwards, reeling in pain. I ran to his side, desperate to see that he was okay. Blood poured from Trent's nose. Before he had time to recover, the boy with brown hair kicked Trent in the side, sending him falling to the ground. He aimed another three kicks at Trent's gut as he lay

188

curled up on the ground.

"Oh come on now, boys," Parker's greasy voice taunted. "We don't want to kill the poor fella. School won't even be worth going to if we don't have this guy around. What would we do with all our free time?" Parker crouched down beside Trent who was gasping for air. "Here's your precious charm necklace." He dropped the charm on Trent's bloodied face. "We'll see you tomorrow, Zero." Parker shoved Trent's face into the ground as he stood up. He laughed as he and his two friends walked back toward the city.

Frantically, I crouched down beside Trent, desperate to help him as the scene faded away, returning me to my spot on the tree.

"Ava?" Trent's voice asked with a trace of panic. "Are you okay? Are you *seeing* something?"

Relief washed over me as I took in Trent's whole, undamaged face, though the anger at what I had just witnessed burned inside me with ferocity. "Who the heck is Parker?" I spat the question.

Trent's face paled. "Parker? How do you know about Parker? What did you see?"

"I saw some thug bullying you with his two wimpy friends, that's what."

Trent laughed uncomfortably. "Ava, as much as I appreciate your indignation on my behalf, what those jerks did to me isn't unusual. It's class discrimination at its finest. People who are a higher social standing can basically do whatever they want to Zeros. Everyone I went to school with thought I was powerless, so even though I was technically a Two, I was treated like a Zero. That's just how it's always been. Well, until Meraki came along, at least. After I started dating her, most of them left me alone. Perks of being with the girl everyone else wanted, I guess." Trent rolled his eyes.

Though I hated myself for it, I felt the slightest softening toward Meraki at this information. I didn't like her, and I certainly didn't like her with Trent, but if it made life easier for him, I'd be the first person in line to congratulate them at their wedding.

"That's horrible. Is it really like that for Zeros everywhere?"

"Pretty much, yeah."

I thought about that for a moment, letting the anger feed my desire for being a part of the Miners. "Well, there's only one thing to do about that then, isn't there? Let's get to the practice room."

My practice group today consisted of Katherine, Teresa, Trent, Trevor, and Meraki. In other words, it was bound to suck. Katherine and Teresa were two of the most difficult challenges for me. Katherine had the very unique ability of slowing down time for everyone besides herself. Essentially, it allowed her to be faster than I was, so I didn't have that advantage in any of our fights. And Teresa was just plain frightening. Her red hair was a serendipitous reflection of her greatest ability—producing and controlling fire. She could hurl large balls of fire at me that were immune to my telekinesis. Instead, I could outrun them or use my shield to block them.

With quite a bit of practice, we had discovered that I could indeed produce a shield. I was so grateful I'd unknowingly discovered it that day to protect the mother and son from Tenebris' terrible whipping. It had taken nearly a week and a half of practice before I could produce a shield that was anywhere close to being as reliable as my shields had been that day. I was fairly certain defending others when there was a real need is what drew out the best results from me, but it was also the most difficult to master. At this point, I could somewhat reliably produce a shield that would protect myself, but anytime I tried to produce one to cover someone else, it would only last a second or two before snapping back to me.

I stood on one of the mats and began to stretch with the group. Trent stood next to Meraki, of course, but his behavior was odd. In fact, it had been since the day I'd walked in on them making out. He was still friendly to her, but there was a formality to it, as if they'd taken several steps back in their relationship and were still in the beginning stages that were full of tentativeness. He also maintained a careful no-contact barrier between them. I hadn't even seen them hold hands lately. It was clear that Meraki blamed me for the change as she mostly avoided talking to me and would shoot daggers at me with her eyes any time she looked my direction.

"Alright," Katherine said. "Jameson designated me as the

191

training session leader today, so I'll be making the assignments. Ava, you are to begin working on your shield with Teresa." I groaned inwardly. Teresa was sure to be extra brutal today. Last time I'd worked with her, my shield had improved dramatically— a fact that caused her a great deal of annoyance. "Trevor and I will be working on strength training and Trent and Meraki will work on hand-to-hand combat. We'll switch things up in half an hour."

I didn't miss the fact that Katherine had paired herself with Trevor. Though I'd been keeping it quiet, I happened to know Katherine and Trevor were together. Two weeks ago, when Katherine handed me her earrings before we began training, I saw a vision of the two of them kissing goodnight in front of Katherine's bedroom door. They never gave any indication to the rest of the group that they were a couple. Not even Elsie seemed to know when I casually asked if her sister was seeing anyone. I figured it wasn't my place to go blabbing about it when I'd found out by completely involuntary means.

"You gonna stand there all day?" Teresa's uncharacteristically feminine voice interrupted my thoughts.

"No, sorry, let's get going." I walked over to the empty space at the back of the training room that was free of equipment—the power area, as we called it. Whenever any of us used our abilities, things tended to get messy. It was best to operate in a relatively open space. I stood with my back to the long mirrors, facing Teresa. Her large, muscular body was intimidating.

"Ready?" she growled.

"You get a lot of satisfaction out of throwing fire at my head, don't you?" I asked. Teresa smirked but didn't answer. "Yes, I'm ready," I sighed, trying to concentrate on my shield. By far, it was the most difficult ability for me to use in Cyrus. I hadn't ever come close to being able to produce a shield in the human realm any time I'd tried.

A ball of fire hovered over Teresa's extended palm. She watched me, trying to decipher a weak area to attack. I don't know why she bothered—everywhere felt incredibly vulnerable. Her palm flicked forward, sending the ball of fire toward my right thigh. I swiped my hand in front of my leg. My blue, rippling shield appeared just in time to catch the ball of fire, which disintegrated as soon as it connected with the shield.

Teresa's face fell in disappointment which quickly turned to anger. She produced another ball of fire and hurled it toward me without hesitation. The ball flew toward my arm, but I blocked it with ease. She exhaled heavily and threw another, then another, then another. We danced around each other, spinning in a wide circle, her attacks coming more rapidly and viciously, one after the other, but I continued to successfully block her attempts. She let out a cry of exasperation and then hurled the largest, most ferocious ball yet. It spun toward me, the flames a wild mix of orange and blue. I spread both palms in front of me, exerting a tremendous amount of effort, but the flames disappeared before they ever connected with my shield.

Teresa fell to her knees, panting. I, too, doubled over and tried to steady my breathing. "What did you do that for?" I managed to squeak out. "My shield was ready. I could have handled that."

Teresa's eyes flashed. "I wasn't sure. I didn't want to hurt you. Not permanently, at least." She gave a half smile. I was stunned. This was the only time Teresa had ever shown a shred of mercy for me in training.

"Oh, thanks, I guess." I felt uncomfortable at her sudden gesture of goodwill. "Those flames were impressive."

Applause from the other end of the practice room drew my attention. Warren walked toward us in his usual black t-shirt and jeans, clapping slowly. "Very impressive, Ava and Teresa. You two are quite the force to be reckoned with. You're going to be invaluable when we make our attack." His grin was wide, his eyes playful. "What do you say we up the stakes a little?" He walked over to another training area where a dummy stood with several knives in its chest. He yanked them out, gathering them in his hand.

"Are you insane?" Trent yelled, running over to where we stood. "Put them back, you idiot. You have no way of controlling a thrown knife—not the way Teresa can make her fire disintegrate. You could seriously hurt Ava." The fury was plain on his face.

Maybe I was feeling a bit reckless or maybe I was overconfident in my skills, but either way, I was eager to test my limits. "No, no," I called out. "It's fine. I can block them."

"Are you trying to get yourself killed?" Trent asked, his anger directed at me now. "Are you really dreading the talk with your

194

dad that much?"

Childishly, I stuck my tongue out at Trent. "Bring 'em over, Warren," I affirmed.

"Excellent," Warren smiled. "Don't worry, Trent. Ava's got this. Plus, when we do face off with Tenebris and his guards, you can bet they won't be holding back like we all do with each other. She needs some real practice."

Katherine and Trevor jogged over to stand by Trent, their arms crossed over their chests. Meraki remained on the mat where she had been practicing, her expression indifferent.

"You put even one scratch on her and I'll kill you myself," Trent breathed, glaring at Warren.

"Feeling a bit melodramatic today, are we?" Warren rolled his eyes. "You ready, Ava?" he asked, standing where Teresa had before.

I took a second to clear my head and focus. This wasn't playtime anymore. "I'm ready," I said through gritted teeth.

Warren threw the first knife. It spiraled through the air, the blade glistening as it caught the light. Both my hands shot out in front of me, creating a massive shield that expanded well beyond my body, keeping the sharp blade a safe distance from me. The knife struck it. I could feel it, just a tiny bit, as if the shield was an extension of my body, but it didn't hurt; it was like the slightest pinprick.

"Very good," Warren smiled. "Here comes another." He hurled the next knife with more force. I barely extended my shield in time.

"Cool it a bit, will ya?" Trent asked through clenched teeth. "She's already exhausted from fighting Teresa."

Warren ignored him, throwing knife after knife with increasing speed. Every time, my shield shot out in front of me, protecting me flawlessly, though my mind burned with the effort. It was similar to the burn in my arms when doing push-ups only in my brain instead. I kept pushing through the exhaustion, catching each knife that came my way.

Finally, Warren ran out of knives to throw.

"Okay, that's enough practicing for one day," Trent said, edging closer to me.

"That was really amazing, Ava. You're getting stronger for sure. You're going to be the best fighter we have," Warren said as he picked up the knives from around the room.

"Thanks," I smiled. "I'm exhausted now. Can we be done?"

"Sure thing," Warren said, giving me a small smile. But then, unexpectedly, he turned and flicked a knife at Trent, who stood a mere ten yards from him. Without pausing to think, I immediately extended my shield out from me, throwing it in front of Trent instead. To my surprise and relief, it worked, staying in place with little effort. The knife hit the shield with a thud and dropped to the ground in front of Trent whose eyes were wide with surprise.

My shield snapped back to me, then disappeared.

It was my turn to be furious. "You complete and total idiot, Warren!" I shrieked. "What were you thinking? He could have been seriously hurt! You didn't know if I'd be able to protect him. You know my shield has been unpredictable in protecting other people!"

"Easy, Ava. I knew you'd be able to, just like you protected those people in the square. You only needed a little push," Warren said, a smug smile on his face. I wanted to slap it off him.

I glared at him, my voice lowering to a dangerous hiss. "Let's get something straight, *Warren*," I sneered his name, "if you want me, Trent, or Meraki to stick around, that better be the last stupid stunt you pull. You might be an impressive fighter, but you know as well as I do that your plan will fail without our help. One more move like that and we're done. Understood?"

Finally, the smirk left Warren's face. He glowered at me. "Yep, understood," he said. Then he turned and stormed out of the room.

I ran over to Trent. "Are you okay?"

He glared at me, barely able to contain his fury. "No, Ava, I'm not okay. How could you be so reckless? Why would you let a maniac like Warren chuck knives at you? Are you completely mental?"

"Who cares about that," I said incredulously. "I'm talking about him throwing a knife at you! You were totally defenseless. It was the dumbest, most irresponsible—"

"Save, it Ava," Trent cut me off. "You're no better than he is. I'll see you in a few hours to take you back to your dad's." Trent shook his head, then turned and stalked back to Meraki. They left the room together without another glance in my direction.

I looked at Katherine who had the same angry expression Trent had worn. "You were being pretty dumb," she agreed. "I know you've got a lot of emotions going on and all, but there was no reason to go and take a risk like that, especially with someone who cares about you so much in the room."

"Yeah, but… what? Who cares about me?" I asked, confused.

"I'll see you later, too." Katherine gave a small shrug and a half smile before following after Trent, Trevor at her heels. Teresa, too, left the room without a word.

I kicked a punching bag next to me. It swung back with more force than I expected, catching me in the gut. I coughed and sputtered, glad that no one was around to witness that episode.

I didn't know what possessed me to agree to let Warren conduct his little experiment. In all fairness, everything turned out fine, but I guess I could see Trent and Katherine's point—it was rather reckless.

Annoyed with myself, I put on some boxing gloves and went to work on the punching bag, paying it back for the shot to the gut. Soon, I was dripping in sweat and breathing heavily. I pushed myself harder, trying to waste time, trying to erase the looks of disappointment and anger Trent had given me, trying not to think about how miserable seeing Dad was sure to be. The burn in my muscles was enough to distract from the mess of thoughts that was my head.

After close to an hour, my body gave up on me. Too exhausted to head to my bedroom here in headquarters, I used my telekinesis to pull over a towel from a rack across the room. I laid down on the sweaty mat underneath the punching bag, cushioning my head with the towel, and fell asleep.

Chapter 19

Confrontation

I woke up to a sharp jab in the ribs. "Ouch!" I complained. I sat up too quickly and knocked my head on the punching bag. Man, that thing was out to get me today.

Trent gave a low laugh as I rubbed the sore spot on my head. "Morning, Sleeping Beauty," he teased. His tone was light but his eyes were tight; I guess I wasn't completely forgiven yet.

"Sorry about earlier," I said, looking at the mat and massaging the sore spot on my ribs rather than meeting his eyes. "I know I was being dumb, and I'm sorry it ended up putting you in danger."

Hesitantly, I chanced a glance at Trent's face. He didn't seem nearly as bothered as he had been earlier. He looked me over, evaluating my sincerity. Apparently, he chose to believe me. "It's okay," he exhaled, "just promise you won't be so stupid again."

"Well... that's a tough promise to make..." I smiled. Trent did not. "Okay, okay. I promise. Sheesh, take a joke."

Suddenly, the day caught up to me. "Oh my gosh, what time is it?" I said, jumping up from the mat. As I did, I saw my reflection in the large mirrors. I looked like the most recent survivor of a vulonine attack. My face was pale with dark circles under my eyes. My sweaty hair had clumped into an unattractive mat that stuck to my left cheek, and a dried string of drool hung down from one side of my mouth. Nice.

"It's time to go. I've been looking for you for a while. I didn't think you'd stay here for so long, though I should have figured you would, being all stubborn like you are."

I pulled a face at the jab. Trent laughed.

"Come on, then. Let's get going," I said, reaching out to grab his hands.

"Right, of course," Trent said. "But first, I have to know. Do you always look this beautiful when you wake up in the mornings?" He coughed, trying to hide a laugh.

"Oh, shut up, or I'll find another Traveler to take me home." I threw my elbow into his ribs. Trent laughed again and dodged my blow.

"Good luck with that," he said, but he took my hands anyway and we were off.

We landed in my living room back home. I looked at the clock. Considering what time Dad's flight was supposed to land and how long it took to drive here from the airport, I had about fifteen minutes before he would be pulling in the driveway. One thing was for sure, a shower was necessary—a quick shower.

"Thanks for taking me home, Trent. And I really am sorry about earlier. I won't let it happen again," I said, trying to convey how much I meant it with my eyes.

Trent stared at me for a minute. I began to feel uncomfortable under his scrutiny. "What is it?"

"It's nothing," Trent said, his eyes shifting shyly to the floor.

"Well, it's just... you really are kind of beautiful, Ava. In a very *real* way," he said.

I snorted. "Right, sweaty hair and drool on my face. I'm America's Next Top Model," I joked, realizing he probably had no idea what I meant.

Trent smiled. "Good luck with your dad. I'll come get you tomorrow after you're done with school."

"Sounds great. Don't be late!"

Trent chuckled. "I'll be here at 2:45 sharp." He winked.

"Excellent."

Trent still stood there, unmoving. I did too. A couple seconds of silence passed and we both laughed at the awkwardness.

"Well, bye then, Ava," Trent said. Then he disappeared before my eyes.

I stood frozen for a moment, still contemplating Trent calling me beautiful. Well, "kind of" beautiful, anyway. Then I remembered Dad would be home soon.

I flew up the stairs and jumped in the shower. This would have to set a new record for fast showers. When I finished, I dressed in a rush and blew my hair dry. Just as I was putting the hair dryer under the sink, I heard the front door open.

"Hey, sugar bean!" Dad called from downstairs. "Where are you?"

It was good to hear his voice again. I had missed him, but I wasn't ready for this. I took a deep breath, trying to slow my hammering heartbeat.

"I'm up here!" I called back, walking down the stairs at a choppy pace—I had to force my feet to move forward.

Dad was waiting for me at the bottom of the stairs, arms open wide. I was surprised to see he'd grown a beard while he was away. He wrapped me up in an enormous hug as he said, "Oh, I missed you, Ava! I am never, ever, ever going on another trip like that again. It's too hard to be away from you."

"Yeah, right," I rolled my eyes, pulling back so he could see. "How many times have you said that before?"

He laughed. "Okay, fine, but at least not for a good long while. I need time to catch up with my girl. What's new with you?"

That was a loaded question—only everything. But I wasn't ready to open that can of worms. "Oh, nothing much. How about you go take a shower, shave that nasty rat off your face, and I'll order us a pizza. We can talk over dinner."

"You don't like the beard?" Dad said, touching it elegantly, a smolder on his face that was worthy of the cover of a magazine. I rolled my eyes again.

"Not even a little. It was worth a shot though," I said, winking. "What kind of pizza do you want?"

"Eh, anything works for me. Just no anchovies. I've been living off of fish for the past four weeks. I don't know if I'll ever be able to eat it again." Dad pulled a face.

"Well darn, anchovies are my favorite topping," I said dryly, "but I suppose I can take a night off for you."

"That's my girl," Dad chuckled, then kissed my cheek. "I'll

be right back down." He picked his bags up off the floor and climbed the stairs to his room.

"No rush!" I called, heading to the kitchen to order our food.

The pizza guy showed up about twenty minutes later. I tipped him as dad came down the stairs, clean shaven once more. Perfect timing.

I set the table and we sat down to eat. Dad must have been really hungry because he ate three pieces before saying a word. The entire time, I fought to keep myself in my seat rather than bolting from the room. This was a conversation we needed to have. I had to keep telling myself that.

"So really," Dad started, "what happened while I was away?"

I paused, trying to phrase things carefully. "A lot of the normal stuff. You know, school, homework, housework. I've also been spending a lot of time with a new friend. His name is Trent."

"Trent," Dad mused. "A boy. Interesting. That would explain why you've looked like you're covering up a murder ever since I walked through the door."

I blushed. I didn't realize I'd been that obvious about hiding something. "Come on, Dad. It's not like that."

He laughed. "Okay, then. It's not like that. So where did you meet him? School?"

I took a deep breath. I hadn't expected to arrive at the topic so quickly. "I met him at track practice, but he doesn't go to my school. He was there watching." This was technically true. Though I'd seen him a few times before that, track practice was the first time we introduced ourselves.

"Is he from a rival school? Were they scoping things out? I'm sure you made 'em nervous if he was," Dad winked.

I gave a shaky laugh. "Well, not exactly. He does go to a different school, though... A school in Cyrus, actually."

I looked at Dad steadily, my nerves suddenly gone, a new confidence taking their place. I watched as his face first turned white, then red, then purple.

"Excuse me?" he stammered. "What did you say?"

"I said he goes to a school in Cyrus. He's a Cyrun, Dad. You know, the place you lied to me about all my life," I accused.

"What do you— That's not— Cyrus? You know about Cyrus?" he shrieked. This type of reaction was very unlike my dad. If I wasn't so angry, I probably would have been concerned for his health. He was no spring chicken anymore.

"Yes, I know about Cyrus. I've been there with Trent, and I know it wasn't destroyed. There was never any war. You lied about all of it to keep me from trying to go, and I want to know why," I demanded, my voice rising.

Dad's face remained a deep, reddish-purple. He raised his tone to match mine. "I have my reasons and they are very good ones! I did all of this to protect you. Cyrus is not a safe place for you, Ava. You might imagine it to be some fairy-tale land where you can use your powers without restriction, but it's far from it. It's a place where no one is free. And it is especially dangerous for you. I absolutely forbid you from ever going there again," Dad yelled, his fist slamming on the table.

"What do you mean it's *especially* dangerous for me? No it isn't. I'm one of the most powerful Cyruns—I have six abilities. I can protect myself," I said defiantly.

"Six? You have six powers?" Dad asked, distracted from his anger for a moment. "When did all that happen?"

"I've discovered two—well sort of three—new powers in Cyrus. I can shapeshift into a wolf, produce a defensive shield, and my precognition abilities have disappeared but were replaced by visions from the past," I explained hurriedly, hoping he might calm down enough to provide me with some real answers.

"Wow, that's incredible, Ava. I knew you were talented, of course. I always suspected there might be more to you than the powers we knew about," Dad smiled slightly, though his face was still rather red. He took a deep breath. "Who is this Trent boy anyway? How is he Traveling between realms?"

"Trent is a Traveler. He's been taking me to Cyrus after school every day, and I've been staying there on the weekends," I explained. "Now please, tell me why you've lied to me. Tell me what you mean about Cyrus being dangerous for me. Is Mom really dead? Or did you lie about that too?"

"Avalon, my darling," Dad said, leaning over to touch my cheek. "I'm sorry I didn't tell you the whole truth. I'm sorry you've been so angry with me. Most of what I told you is true; Cyrus may seem like a peaceful place because there are no outright wars being fought, but it is far from being free of conflict.

206

There are battles happening there every minute of every day. It's all one big battle of will. And yes, people are dying from it. The true essence of Cyrus is being destroyed, just as I told you all those years ago. It may not be the literal destruction I led you to believe, but it is every bit as devastating. And I'm afraid what I told you about your mother is also true. She did die in Cyrus a couple of years after she left you here with me. I wish that had been a part of the lie, but she's gone, Ava." Dad looked at me with sympathetic eyes.

I didn't say much. It was difficult to accept that my mother was truly gone, but I couldn't honestly say I'd had much hope she was living. Though Dad's lies were large and sweeping, I didn't think he'd lie about that.

"You still haven't said why Cyrus is supposedly 'particularly dangerous' for me," I stated emotionlessly.

"I'm afraid I'm not going to be able to explain that to you— at least not right now."

I opened my mouth to protest, but he put his finger over my lips to silence me. "Please, Ava. I'm your father. I love you more than anything in this whole world—or Cyrus, for that matter," he smiled crookedly at his joke, his brown eyes probing. "Can you please trust that I'm doing what I believe is best for you? I always have. There are things you don't understand. There are reasons you and I are here, not there. Please, Ava. Don't go back. Stay here with me. Stay safe."

"If you tell me what you mean, I might consider it," I said, though that was far from the truth. I was going back to Cyrus, one way or the other.

Dad's head dropped, his shoulders slumped. When he finally raised his eyes to meet mine again, they were wet with tears. "I can't, Ava. I wish I could, but I can't. Please trust me."

"I'm sorry, Dad, but I have to do what I feel is best for me. If you won't let me Travel back and forth the way I have been while you've been gone, I'll stay in Cyrus permanently, at least for the foreseeable future."

A look of pain mixed with anger flashed through Dad's eyes. "You are my daughter, Ava. You're only seventeen. You're still a minor and you will do what I say. You are welcome to practice and use your abilities in discrete areas and here at home if you wish, but you are not allowed to visit Cyrus anymore. I forbid it. You have school and other responsibilities here that need your attention. I will not let you give up on your life. Cyrus is too dangerous for you. You're staying here," he said firmly, his pointer finger slamming into the table.

I didn't want to cause my dad pain. I didn't want to fight with him. But he was being completely unfair. He wouldn't tell me the truth about his secrets and lies. He wouldn't let me Travel to be a part of the world where we both belonged. I couldn't walk away from it all now, not when I had a chance of making a difference for people in Cyrus. People like Trent needed a life that was fair, not one dominated by Tenebris. Though it pained me, I had to stick up for what I believed to be right.

"I may not fully understand your reasons for keeping the truth from me, but I've been to Cyrus. I know what it's like and you're right, in many ways it is a horrible place. That's exactly why I have to go back. I believe I can make a difference. Maybe enough of a difference that we might be able to return together someday—"

"That will never happen," Dad said flatly.

"Regardless, I'm going back. It is my home. It's where we both belong. Trent will be back to get me tomorrow afternoon. I'll pack enough to get me by for a few months. If you'd allow it, I'd love to come back and visit for Christmas." I said it coldly, matter-of-factly, though internally, it felt like my heart was shattering. I loved my dad. I didn't want things to end like this.

"Ava, my baby, please don't do this," Dad said, choking over his tears.

"Come with me," I begged him. "Or at least let me go on good terms."

He paused, seeming to want that as much as I did. "I can't, Ava. I wish you'd trust me. You shouldn't be in Cyrus. I shouldn't be in Cyrus. We belong here, together. You're safer here."

"Sorry, Daddy. I'm going back," I said. I stood up and rounded the table. I kissed the top of his head before heading up to my room.

I cried into my pillow for hours before finally falling asleep.

CHAPTER 20

HOME

My duffle bag was ridiculously large for the small amount of clothing I was bringing along. It was more difficult than I thought it would be to find clothes that wouldn't betray their human origin.

Trent would be here in just a few minutes. I sat on the edge of my bed, looking around my room, trying not to feel too nostalgic. It wasn't working. I was going to miss the purple walls, the posters hanging on them, the soft brown carpet, and my incredibly comfortable bed. The mattress on the floor I had at headquarters did not compare.

There was a knock at the door. It was going to be Dad, trying yet again to convince me to stay. He'd tried about ten different times already.

"Come in!" I called.

"Hey, sweetie," Dad said as he entered the room.

"I'm still going, Dad," I said, annoyance obvious in my voice.

"I know. If my previous attempts to persuade you didn't work, I knew this time would be no different." He smiled a painful smile that prodded at my broken heart. He took a seat next to me on the bed. "I just came to give you this." He held up the ring on a chain I'd found all those weeks ago. I hadn't told him about the vision I'd had, and I didn't plan to. Not now, after all the pain I was causing him.

"Thanks, Dad. It's beautiful," I breathed, touched at the gesture. I was an awful daughter to be hurting him this way.

"It was your mother's engagement ring. I figured you should have a piece of both of us as you head back into our world."

A genuine smile—the first I'd had since the fiasco that was our conversation last night—broke across my face. I reached over and pulled him in for a hug. I rested my head on his shoulder, breathing in his aftershave. I didn't even know it was possible to ache for someone so much. "I'm going to miss you, Dad."

"I wish you wouldn't go. You don't have to. You can stay here. You can stay safe. Please."

"I thought you said you weren't here to try and convince me to stay," I said, backing up to glare at him.

"I know, but can you blame me? You're taking away everything that means anything to me, Ava." He paused while my heart twisted in pain. "Please do come back for Christmas. I'd love to see you then," Dad said, his voice strained with emotion.

"I will, I promise. Nothing is going to happen to me."

"You don't know that. You don't know how dangerous Cyrus can be." Dad breathed deeply, closing his eyes.

"I also know that I have to stick up for what I believe is right."

Dad smiled and opened his eyes. "You've always had a strong conscience. I admire you for that."

"Thanks, Dad."

Dad turned and pulled something new out of his pocket. "This was my brother's. It's a pocketknife he gave me awhile back." He extended the object out to me. The exterior was made of wood with a small sheep carved into the handle. "If you have time and are able, I'd appreciate it if you'd try and track him down. His name is William Longfellow. Most people know him as Will. If you find him, can you please give him this letter?" He handed me a sealed envelope. "And promise me, Ava, you won't open the letter yourself. It's for my brother. I'd appreciate it if you'd respect that."

I took the letter from his hands and put it in the front pocket of my bag, along with the pocketknife. "I promise not to read it, and I'll do my best to find your brother. Does he know about me? Should I introduce myself as his niece?"

Dad's eyes crinkled in a sad smile. He reached out and cupped the side of my face. "No, he doesn't know about you, but I'm sure he'll see you as the wonderful gift that you are. He'll be so happy to meet you."

There was a knock on the front door. Trent was here. It was really time to go. I wouldn't see my Dad for over a month. Being away from him wasn't the issue—it was the circumstances around my departure that stunk. I hated doing something I knew he was so against.

I stood from the bed. "Bye, Dad. I'll see you again soon. I love you more than anything."

Dad stood as well. "I love you too, Ava. And while I don't approve of what you're doing, please come back as often as you'd like."

"Thanks, Dad. I'll see what I can do." I leaned in for one last hug. He hugged me back tightly and gave me a kiss on the top of my head. I grabbed my pathetic bag and clunked down the stairs with it trailing behind me.

Trent's smile as I opened the door immediately faded as he took in my broken expression. "Was it really that bad?" He asked with concern.

"Worse than you could possibly imagine," I sobbed, wiping tears from my cheeks. "Can we just go please?"

"You sure that's what you want?"

"I'm sure," I said, my voice thick with tears.

Trent took my bag in one hand and held mine in the other. My feet left solid ground, tearing me away from my father and my home. The last piece of my heart shattered, sending a crippling pain throughout my body.

We landed in Trent's backyard. I was surprised—I thought we'd go directly to headquarters. "What are we doing here?" I asked.

"I thought you might want a little time to yourself before having to face everyone else."

He was so thoughtful. "Thanks," I said as the emotion welled up inside me, bursting out in sobs and sniffles. Trent gently guided

213

me over to the garden bench. He wrapped his arm around me in comfort, letting me cry into his blue shirt.

It took several minutes of ugly crying before I could calm down. Once I did, I still didn't move. I just sat there, leaning against Trent, trying not to think about how awful this whole situation was. Why couldn't my dad have just told me what he meant? Why was Cyrus so dangerous for me? Why didn't he come with me? I thought I knew the answer to the last part—my mother. He didn't want to return because of how badly she'd hurt him here. He wanted nothing to do with this realm, that much was obvious.

After several minutes of silence, Trent gently nudged me into a sitting position so he could see my face. "Okay, you're killing me, Ava. What happened? Why are you so torn up?"

I looked him over, not eager to relive the whole disaster, but I did anyway, for his sake. I suppose I did owe him some sort of explanation for acting like a total nut-job.

"Are you sure you made the right decision by coming here? If it hurts you both so much, why didn't you just stay?" he asked when I'd finished.

"Because I can't sit back and do nothing, letting an entire world of people remain slaves to an unfair master when there's even a tiny possibility that I might be able to do something about it. Not many people can resist a direct command from Tenebris, but I can. It would be wrong not to act when I could put a stop to all of this. You could be free, Trent, to be whatever you want to be. Your 18th birthday is coming up. I cannot stand the thought of

214

you suffering for your entire adult life because of a corrupt system. Plus there's the census to worry about. Your whole family is in danger. Obviously, Tenebris has an affinity for going above and beyond in his punishment of people. I won't let that happen to you and your family. Praesidium has got to go."

Trent was staring at me in confusion.

"What?" I asked.

He shook his head slowly. "You're sort of amazing, you know. If anyone else was in your shoes and came to Cyrus, discovering they had six abilities, which practically makes them part of the royal family, they'd want nothing to do with the plight of the little guys. I mean, kids at school who have two powers treat me like dirt because they think they're so much better than me, the Zero. But the thought doesn't even seem to have crossed your mind. And not only that, you're sacrificing your relationship with your dad to do it all."

I blushed at his compliments. He was blowing things way out of proportion. "First of all, you're not a 'little guy'. You're a Traveler for crying out loud! The same opportunities I could have, you could have too. You said Travelers are highly respected—"

"Not like an Elite," Trent interrupted.

"Same difference. The point is, I'm not doing anything out of the ordinary. I see an injustice, I have something I can attempt to do about it, so I'm going to. That's all there is to it."

"Still amazing," Trent said under his breath, shooting a sideways glance at me.

215

I nudged him playfully with my shoulder. "Stop it," I said. "Now let's get back to headquarters. If there's one thing I've decided after all this mess, it's that I'm not burning bridges with my dad for nothing. If we're going to act, we need to do it soon, while we know I'm still immune to Praesidium. We need to talk to Warren—it's time he told us the whole truth about himself."

Chapter 21
Coming Clean

The caves were quiet when we arrived; there was no one in the kitchen, game room, or practice room.

"Warren is likely in his bedroom if he's not around here. Probably best so we can talk to him in private first," Trent said, leading the way down the southern tunnel which Warren had to himself, of course. He and Trevor had the biggest rooms.

I knocked on his door. We waited for a minute, but no answer came. I knocked again. "Warren! It's Ava and Trent. There's something we really need to talk about!"

There was some shuffling on the other side of the door, then Warren's face peered through a small crack, his expression conveying his annoyance.

"Uh, you okay in there?" Trent asked.

"Yeah, sure. What's up?" Warren shrugged.

"Can we come in for minute?" I asked. "I have something important to talk to you about."

Warren glanced over his shoulder. "It's not really the best time—"

"Just let them in," called a crystal voice behind Warren. "I've got to get going anyway." Meraki yanked the door open, stepping out into the hall. That was unexpected. Both Trent and I were frozen in shock.

Meraki gave me a cold look, then turned and glared even more frostily at Trent. I didn't think it was possible to convey so much hate in a single stare, but she had found a way. "See you both later," she trilled as she stormed past us down the hall, her hips undulating as she walked away.

I glanced up at Trent who was staring after her, open-mouthed. Though I hated the girl, I still felt sorry for Trent. He was obviously blindsided by what had just happened. "You okay?" I asked him quietly.

He looked down at me and unexpectedly smiled. "Yeah, fine. Just... wow," he mouthed the last word, his eyes wide.

"You guys came here for somethin', right?" Warren asked grumpily.

My tone was cold. I hated Meraki, but I hated Warren as well for hurting Trent like that. "Yes, we came to ask you about your father, actually."

"My father?" Warren asked, confused.

"Yes. The first day we met, I had a vision about your father—"

"I've been wondering when you'd ask me about that," Warren interrupted, a stupid grin on his face.

"Wait, you knew?" I asked, caught off guard.

"Not that day, of course, but Amos gave me a heads up."

Amos—how had I forgotten? Of course he would know something was off. He couldn't read minds, precisely, but he had the ability to read the tenor of someone's thoughts. Any time the whole "human world orphan" issue came up, he would be able to sense I didn't trust what Warren was saying.

I pretended not to be surprised and continued on. "Well, yes, I had a vision, and I know your father is Tenebris."

Finally, Warren looked appropriately abashed. "Aren't you just clever," he sneered, rubbing both hands down his face in stress. "Guess the cat's out of the bag. We need to round everyone up. Time for a meeting. I think it's best everyone hears this story at the same time."

After a ten minute search, we were able to track everyone down except Meraki, who had already gone back to her parents' store.

We met in the game room, which was beginning to feel more like a conference room than anything. Warren sat up front with me next to him. I felt stupid there, but the team had officially voted me second-in-command of the Miners two weeks ago, so from now on, I sat next to Warren at these meetings. Though I'd worried what Jameson would think, he told me he was thrilled not to be second anymore. Apparently, he'd only done it because nobody else would step up after Fox died. He would still be managing our training, though.

"Thanks for coming together, guys," Warren began.

"And girls!" Elsie chimed in.

"And girls," Warren amended, rolling his eyes. "There's something about me that I probably should have told you all a long time ago. Because of our beliefs and our cause as a group, I've been afraid of your reactions, so I've kept this information about myself a secret. Avalon has just approached me about the situation, which she uncovered via one of her visions.

"I have led you all to believe I was raised an orphan in the human realm, just like most of you. This is not true. I was born here, in Cyrus. I was raised by my mother, Isabella, until I was seven. At that time, she was killed by King Tenebris personally. He also tried to kill me at the time."

"Dude, that's messed up," Damion said from his arm chair. "I'm sorry."

"Thank you," Warren nodded toward Damion. "Unfortunately, that is not all." He paused. "My father was—and is, I suppose—King Tenebris himself."

The expressions of shock and disgust were plain on everyone's faces.

"That blows, man," Jameson said angrily. "Why didn't you tell us earlier?"

"Seriously? You probably should have mentioned that before," Teresa agreed.

"So that's why you hate him so much," Katherine mused. "Makes, sense, of course. Not that we don't all hate him, but I've noticed he holds a special place of hatred in your heart. He killed your mom? Why?"

"I think I know," I chimed in. "As Warren said, I had a vision the very first day we met. I touched the bracelet he's wearing." I motioned to the leather strap on his wrist. "It was your mother's, wasn't it?"

Warren looked at the strap, fingering it sadly. "Yes, it was hers. I went back to her body later, after I was sure he'd be gone, and took it—you know, as a momento. She never got a proper burial."

"I'm sorry," I said sympathetically.

"Nothing to be done but fight back now, is there?" Warren said, a sad smile on his face. "Carry on with the details of your vision. I'm interested."

"First, I saw your mother giving birth—we can skip those details." There were several grunts of consent, particularly from the boys in the room. "Then, I saw her take you as a baby to your father's prison cell. I'd assume that was during the time his brother had been keeping him locked up. Tenebris denied you were his child and told your mother if she ever tried to claim you were his, he'd... have her killed.

"The next scene was of the two of you in a tent, the day she died. Tenebris came. He said he'd warned her not to say anything about you and that there had been rumors going around the kingdom. He said a child from a peasant like her would never be respected enough to be king. You ran out from the tent to protect her. He killed her with a dagger. He tried to kill you, too. He commanded you to stop running, but the command didn't bind you like it does everyone else—you kept running. That was all I saw."

"I remember it like it was yesterday," Warren said, his tone haunted. "She was so perfect. She didn't deserve it."

We all hung our heads in sadness and respect for Warren's grief. Though I felt it had been necessary, it was much more difficult to reveal to him what I'd seen than I thought it would be.

"So that's the real reason you can resist Tenebris," Trent began. "Because you're part of the royal bloodline, not because you come from 'the human realm' as you've told all of us."

"What are you talking about?" Amos asked, confused. His wild, brown hair added to his frazzled look. "What does that have to do with anything?"

"He's right," Warren said, "though I'm surprised you know about that. How do you?"

"My grandad was a guard at the palace. He overheard discussions when Tenebris—the second son—was born into the family. Apparently, having two children hasn't happened often in royal family history because they try to avoid it."

Trent turned to speak to the whole room instead of only Warren. "You see, Praesidium gives our king or queen the ability to control the people of Cyrus, as we all know. What many don't know is that it was created by blood magic. This means Ganton, through Praesidium, can pass his powers on to any person who shares his blood. It also means that Praesidium has no power over any person who is a blood relative of the royal line. Because of that limitation, the royal family has intentionally had only one child whenever possible. They don't want a bunch of people in the kingdom who are immune to Praesidium's powers. It also helps minimize fighting or claims to the throne if there's only one clear descendant.

"Traditionally, if a second child is conceived in the family, the pregnancy is aborted before the child can be born. Queen Trisha refused when she found out she was pregnant with Tenebris. King Simon was furious but didn't want to force his wife to comply in this particular situation, so Tenebris, obviously, was born.

"As we all know, when King Simon died and King Trinnen took the throne, he threw Tenebris in prison in an attempt to negate the threat he posed to his power. The kingdom was shocked and didn't understand, not knowing Praesidium's limits. According to my grandad, Trinnen threatened to kill Tenebris but agreed to let him live in confinement only if he swore never to have children of his own. I would assume that is another reason he was so concerned when he found out about you," Trent said, motioning toward Warren. "Tenebris knew if Trinnen ever found out, he'd be killed for passing on his immunity to Praesidium to a new generation."

"That explains a lot," Elsie said. "Like why the rest of us who have lived in the human world haven't stayed immune to Praesidium like you have, Warren."

"Exactly," I stepped in. "Which brings me to my next point. I think we need to move up the time schedule of our attack on the castle. We don't know how long I will be immune to Praesidium. Most of you have lost some of your immunity. The only person who hasn't is Warren, and evidently, his immunity is totally different than ours. We need to act quickly so that I can help as much as possible. I don't think Warren will be able to face Tenebris alone."

"Hold up for a second," Amos cut in. "How fast are we talking here?"

"Within the week," I said firmly.

Several whistles and grumbled complaints circled the room. The only exception was Jameson who gave an enthusiastic, "Alright!" He was always eager for a challenge.

"No way!" Amos exclaimed. "We've been counting on months to prepare and you're trying to cut us back to days? You're going to get us killed!"

"I agree, that's much too fast," Katherine said, standing from her seat. "We'll be unprepared and clumsy. Not to mention the fact that we still don't know how to get around Praesidium's defenses."

"That's not true. We're very well prepared. We do combative training daily," I disagreed, "and we will have a plan—a good one. That's what we're going to focus on for the next week. We'll do reconnaissance and—"

"Enough," Warren said calmly but firmly. The noise around the room came to a stop. All eyes were on him as he stood, looking at each of us in turn, deliberating.

Warren took a deep breath before saying, "I think Ava is right—"

The noise erupted again. "Yes!" I heard Jameson call. Trent shifted nervously, but his face remained calm. The rest of the room looked angry.

"I said enough!" Warren yelled this time. Again, the noise died down, a little less quickly. "We have to strike while our opportunity is greatest. Ava has been a fantastic addition to our team, which is why, I believe, you all voted to have her as second among our group. We cannot afford to miss the opportunity to utilize her abilities to the fullest."

Warren's speech made me feel like a tool to be used rather than a person to be valued. I'd take it, however, if it meant getting my way.

"Now, I suggest you all eat a good dinner and get a good night's rest. We put our plans in action starting tomorrow. We'll meet here immediately following breakfast to discuss strategy," Warren said. Then he stood and left the room.

Nobody said anything to me as they walked out, though most of their glances my direction were cold—except Jameson who had an enormous smile on his face.

"Nice work, Ava," he said with a wink as he left the room. I gave him a weak smile in return.

"Well," Trent let out a long breath as he came to my side, "that was an interesting afternoon." He chuckled, then took my hand to pull me out of my seat.

"Thanks," I said, blushing slightly. "Everyone hates me, but if it results in success in the long run, who really cares?"

"Right," Trent gave a half smile, not convinced it wasn't bothering me. "Don't worry, they'll come around. What d'ya say we make ourselves a couple of sandwiches and then head up to our tree for a bit?"

I beamed. "Our tree? And where would that be exactly?"

"Like you don't know," Trent winked, then he walked briskly out of the room, shooting a teasing smile my way. My heart jumped in my chest. I followed after him to the kitchens, where we threw together a couple ham and cheese sandwiches and then left headquarters. We could have Traveled there, but Trent said he'd prefer the walk tonight.

It was dark outside, and the sky was perfectly clear. The stars were beautiful. The moment felt intimate, though I wasn't sure why. Maybe it was the peaceful night. Maybe it was the heat I could feel off Trent's skin as we walked close together. Maybe it was the fact that we felt comfortable enough together without having to say anything. Maybe it was everything combined.

When we got to the tree, Trent gave me a boost up to the closest limb. I climbed up a few more branches until I found a spot that looked comfortable and big enough for the two of us. Trent pulled himself up after me. He sat next to me, and I handed him his wrapped sandwich from my jacket pocket. "Thanks," he said.

I watched as he looked up into the night sky. He seemed more relaxed than I could ever remember seeing him, though I wasn't sure why, considering the crazy day it had been. We did essentially catch his girlfriend with another guy, after all.

"You okay, Trent?"

He looked down at me, as if surprised to remember I was next to him. "I'm great! Really great, actually. But I am worried."

"About what?" I said around a bite of sandwich. He smirked at me talking with my mouth full.

"My parents got notice of their census appointment today. The surveyor will be coming in ten days."

"Well, hopefully by then, Tenebris will be history anyway," I said lightly, though internally, I was worried sick. What if we weren't successful? What would happen to Trent? What would happen to Em and Sam?

"That's the main reason I agree with your condensed timeline. Besides, we've had enough waiting around. I have a feeling no matter how well trained or how well planned we are, things are going to end up going to pot anyway, so we might as well get on with it." He chucked his top crust into a bush nearby.

I waited for him to say something, hoping he might bring up the situation with Meraki. He didn't, and I wasn't known to be the most patient person in the world.

"So, do you want to talk about what happened with Meraki today? It was kind of a shock," I said tentatively. With almost anything, Trent was very open with me. That was not the case with his love life, not that I'd ever wanted details before now.

Trent looked at me, considering. "There's really not much to tell. She's at perfect liberty to be with whomever she wants." He paused, looking at me shyly this time. "I broke up with her about a week ago, actually."

Instantly, I was flying. Trent and Meraki? Broken up? My heart was doing backflips. I pretended to be concerned for Trent's benefit. "Why? What happened?"

Trent hesitated again, his expression uncomfortable. I could think of only one reason he might be acting this way, and it sent my heart hammering in my chest. I smiled at him encouragingly. "You can tell me," I promised.

He met my eyes and his discomfort seemed to slowly melt away. "Truth is, I like you, Ava, maybe even since the first day I saved you from that dumpster and helped you when you were hurt. I knew you were different right then and there—you'd have to be, risking your life to help people you didn't even know.

"Then there was the boy who was almost hit by a truck. You risked exposing yourself in front of all your teammates to save him." He paused and took my right hand in both of his. My heart pounded faster in my chest. "Since those moments, I've gotten to know you personally. You're passionate, caring, feisty, talented, intelligent, beautiful, funny, and fearless. You're totally unlike any other girl I've ever known. I guess it was all enough to break Meraki's hold on me. It didn't happen immediately, but even the first day you were in Cyrus and she was at my house, I started to wonder what I saw in her besides her beauty. Within a couple days, any feelings I had for her were completely gone. I don't think I ever did have real feelings for her; I think it was all her ability to infatuate me with her looks. I suppose having true feelings for someone else is enough to break her hold."

I could hardly believe what I was hearing. It felt too good to be true. It was what I'd been hoping for every minute since I got to know him.

"That first night you took me back to the human realm—" I stopped, feeling shy.

"Yes, I remember," Trent smiled, tucking a strand of hair behind my ear. My heart skipped a beat at his touch. "Go on."

I bit my lip. "Were you going to kiss me?"

Trent chuckled. "Yes, I was trying to kiss you. But you pulled away from me?" He finished it as a question. "I guess that leads me to ask, do you have any feelings for me? Sometimes it seems like you might. Other times it feels like I'm just hoping you do." He dropped his eyes.

I was nervous. I had never tried to tell anyone I had feelings for them—well, except that one kid, Skyler, in like 2nd grade through a note, so I don't think that counts.

"Yes," I exhaled. "I have feelings for you too—more and more every day, actually," I smiled crookedly. "And it has been really suckish to watch you with another girl who has supermodel powers, by the way."

Trent was beaming. "Really? Then why did you pull away that night?"

"You had a girlfriend, and I barely knew you. I'm not the kind of girl who goes around kissing any random guy I find attractive, you know. The better question is, why didn't you ever try again if you've liked me all this time?"

Trent considered as his thumb drew patterns on the back of my hand. The simple gesture gave me goose bumps. "I'm not completely sure, but I think it comes down to two things: I felt guilty about my feelings for you because of Meraki and even guiltier I'd acted on them without properly ending things with her first. Second, you flat out rejected me," he laughed, "so I wasn't exactly keen on the idea of putting myself out there again until I was more certain how you felt."

"Makes sense," I said happily.

I was unsure where we went from here. Trent seemed to be thinking something similar. His eyes flashed back and forth from my eyes to my lips. My heartbeat accelerated. He was thinking about kissing me again. Was I ready? *I don't think I'm ready!* He moved in closer, his eyes closing.

I put my fingers to his lips, stopping him. His eyes opened, confused. "Can we just... wait?" I asked. "It doesn't feel like the right time. It seems like something we're supposed to do because we just talked about our first botched attempt. I want to wait until it feels like something we want to do. You know, when the moment's right."

Trent laughed and shook his head slightly, moving back. "Whatever you say, Ava, but just so you know, kissing you *always* feels like something I want to do." He winked. The butterflies in my stomach intensified.

We spent another half hour or so in our tree, enjoying the clear night, the stars above, and our newly declared feelings before going back to headquarters. Though my day had started horribly and I still felt sick whenever I thought of my dad, my heart was on cloud nine.

CHAPTER 22

BROTHERS

Trent walked me back to my room later that night, pausing as we reached the door. "Thanks for tonight," I said. "It really helped clear my head after the bad morning I had."

Trent smiled. "I'm glad. Sleep well tonight, Ava. I'll see you in the morning." He leaned forward and kissed my forehead. I nearly collapsed on the spot.

Before I was coherent enough to gasp, "Goodnight!" at Trent's retreating figure, he was likely out of earshot.

Sleeping was not an option—I was way too wound up. Instead, I sat cross-legged on my little mattress and tried to process the day. I could hardly believe how happy Trent had made me tonight, but I still felt a cloud of despair whenever I thought of my dad.

With that in mind, I reached over to my duffle bag, which was on the wooden chair, and dragged it over until it sat in front of my mattress. I opened the front pocket where I'd stashed my uncle's pocketknife and the note intended for him. I pulled the letter out first. An overwhelming desire to open the note overcame me. Perhaps it would provide some answers to my father's secrets. I very nearly tore into the envelope, but shoved it back in the pocket instead, choosing to obey my dad's wishes.

I fished for the pocketknife—pulling it out to examine the beautiful craftsmanship of the handle—when a vision overcame me. I welcomed it, hoping it might give some answers.

I was first met by a horrifying scene. I found myself in a thick part of the forest. A teenage version of my father lay on the ground close by, a ferocious animal at his feet, looming over him. The creature looked like a large wolf, yet there was something distinctly feline in its shape and hypnotic movements. Its fur was coarse and black. Its green eyes gleamed over exposed, yellowed teeth. The creature snarled and lunged at my dad, who rolled over swiftly, the beast missing his side by inches.

"Carmichael!" a voice called from the distance. I turned to see a slightly older boy, probably about seventeen, sprinting toward the beast. As he drew closer, he thrust out his palm, where a green light shot forward, hitting the beast in its side. The creature yelped in pain and stumbled sideways. The boy closed the distance between himself and Mike, kneeling at his side. "Michael, are you okay?"

Mike began to sit up, wincing as he did. He brought his right arm across his body to show the older boy. He drew in a sharp gasp—Mike's arm was gouged and bloody. "We need to get you home!"

The creature—recovering from whatever attack had been made against it—crawled toward the boys, its ugly head bowed low, baring its teeth.

Without a moment's hesitation, the older boy thrust out both

233

palms, pushing forward green patches of light, which stunned the beast in quick succession. With every strike, the creature cowered in pain, retreating, until it finally turned completely and sprinted away.

"Thanks, Will," Mike grunted. "I thought I could control it. Guess I was wrong."

Will shook his head. "You have got to stop experimenting with your powers like this. Magical creatures are not the same as regular animals." Will extended his hand out to Mike, helping him to his feet.

"Good thing you're always around to save me," Mike smiled weakly.

"I suppose that's what brothers are for." Will gave Mike a smile of comradery, then supported him as they hobbled off together.

The memory faded and reformed. I stood in a dingy pub with wooden tables and dim lights. A fire in a large fireplace burned at one end of the wide room. My dad, with his head in his hands, sat at a small table next to the fire. Will sat across from him. Two large, empty mugs sat in front of the pair of brothers. I hurried over to their sides.

"What do you mean she left you? Rose loves you! She would never do that," Will exclaimed.

"She's gone, Will, for good. 'S nothing I could do or say to make her stay." Mike's words were slurred and his eyes were unfocused as he painfully lifted his neck to look at his brother.

How odd, I'd never seen him drink in the human realm—not even a beer. He told me alcohol didn't sit well with him. I could see, now, that was very true.

"I'm sorry, brother. Did she say why?"

"—nuther guy. She's gonna marry another guy," Mike winced as the words came out. His upper body slumped across the table as he fell over.

"Come on, now, Mike. This isn't like you. If you love her, fight for her! Don't sit in this grimy old pub drinking your sorrows away. You're a better man than that."

"It's useless. 'S too late. She's gone," Mike mumbled without attempting to lift his head.

Will leaned back, sucking in a sharp breath as he clasped his hands behind his head. "What's useless is trying to talk to you in this state, but I need to, Michael. I've got something important to tell you." Will reached for a side pocket in the leather jacket he wore and pulled out a scroll. He unrolled the parchment to show his brother. "I've been summoned to guard the palace, Mike." Will's eyes were alight with excitement. "Can you believe it? King Trinnen has heard about my abilities and wants *me* to join his ranks."

Mike's head flew off the table, his expression angry. He seemed more attentive in that moment than he had the entire length of the conversation. "No!" He slammed his fist on the table "You can't go, Will. The king is a wicked man. He's not worth protecting!" Mike jumped to his feet in anger.

235

At Mike's behavior, many people in the bar turned their heads and fell silent, watching.

Will stood and put his hand on his brother's shoulder. He pushed him back down in his seat. Mike staggered and then sat, caving under the pressure from Will. "Quiet, Michael. It is not wise to speak ill of the king so openly. King Trinnen does what is necessary to keep the people of Cyrus safe. I will go and fulfill my responsibilities to our kingdom."

"You're a fool, Will. You're jus' another pawn in his game. He's evil! Vile!—"

"Mike, please," Will glanced around self-consciously at the angry stares the brothers were receiving. "Control yourself. I'm going to take my place as I should. Before I go, though, I want you to have this." Will pulled out the pocketknife I now had from his jeans and offered it to Mike. Mike stared at the object with disgust before he knocked Will's hand, sending the knife flying.

"I don' wan' your stupid knife. Have a nice life, brother." Mike struggled to his feet and stumbled through the crowds to the door. He threw it open and staggered out into the brisk air.

Will stood and picked up the knife from the floor. "Sorry for my brother's behavior," he declared loudly to the pub. "Forgive him, he's not thinking straight. He's suffering from a broken heart." Will crossed the length of the room in a few longs strides, then followed after his brother.

The memory retreated, morphing into a new one that was nearly unbearable to witness. I stood in a musty smelling dungeon.

Hay and rat feces were strewn about the floor. My father was chained to a post and knelt on his knees. The shirt on his back was ripped to shreds, and his back was bleeding profusely. Behind him, Will—dressed in a royal guard's uniform—held a lethal whip in his hands. Tears poured down Will's face as he raised the whip with trembling arms and brought it down on his brother's back. Mike cried out in agony so intense I thought my heart would stop then and there. Never before had I understood the meaning of a broken heart. I was gaining a painfully complete understanding here, in this wretched moment from the past.

Will hesitated, obviously fighting an internal battle that raged with force, the tears pouring down his face at an alarming rate. I was reminded of what my father said yesterday—that the people of Cyrus were fighting a battle of will every day.

"I said 30 lashes, Officer Longfellow. You still have five to go. Get them done. Now!" I turned to see a man dressed in black with a red velvet cape hung around his shoulders. His resemblance to Tenebris was nearly identical, with the exception of a brown goatee and slightly lighter hair color. I knew immediately that I was looking into the cold face of King Trinnen, Tenebris' older brother. Around his neck hung Praesidium, which glowed a vibrant red at his most recent command.

Behind me, I heard another crack of the whip. I didn't dare turn around—the sound from my father was already too much to bear. Instead, I watched King Trinnen's lips turn up in pleasure at my father's pain. I lunged at the awful man, desperate for some

237

sort of revenge. I flew right through him, of course, falling to the floor, unable to cause harm in a memory.

I remained crumpled on the floor, covering my ears and squeezing my eyes shut, trying to block out the horror taking place in front of me. It was no use. The whip was too loud, the cries from my dad piercing. I felt every blow twist my heart and cause my stomach to heave.

Finally, mercifully, the last crack of the whip rent the air. Hesitantly, I opened my eyes and turned to face my father. He was slumped over, unmoving. Will dropped the whip, sending it clattering to the ground as he fell to his knees. He sobbed into his hands.

"I'm sorry, brother," Will's voice said feebly through his tears. "So sorry."

"Silence!" King Trinnen cut across Will's apology. "Untie the criminal and bring him to face me."

Will stumbled forward on his feet. With shaking hands, he loosened his brother's ties and, as gently as he could manage, helped Mike to his feet. As Mike turned to face the king, his face was ashen and his breathing labored.

King Trinnen's face broke into a wicked grin. "Now, Carmichael Ross Longfellow of Cashmere, I hereby sentence you to banishment from Cyrus. You are to spend the rest of your days in the human realm. You are forbidden to ever enter this realm again." As he said it, Praesidium glowed more vibrantly than I had ever seen it. With the weight of Trinnen's commands, Mike slumped forward and bowed his head. Silent tears ran down his face.

King Trinnen stepped closer to Michael, then slapped him across the face. "I will be back in a few minutes with a Traveler who will take you to the human realm. Officer Longfellow, lock him up in one of the cells, then depart for your assigned post immediately. No wasting time on your sweet goodbyes." King Trinnen's eyes gleamed malevolently as he swept past the pair of brothers to a door at the end of the dungeons.

The horrific scene ended and was replaced by new surroundings. I stood in an ornate white and gold room—the very opposite of the place I'd just been. The walls were adorned with golden pillars, which were carved with intricate patterns and large stretches of marble. The floor was also marble with a long, thin expanse of red carpet that ran from the wide doors at one end of the room to a large podium. Two majestic thrones sat atop it, one slightly larger than the other, with another gold door behind the pair of seats. On the two thrones were King Tenebris—dressed in a purple uniform adorned with several medals—and the queen, who wore a simple yet elegant blue gown. Her golden hair moved in large ringlets down one shoulder. Her face was strikingly beautiful, though she wore heavy makeup that I personally felt detracted from her natural beauty. The pair of royals sat silently and watched the large set of doors on the other side of the room.

At that moment, the doors opened. Two guards in red uniforms stepped through, with a man dressed in a white uniform

239

behind them. The guards in front stepped aside while the one in white continued forward. As he drew closer, I recognized him as an older, more wrinkled Will.

Will approached the base of the podium and bowed.

"Thank you. You may rise," Tenebris said without emotion.

"Your Majesty," Will rose to his feet. "I come to you today with a request. My daughter is ill—severely so. I fear she doesn't have much more time to live. I have served you faithfully for many years and your brother Trinnen before you. I have dedicated nearly 20 years to this kingdom. Now, I request your permission to be relieved of my duties so that I may return to my home and family to spend the remainder of my daughter's days by her side." Again, Will bowed humbly.

Tenebris watched Will thoughtfully. The queen's hand covered her heart. She looked at Tenebris with pleading eyes. "Let him go. Please," she whispered.

Tenebris considered the queen carefully, then turned his attention back to Will. "Very well. You shall be missed, Commander Longfellow. You have served this kingdom honorably and have certainly been one of my most loyal officers. I regret your departure, but see that you have made up your mind on the matter. You are hereby relieved of your duties as a palace guard. Please don't be a stranger. You and your family are welcome back any time." The king's lips twitched in what I imagine could pass as a faint smile.

Will's smile, on the other hand, was radiant. "Thank you, your

Majesty. I truly appreciate your understanding. I will pack my bags and be gone by nightfall." Will bowed once more before walking briskly back down the red carpet to the doors, a definite spring in his step.

The scene disappeared and reformed. I stood in a dark alley. The weather was cold and the street was wet. A few paces to my right, a hooded figure stood, peeking around the edge of a brick building in the direction of a large centaur statue. I walked forward to see the person's face, but was interrupted by a voice behind my back.

"Good evening, Mr. Longfellow." Startled, I spun around and was met by a young face. A second figure stood in the alley, though I was certain he hadn't been there a moment before. His face was obscured, partially, by the hood of his red jacket, but I could tell that he was young—probably 15 or so. He wore red sneakers, jeans, and a confident smile.

The hooded figure also turned to face the newcomer. Under the hood, I recognized Will's face once more. He rushed forward to stand in front of the boy. "Hello. Are you Fox Springs? The Traveler?"

The boy smirked. "Depends who's asking and why. As I understand it, you were once a palace guard. I hardly think confessing to be an unregistered Traveler would be a wise move, considering." The boy leaned back against the brick wall of the building, seeming unfazed.

Will's voice was frantic. "I was a palace guard, yes, but I

haven't been for weeks now. I need a favor, that's all. My brother was sent to the human realm many years ago. I simply want you to give him this knife," Will held out the carved pocketknife, "and this note." He shoved the two objects toward the boy who eyed them skeptically and made no move to take them.

"If I were able to do what you were asking, I'd need some sort of payment as an incentive. Surely you understand."

"Yes, of course. You want money? I've got money." Will scrambled in his inside jacket pockets and pulled out a pouch. "There are fifty gold pieces in here. They're all yours if you can help me."

The boy held out his hand for the bag. Will gave it to him. "Excellent. And what's your brother's name?"

"Carmichael Ross Longfellow. He usually goes by Michael or Mike. He told me he was going to the Americas. He likes places that aren't too busy, so I'd stick with smaller towns in your search."

Fox Springs smiled smugly. "Finding him won't be an issue. I'll send you a message when I've completed your task at which time I expect the other half of my payment."

Will was taken aback. "The other half?"

"Yes, another fifty pieces of gold. Is that a problem? If it is, I'm sure you'll be able to find someone else." Fox Springs moved to return Will's items.

"No, no problem. Another fifty pieces. You've got it."

"I'll be in touch." And with that, the boy disappeared.

The scene receded and I found myself in my room at headquarters once more, my head spinning, my breaths coming in shallow gasps. I couldn't get past the horrible image of my father being beaten senseless by his own brother, who was clearly agonized by his actions that were beyond his control. Trent once told me King Trinnen was better than his brother, Tenebris. I found that extremely difficult to believe after the scene I had just witnessed. Nausea rolled through my stomach. I leaned over the edge of the mattress, afraid I might actually throw up.

After several minutes of deep breaths, I calmed myself down enough to process the images in their entirety. This much was obvious—the bond between my dad and his brother ran deep. Circumstances had forced them apart in various ways, but both still felt loyalty and love for the other. I itched with curiosity as I stared at the letter from my father, which lay on top of my open luggage. I knew I wouldn't open it, though—not after what I'd just seen. I felt an intense desire to protect both my father and unknown uncle, and that included guarding their secrets.

One more piece of my life's puzzle also snapped into place—the reason Dad said he couldn't come back to Cyrus with me. He was banished. He literally could not return as long as Praesidium existed. I also better understood the reasons for his lies. I couldn't blame him for hating Cyrus. The treatment he received here was abhorrent. Of course he wouldn't want me to return.

Another interesting moment was meeting Fox Springs. He seemed... sly. Perhaps his name was supposed to be indicative of that quality. How I would have liked to meet him when he was part of the Miners. It was sad to think of him dead now. He was so young.

I flopped down on the mattress, hating myself for jumping to conclusions about my dad. I thought he was afraid to return to Cyrus. I thought he was being a coward. I should have known better—my dad had always been strong, tough, and a fierce defender of what was right. Though I know he was terrified for me to come back here, I also think he's probably proud of the things I'm trying to accomplish. Though I still regret not leaving on better terms with him, the thought brought some peace to my convoluted heart and mind.

CHAPTER 23

RESTLESS

The clock ticked slowly through the night. I didn't catch even a minute's rest. When it was finally six o'clock, I decided it would be acceptable to wake Trent and tell him about my vision.

I crept down the west corridor hoping not to wake anyone. I approached the wooden door covering Trent's small room and knocked lightly. A moment later, it swung open to reveal an already dressed and alert-looking Trent. He smiled his charming smile.

"Good morning, gorgeous," he greeted me.

I blushed slightly. "Good morning. Can I come in?"

Trent glanced behind himself nervously. "Yeah, I guess that's fine." He stepped aside to let me through. His bedroom mirrored mine exactly—a mattress on the floor, a wooden chair, and a plastic set of drawers for his belongings, which contained one pair of jeans and two t-shirts. Trent didn't keep much here since he tried to sleep at home as often as possible.

The door closed behind us, and I instantly understood his nervous behavior. We were alone—completely alone. In a private room. And an hour before anyone expected us to be anywhere. My stomach twisted. That's not why I was here.

Trent stood at the door, his arms crossed behind his back.

"Sorry, I didn't mean to barge in on you," I apologized. "I just have something I want to tell you before the meeting. It's about a vision I had last night."

Trent visibly relaxed as he understood my unexpected appearance. "Sounds interesting. Go ahead and have a seat." He motioned to the wooden chair. Trent sat on his mattress with his back pressed against the rock wall.

I dove into my visions, trying to remember every detail. The scene in the dungeons was particularly painful to re-live but important for Trent to understand, so I pushed forward, nausea and hatred for King Trinnen turning my stomach.

When I finished, Trent looked surprised. "That's quite the story. Sounds like there's a lot about your father you don't know, but I guess it helps clarify a few points."

"It definitely raises as many questions as it answers," I agreed. "Look, Trent, before I left my house, my dad gave me this knife and letter." I removed the two objects from my pants pocket and held them out. "The knife is the object that held the memories. He asked me to find his brother and get them to him."

"That would be awesome if you could track him down, Ava. Sounds like something to look forward to once we have this whole mess with Tenebris behind us."

I didn't miss Trent's meaning. He understood I was excited about finding my uncle, but he was clearly saying it was something that should wait. I frowned. "Maybe we should be trying to find him now. He might know something that could help us. He did work for Tenebris after all."

"Yeah, but so do a lot of guards. The royals have always been careful not to reveal too much to their servants. I doubt he'd know anything that could help." Trent said it like it was the end of the discussion. I wasn't ready to give up so easily, but I decided it could wait.

"Fine. Let's go get something to eat. The meeting will be starting soon." I stood from the chair and walked out of the room without bothering to wait for Trent, though I could hear he was following close behind.

Breakfast was a quiet affair. I was angry with Trent, and he was obviously frustrated by my anger. We hurriedly dumped our dishes in the sink, and then entered the game room. We sat on the loveseat but at opposite ends of the small couch.

All of the Miners slowly trickled into the room over the next five minutes. Most were quiet, still groggy from an early morning, but Elsie and Katherine were in a heated argument as they entered the room.

"—should just ask Trevor to carve me out my own space. I am so sick of you stealing all of my stuff," Katherine huffed as she entered the room.

"Go for it! No one's stopping you. In fact, save him some trouble and just move into his room, why don't you?" Elsie shouted. "Then I wouldn't have to be woken up at all hours of the night when you two finally decide to stop making out!"

Katherine's face went from a deep red to purple as she

stuttered for a retort. Trevor—who had been sitting across the room—jumped up and went to Katherine's side. He put an arm around her and gave Elsie a hard look. Elsie seemed to realize her enormous slip and gasped, covering her mouth with both hands.

"I am so sorry, Kat," she breathed. "I didn't mean to— I wasn't thinking— that was really stupid—"

I glanced around the rest of the room. Surprise was evident on everyone's faces. So I guess Elsie was simply pretending not to know when I asked her about Katherine's love life, but the rest of the group clearly had no idea.

"Just shut up, Elsie," Katherine said, turning into Trevor, her face still bright red from embarrassment. "Let's sit down," she mumbled. Trevor took her hand and led her over to the spot where he'd been sitting before.

"Oh come on, people," Warren said as he walked into the room, Meraki slightly behind him. They were holding hands. She gave an icy glare in my general direction, so—forgetting my anger with Trent—I slid over and took his hand. He smiled down at me. "This isn't grade school. Nobody cares who you're dating. Obviously we have several couples in the room." He lifted his hand that held Meraki's and looked pointedly in mine and Trent's direction. "We can all learn to cope with it. Now let's get on with the meeting. We have a lot to get done today."

Warren took his place at the front of the room. With a sigh, I heaved myself off the couch and joined him at the front. I watched as Meraki took the seat farthest from where Trent sat. I was okay with that.

Warren cleared his throat. "As you are all aware, the team has decided to move up our attack on Tenebris."

"Some of the team, you mean," Amos grumbled.

"Shut up, Amos." Jameson chucked a pillow at Amos who took it straight to the face. Normally, that wouldn't hurt, but with Jameson's super-strength abilities, it was probably rather painful. Amos stood, red-faced, to retaliate, though I'm not sure why. No one was crazy enough to pick a fight with Jameson. In addition to his super-strength, he had enhanced fighting abilities. Warren looked at them both with raised eyebrows. Amos hesitated, then sat back down with a huff.

"We will attack seven days from today," Warren continued. "Remember that capturing Praesidium—not necessarily killing Tenebris—is our primary target. However, if any of you do get the chance to take out my dear old dad, go for it.

"There is much to be done to prepare. I've spent most of the night drawing up training and observation schedules. Every day leading up to the attack, each one of you will participate in four hours of combative and/or magical training as well as four hours of reconnaissance work. There are several areas around the palace where our existing intel is weak. This schedule," Warren stood to post a large, poster-sized paper on the wall, "will detail when and where you are expected each day. It also details who is the team leader for each reconnaissance or training session. If you are assigned to be a team leader, you are responsible for the safety of each member of your team. Do not take the responsibility lightly. When the meeting is adjourned, you can look over the schedule more closely. If you are unable to meet these commitments, you will be dismissed from the team, effective immediately. Any questions?"

The expressions around the room were stony. It was obvious most of the group was unhappy with Warren's leadership style, but I was grateful he was drawing a hard line. Now was not the time for arguments. We needed to get serious and get things done.

"Next item of business," Warren carried on. "I'm hoping we can come up with some ideas or solutions to this problem as a group. We have not been able to do any reconnaissance work inside the castle. Any previous attempts have been utter failures. I feel it is vital we get a better look at life for Tenebris on a day-to-day basis. I believe this could reveal the key to stealing Praesidium.

"Now, I have a thought. The annual Cyrun Royal Ball is coming up in just three days. As we all know, it's an important event for those closest to the king. This is likely our best opportunity to penetrate the castle, though security is sure to be even tighter than usual. Any suggestions for how we make the breach?"

The room was silent. Everyone looked at each other, hoping someone might have an idea. Nobody did. Except me.

"I had a vision last night," I began. "It was about my father's brother who was a well-respected guard for King Trinnen and then

250

King Tenebris. He left on good terms, and Tenebris specifically said my uncle was welcome back to the palace any time. Perhaps if I was able to find him, I could convince him to help us. I have reason to believe he hates Praesidium and the king as much as we do."

"Are you insane?" Damion was the first to speak, his blue eyes critical. "It's way too dangerous to bring in an outsider this close to our date of attack, let alone someone who has served the king for years. He'll report us immediately. We'll all be arrested and killed."

"I agree. That's crazy," Teresa said.

"He could be our only chance! He would know loads about the palace schedule, the guards and their rounds, and King Tenebris himself. His knowledge could be invaluable," I defended.

"You're so naive, Ava," Amos said. "Most people in this stupid kingdom are unwilling to lift a finger against the king. What makes you think your uncle would be any different?"

"I think it's a great idea!" Elsie chirped. Everyone looked at her with the same ludicrous expression they were giving me. Katherine's eyes burned with frustration. "Ava is totally right. Her uncle would be an awesome resource. Ava is smart—she won't go blowing every Miner secret the second she walks through her uncle's door. She'll play it safe until she has a better idea of where he stands before she gives anything away. Plus, either way, she doesn't have to mention who we are or where our hideout is.

Worst case scenario, she puts herself in major trouble, but we all know she can probably handle her uncle, even with his guard training. I say we let her go for it."

The room turned to utter chaos with insults being thrown every direction. I gave Elsie an appreciative smile which she returned.

"Enough!" Warren called out. The room grew quiet with several reluctant huffs. "I think Ava and Elsie are right. We will set certain parameters Ava must agree to, of course, but this could be the break we've been hoping for."

"Thank you!" I cried. "I will not let you guys down. I swear to be very careful and not reveal anything about us until I get a feel for my uncle's loyalties."

"That's all good and everything, but we need to decide on specifics that remain a secret no matter what," Damion said.

"I agree," Warren nodded. "You may not mention how many of us are part of the Miners or anyone by name, you cannot tell him even a general idea of where hideout is, you cannot reveal anyone's magical abilities besides your own, and you cannot tell him when we plan to attack. If you can agree to keep all of those details to yourself, you may attempt to find him. Any clue where he may be?"

"I have an idea," Trent spoke up. "Ava was telling me about her vision this morning. She described a meeting her uncle had after he was released from his service to the king with the Traveler Fox Springs." The room seemed to grow stiff at the mention of the

252

Miners' lost member. Trent cleared his throat uncomfortably before he carried on. "She described a statue of a centaur that was visible from the edge of the alleyway. I'm familiar with the place she described. It's in Cashmere, so her uncle was there not long ago."

"Yes, my father is from Cashmere," I said excitedly. "King Trinnen mentioned that. My uncle probably stayed in the province where they grew up."

"Sounds like a solid lead," Warren agreed. "Follow it and see where it takes you. Trent, you'll go with Ava. I can't give you more than today to try and track him down. I need you, Trent, to help get people to their reconnaissance assignments, and you both need to train with the team, so work quickly."

"Understood," I nodded.

"Well get going then," Warren said impatiently, motioning for us to stand.

"Oh, sorry, I didn't realize you meant now. Ready, Trent?"

"Guess I have to be." We stood, and he took my hands.

CHAPTER 24

CASHMERE

We appeared in front of a bronze centaur statue with a pool of water at its base, just like I'd seen in my vision.

"You did it!" I jumped and wrapped my arms around Trent's neck. "I can't believe I'm going to meet an extended family member! I've never done this before. Do you think he'll like me?" I dropped my arms and stepped back.

Trent laughed and ruffled my hair. "You're silly. I'm sure if what you told me about your vision is true, he'll be ecstatic to meet his brother's daughter. And I'm sure he'll appreciate a reply from his brother after all this time. You still have the knife and letter, right?"

"Right here," I said, patting my pants pocket. I realized it was not the best pair of jeans to wear when meeting family for the first time. They were old and raggedy. My shirt, too, was a bit tattered and rather plain—a simple magenta t-shirt.

"You look great," Trent smiled, guessing my train of thought. "Stop worrying. Now let's see if we can figure out where your uncle actually is. The pub is supposed to be the gossip center of town. I'd say that's where we begin." He pointed to a dingy looking wood building that stood at the end of the street, passed the long rows of shops.

As we opened the door to the pub, I was met with a distinct sense of familiarity—this was the place my dad and Will had come for drinks. It was as dark and dank as it had been in my vision, with a fire lit in the fireplace, despite the stuffy atmosphere inside.

Trent took my hand and dragged me toward the dirty bar at the front of the pub. We each took a seat and were met with unfriendly glares from the pair of men sitting to the left. The bartender—a portly, balding man with wrinkled skin and a limp in his step—approached us and asked what we wanted to drink. I looked at Trent with alarm. I'd never had a drink in my entire life. Kids back home were sometimes into that kind of stuff, but I had never been interested.

"Two beers would be fine," Trent answered.

The bartender shuffled a few paces and filled two dirty mugs. I stifled a gag. He slid the mugs down the bar to us without another word.

Trent passed me a drink, which I hesitantly lifted to my nose. Cautiously, I sniffed. Bad idea—it smelled disgusting.

"You don't have to drink it, Ava," Trent whispered as he tried not to laugh. "In fact, I think it would be best if neither of us did. We want to be sharp."

Still, Trent lifted the mug to his mouth, though the level of his drink hadn't changed when he set the mug back down. I followed suit and pretended to take a sip as well.

"So, you gentlemen from the area?" Trent asked the two men sitting next to us conversationally.

"Yeah, what's it to ya?" the man closest to us grumbled. The other didn't bother to acknowledge us.

"We're hoping to get in touch with an old family friend, but we're not sure where to start. We thought he might be from this province. His name is Will Longfellow. Ever heard of him?"

"'Course I have. The Longfellow family has lived here for generations. They're out in Burgeon." The man gestured over his shoulder.

"Thank you. We'll head that direction as soon as we're finished here."

The man gave Trent a look that clearly said, "I don't care."

Trent stood and placed a few silver coins on the counter next to our mugs. "Let's get going," he whispered.

I was all too happy to follow him outside, thinking of my dad's drunken stumble out this same door many years ago. Though most of the memories I had of him in Cyrus were sad, I couldn't help but feel a greater connection to him now that I was here, in the town where he grew up.

"So... Burgeon. Any clue what that means?" I asked Trent as we hurried down the city street, past the centaur statue.

"There are fourteen provinces in Cyrus. Cashmere is one of them, but there are quite a few smaller towns that normally surround a Province's major city center. The man meant your father lives in the town Burgeon." Trent gestured to a sign that hung on a lantern post, which read, *Burgeon,* with an arrow pointing down a smaller cobblestone street. It seemed to head

256

roughly in a northeastern direction.

"How are we supposed to find him once we get to Burgeon?" I asked. My breathing was becoming labored as I struggled to keep up with Trent's brisk pace—his legs were much longer than mine.

"How's your wolf nose feeling?"

"My wolf nose?" I asked, surprised.

"Yeah. Do you think you could track in a scent?"

"I don't know. I've never tried before. Wouldn't my uncle need to have walked this path recently?"

"Probably. But I'd guess he has. Cashmere is already a small province, comparatively. Any of its surrounding cities are going to be limited in their supplies and resources. If he's caring for a sick daughter, I'd assume he comes to Cashmere often," Trent explained as we reached an iron arch that led to a bridge over a small stream. We crossed the bridge, leaving the city behind.

"Do you think my uncle's scent will still be detectable on the knife after all this time?"

"I'm not sure, but I think there's a good chance. He did carry it around for most of his life, and your father has probably not done much with it since he received it."

"Alright, let's give this a shot," I said, stepping off the cobblestones into the dirt and grass. I reached in my pocket and handed Trent the pocketknife and letter. Then I focused on the warmth of the wolf inside me. I'd been able to give transforming quite a bit of practice since I'd discovered the ability—it came easily now. A shimmering sensation tingled outward from my heart to my head, arms, and legs until I stood hunched over on four legs. I could feel the raw power of my limbs and heard my breaths come in wolfy huffs.

"Good doggy, doggy," Trent cooed, reaching to scratch behind my right ear.

I snarled and snapped at his extended hand. He jumped back in fright, his eyes wide. I chuckled. The sound came out in a low rumble. Trent eyed me suspiciously before he rolled his eyes. "Was that really necessary? You scared the daylights out of me!"

I laughed again, then nudged Trent's hand that held the knife. He opened his palm to let me have a sniff. It mostly smelled like my dad, but there was a hint of something else there. Holding onto that smell, I sniffed the cobblestone path. There was no detectable smell that matched the scent of the knife, but I kept my nose down, sniffing as I trotted down the path, Trent at my heels.

After several minutes, I caught a faint whiff of the scent on the knife. I lifted my snout and looked at Trent.

"You got something?" he asked excitedly.

I nodded and put my nose back down, sniffing again. The scent grew stronger as I continued down the path.

Soon, homes came into view. None of them smelled like the knife, so we continued forward. Occasionally, someone would be outside. They'd look at me in alarm, evidently not expecting to see a wolf walking down the street. Trent would always call out something like, "It's just my friend who's a shapeshifter! You're in no danger!" and they'd relax.

After several more minutes, the scent turned down a side road from the main one we'd been on. We followed it. About a half mile down that road, the scent grew quite strong. I looked up to see the house I'd visited in memories—the house where my father had grown up.

I let out a low whimper to let Trent know we'd found it, then ran off to the side of the road again and concentrated on pulling out my human form. The tingling sensation receded down my arms and legs, back into my chest. In less than a second, the transformation was complete, clothes and all; I was extremely grateful for that detail.

"Pretty cool, huh?" I asked Trent.

"Let's wait and see if you actually found the right place before you go bragging too much."

"There's no way I'm wrong. I know that house from a memory I saw of my dad's. His brother must live in their parents' house. Come on, let's go see!" I hurried forward, eager to meet my uncle for the first time.

I lifted my fist to knock on the front door but hesitated.

"What's wrong?" Trent asked.

Dread welled up inside me. "What if he hates me, Trent? What if he hates my father? What if he's nothing like I imagine and he's actually loyal to Tenebris?" I turned and started down the steps. "This was a bad idea. We should go back—"

Trent grabbed my upper arm, stopping me. "Come on, Ava. It's not like you to be afraid. This is worth a shot."

I looked into Trent's pleading eyes, remembering my dad as he stood on these steps asking my mother not to leave him. Trent was right—I needed to give my uncle a chance. I took a deep breath and turned back to the door. I raised my fist and knocked firmly four times.

I heard footsteps on the other side of the door. My heart stopped as they drew nearer. Finally, the door cracked open. A woman I'd never seen before peered out at us. She was middle aged with long, red hair, blue eyes, and a freckled face. She was slender and wore jeans, a brown, long-sleeve shirt, and a white apron.

"Can I help you?" the woman asked.

"Y-y-yes," I stammered and cleared my throat. "Does Will Longfellow live here?"

"He does. He's my husband. And who are you?"

"My name is Ava Tanner—or Longfellow, I mean. Sorry, I'm not used to using that name. I'm Will's niece."

The woman looked me over with suspicion and surprise. She glanced over her shoulder as a deep voice behind said, "Let her in."

CHAPTER 25

SECRETS OF THE GUARD

The woman stepped aside, opening the door wider. She motioned for us to come in.

The room we entered was small, somewhat dark, but very cozy. The walls were made of dark wood and the floor was covered in light brown carpet. There were a few sitting chairs, a long blue couch, and a fireplace at the far end of the room. There were no lights around, so I assumed there was no electricity, just like Trent's home. The most interesting part of the room, though, was the man who stood behind the red haired woman. I recognized him immediately as my uncle Will. There were definite similarities between him and my father. They shared the same hair color, the same tan skin tone, but Will's eyes were a beautiful blue and his face was longer than my dad's. His nose, too was larger than my dad's angular one. He appeared to be quite a bit older than my father, though in the memories, they'd seemed to be only three or four years apart.

"Hello," the man said, extending his hand in greeting, his eyes guarded. "I'm Will and this is my wife Anna. Please have a seat."

Trent and I walked over to the blue couch that sat along the back wall. Will sat in a red wingback chair next to the fireplace, facing us. Anna did not join us but made her way up the set of stairs.

"I heard you tell Anna you're my niece?" Will asked.

"Yes, I'm Carmichael's daughter, Avalon," I nodded eagerly, "and this is my... friend, Trent."

"I didn't know Mike had any kids." Will eyed me skeptically.

"Well, my father did send me with these." I nudged Trent for the note and knife. He handed them to me swiftly. "Maybe that will help convince you?" I stood and crossed the few steps to where Will sat. He took the knife and note with wide eyes, as if it were too good to be true.

"Th-thank you," he stammered. He took the knife and examined it, then turned his attention to the letter. "This is from your dad?"

"Yes, he asked me not to read it but give it to you directly. He told me it was very important."

"Do you mind if I read it now? Perhaps it will help us both understand more of our present situation."

"Of course, go ahead."

I noticed he hadn't asked why my dad wasn't here with me. He knew, obviously, that was an impossibility. I waited eagerly as Will read the letter. His expression worried me. It changed from one of excitement to one of shock and eventually confused horror.

When he finished, he looked up at me with wide eyes. "If you'll excuse me, please, I'll be back in a few moments." Without further explanation, Will rose from his seat and crossed the small room, disappearing from view. I heard a door open somewhere

262

behind us. I jumped as it slammed shut.

"Could the letter have been that bad?" I looked up at Trent.

"I'm sure it was just different than he expected. Try not to let it worry you too much." Trent put his arm around me and rubbed my arm comfortingly, though his eyes, too, were tight with concern.

Several minutes passed as Trent and I sat in strained silence. There was some movement from the floor above, but otherwise, the house was quiet.

Finally, I heard the back door open and Will re-entered the room with a few long strides. "Sorry," he apologized as he returned to the wingback chair. "Your father was always full of surprises, often unpleasant ones. It would appear that has not changed." Will tucked the letter away in the breast pocket of the leather jacket he wore.

"Can you tell me what my dad said?" I asked, my curiosity growing intensely.

"I'm afraid not. It doesn't really concern you anyway. It was mostly a response to an apology I sent your father two years ago. Thank you for bringing it to me. It brings a great deal of comfort to hear from him after all this time. Would either of you like something to eat or drink before you head on your way?"

I was surprised. Will hadn't been overly friendly or unfriendly in our time together thus far, but his dismissal now was clear. Surely he'd want to spend at least a little time with his previously unknown niece. He hadn't even asked me anything about myself.

"We actually came to ask you a few more questions," I said tentatively. "They're unrelated to my father's letter—questions of our own. Do you have another minute?"

Will didn't answer immediately. Instead, he looked at me with intense scrutiny—it made me uncomfortable. I squirmed in my seat. Trent squeezed my hand lightly.

"I suppose that would be alright," Will said with a sigh, sinking back into his chair.

"Thank you," I began. "So you served as a palace guard for many years, correct?"

"Yes." Will responded curtly.

"My father warned you against becoming a guard. Did you ever come to agree with his position? That it was a cruel job, a dangerous job?"

Will's eyes tightened. "At times."

"When you asked King Tenebris to be released, you left on cordial terms. Have you kept in contact as he said you could?"

"How do you know about that?" Will asked.

"I have a gift that allows objects to reveal certain glimpses of memories to me. The pocketknife showed me some of your history with my father."

Will shifted uncomfortably. "How much have you seen?"

"Enough to know you have good reason to hate the crown."

"Of course I do not. I am loyal to my king and the kingdom," Will said, jumping to his feet in indignation. He said it automatically, as if it was something he'd trained himself to say

264

whenever someone questioned his loyalties.

I stood as well, my temper rising at my uncle's cowardice. "So you approve, then, of being forced to beat your own brother within an inch of death? Not to mention the innumerable other innocent people who have no doubt been terrorized at your hands on the commands of your king. Or the ludicrous social system designed to keep those the king views as less worthy in a pitiful and helpless state. Beggars on the street who are treated like vermin. Kids in school who get beat up because they're a lower social standing than their peers. The complete absence of anyone's free will. These are all things you believe in, would fight to defend?"

Will's face turned white as I hurled my accusations at him. "Your father told you?" The ghost of the past glimmered in his eyes.

"No, I saw it all for myself, Will. I saw my father bloodied and beaten. I saw the tears streaming down your face as you were forced to carry on with his flogging. I saw King Trinnen's pleasure at my father's suffering. He is not worthy of the crown nor is his brother. We seek to change that. That is why we are here—to ask for your help."

"My help? Are you insane? I could never fight against my king."

"I'm not asking you to. I simply want to know two things. First, do you have a way of making contact with the king? If so, would you be able to get me into the palace, even for a short amount of time? Second, do you know anything about the object

265

known as Praesidium?"

Will looked frantically back and forth between me and Trent before he sat down again. He let out a long breath, holding his head in his hands. I followed and took a seat on the couch, trying to reign in my indignation.

"What exactly are your plans?" Will asked, looking up at me with tired eyes.

"I'm afraid I can't give specifics yet—not until I know you'll help me. To put it simply, we seek to free Cyrus of the forced obedience of Praesidium. We are in a unique position to be able to do so."

Will considered for a moment. "So you're saying you want freedom for Cyrus, including a change in the social system?"

"Essentially, yes."

"Then I'll help you how I can," Will said, dropping his hands from his face as he straightened up in his seat.

I was shocked. He'd been so resistant only a moment earlier. I didn't understand his sudden change in heart. "Uh, that's great and everything but why would you agree so quickly?" I was worried this was some sort of trap.

"It's my daughter, Kayley," Will sighed. "She's very sick. For many years, I sought freedom from my position as a guard so that I could spend more time with her and my family, but Tenebris never agreed. The most I got was two weeks during the summer and occasional weekends. Only after I managed to work my way up the ladder and really impress Tenebris did he finally concede, and I believe it had much more to do with the queen's wishes than his own."

Will looked over his shoulder out the large windows as he spoke. "I have hated the crown ever since that day I was forced to beat my brother, but I haven't been able to get out because of Praesidium. They valued me, highly, because of my offensive gifts. Every day I served was an internal battle of self-loathing as I fought to defend the people I hated." Will turned back to face us. "Even now, after years of serving my kingdom, Tenebris has refused medical treatment for Kayley. He sees her as a lost cause, a Zero. He has forbidden any doctor from seeing her. She was born with a birth defect, you see, and has never had a strong mental capacity. She'll be 18 in just two years, and we will no longer be able to care for her. I suppose it's time I take a page out of my brother's book and fight for what I want. If there's even a slight chance you could change things for my family, I'm willing to risk it."

I looked at Trent who seemed as surprised by Will's sudden change of heart as I was. "What do you think?" I whispered to him, though Will could hear us perfectly well.

"I think this could be our best chance and we proceed with caution." He whispered back, eyeing Will skeptically.

"As far as your questions," Will looked at me, a fierce gleam in his eye, "I do happen to have a very convenient way to get you into the castle. And yes, I know a few things about Praesidium— or rather, I know the best place you can learn more."

267

CHAPTER 26

THE KING'S FEAST

"You've got your invitation?" I whispered to Will as we ducked behind a row of large shrubs alongside the path that led to the main palace gates.

"Yes, it's right here," Will said, patting the breast pocket of his red guard's uniform, "though it's not really necessary. The majority of the guards here were once under my command. I should be easily recognized and accepted."

Every time I glanced at his uniform, my heart stopped for a moment until I reminded myself he wasn't one of the bad guys— or at least I was hoping he wasn't.

"Are you ready, Trent?" I asked, looking across Will to Trent who stood on his other side. He looked... amazing. Trent in regular clothes was always great, but Trent in a tuxedo was breathtaking.

"Definitely not. But I'll be pretending otherwise. Thanks for asking." Trent straightened his jacket lapels nervously.

I smiled. "Great, let's get going then."

We glanced around to make sure no one was watching before we ducked out from behind the shrubs onto the cobblestone path, which led to the palace doors. It was lit on either side with small lanterns that glowed vibrant greens, blues, and reds.

The past two days had been spent preparing and discussing strategy with Will and Warren. Warren is the only member of the Miners Will had met besides Trent and myself. Will—being a former high ranking palace guard—had been invited to the annual Cyrun Royal Ball, as he was every year. Trent and I now accompanied him as his oldest daughter, Bridgette, and her boyfriend, Tyler.

Planning without revealing too much information to Will about the Miners had been difficult. Essentially, he knew about my six abilities and that I seemed to have immunity from Praesidium's effect because I'd grown up in the human realm. We had not mentioned Warren's absolute immunity; Warren wanted to keep his heritage out of it. Will also knew Trent was an unregistered Traveler, a fact that I fervently wished we'd been able to keep from him. If Will ended up being a traitor, I knew there was no way either Trent or I would come out of this alive. It could very well be that we'd walk through the massive palace doors and Will would march us straight up to Tenebris. He'd declare our intentions, and we'd be cast into prison, where we'd be tortured for information and then put to death for treason.

Even if this wasn't a setup, there was still the possibility that Will's strong Cyrun connection to Praesidium would compel him to tell Tenebris the truth. The Miners were all somewhat immune to Praesidium's constant pull on Cyruns because of our connections to the human realm, but Will had never left the influence of Cyril for even a minute. We were banking on his desire to help his daughter overriding the urge to obey his master's wishes. According to the plan, we intended to keep Will away from Tenebris as much as possible, hoping to avoid any direct commands.

Our ultimate goal this evening had only become clear after Will revealed some of his knowledge from his time as a guard. We were here to discover Ganton's diary. Will wasn't certain it actually existed, he'd only heard rumors that had been passed down among palace guards for years. There was one room up in the palace library that was constantly guarded by four guards. No guard had ever been inside the room, but King Trinnen and then King Tenebris had visited the room occasionally during Will's time as a guard. The rumor was that Ganton—the creator of Praesidium—left instructions about the necklace in his diary, which was kept in that room. The Miners were convinced the diary had to be real. There was no other purpose for guarding the room so carefully.

Personally, I wasn't sure what to think, but I hoped the rumors were true. Either way, it seemed to me that whatever was kept in the room had to be important for it to be kept so private. Therefore, our goal was to break into the room and find out what was behind the doors. The plan involved several Miner members, though Will was oblivious to that fact.

I pulled at the tight waist of the purple dress I wore, desperate for breath. How did girls ever wear corsets? It felt like I was going to suffocate. Surely my face was turning red.

"You okay?" Trent whispered nervously as we continued up the long path that was lined with palace guards. They watched with hard stares as we passed. Will occasionally nodded to a guard, though the guards never acknowledged him in return—I'd guess it was against protocol.

"My lungs have never been so desperate for relief, but sure, I'm fine," I whispered back bitterly.

Trent chuckled and wrapped his arm around my back. "Well, if it helps you feel better, you should know you look incredible."

I blushed. "Thanks."

Trent gently squeezed my waist as we approached the palace steps. The staircase was long and elegant. The two doors at the top were enormous and manned by several guards in red uniforms that were similar to the one Will wore, though Will's lacked several notable weapons the other guards wore on their belts.

"Invitation?" The guard immediately in front of the right palace door barked.

"Yes, here you go," Will said, digging into his pocket. He retrieved the invitation and held it out for examination.

"You are Mr. Longfellow? And these are your guests?" The guard asked in a monotone.

"I know you know who I am, Carson, but yes, fine," Will rolled his eyes. "This is my daughter, Bridgette, and her boyfriend, Tyler."

"Very well. Step aside for a security check and then you may proceed to the dining hall."

"Thanks, Carson," Will said, stepping around the guard. Trent and I followed.

The inside of the palace was magnificent. Like the throne room I'd seen in my vision a few days ago, the palace was dominated by white and gold with occasional red accents. The floors and walls were made of marble with gold crown molding, gold pillars, and gold banisters on every staircase we passed. The doors to every room were also gold and etched with ornate patterns. The rugs were always some shade of red, reminding me of bloody splotches scattered about the palace—an accurate representation, I suppose, of all the blood on the royals' hands.

"We'll be eating in here," Will whispered, gesturing to the open doors only a few steps ahead. "Remember to avoid conversation with Tenebris at all costs."

The room we entered was incredibly spacious and well decorated. There were several long tables that lined the room in one large rectangle. Bouquets of flowers stood on short pedestals around the room. A waiter by the door directed us to three seats on the far side with our backs to the large windows. We were a little too close to the head table for my comfort—only about five chairs would separate us and the king.

The room was approximately half full as we arrived. Several more small groups and couples poured in after us until every seat was occupied.

A man dressed in a black tuxedo walked through a smaller pair of doors on the opposite side of the room. "All arise for His

Majesty, King Tenebris and Queen Isabella," the man called loudly over the crowd. Everyone stopped talking and stood from their places at the table.

"Isabella?" I whispered to Trent. "The queen's name is Isabella?"

"Yes, now be quiet!" Trent urged nervously.

I was confused—Warren's mother was named Isabella. But Tenebris had killed her. Could it be nothing more than an incredible coincidence that the queen was also named Isabella?

My thoughts were brought to a halt as I watched King Tenebris—wearing a sharp black uniform—enter the room. At his side was Queen Isabella, wearing a strikingly beautiful red dress that hugged her magnificent figure. Her gold curls were pulled back in an intricate twist that cascaded down her back.

As she drew closer, I sucked in a sharp breath. I recognized her. She looked like Warren's mother had in my visions. She, too, had been beautiful. But there was something different about the queen. She wasn't Warren's mother, but her heavy makeup was obviously designed to make her *look* more like Warren's mother had. A chill ran down my spine. How disturbing. Did she wear such heavy makeup for this reason? Was it on Tenebris' orders so that she would look more like the woman he had once loved? The woman he murdered?

As the royal couple approached their seats, two members of the wait staff pulled their chairs out and they sat. The rest of the room followed and took their seats. I felt a tug on my hand. With a jolt, I realized it was Trent, pulling me down into my own seat. I'd forgotten to sit with everybody else. Embarrassed, I shot a furtive glance at the king and queen. Tenebris appeared mildly annoyed. Isabella seemed intrigued. I dropped my eyes to the table, hoping their attention would focus elsewhere.

Fortunately, at that moment, the wait staff poured into the room and approached the tables with large serving trays. A waitress set down a plate of unrecognizable food in front of me. I looked at it with hesitation.

Trent chuckled. "Don't overthink it. It's just fancy food. I'm sure it will be great." To prove his point, he speared a forkful off his plate and popped it in his mouth.

"Do you know much about Queen Isabella? Do you remember the wedding?" I asked Trent in a whisper.

"Not really. I was only six when the marriage happened. Tenebris keeps the queen hidden for the most part, but most people say she's very kind."

"How about you, Will? Do you know her well? Has she always looked like that?" I asked over Trent who sat between us.

Will glanced at the person seated on his other side, then back to me. "That's not really something we should be discussing, Bridgette." The look he gave me clearly said, *shut up!*

Grumpily, I stabbed the piece of mystery meat in front of me and cut off a chunk, shoving it in my mouth. Only after I noticed the woman to my left watching me out of the corner of her eye did I realize my table manners were less than lady like for the current setting. I took a deep breath and tried to act normal for the rest of the meal.

Finally, the wait staff delivered dessert. By far, it was the best part of our dinner, though I still wasn't certain what I was eating. It was some sort of pudding with pieces of cake scattered throughout. By the time our waiter took our plates away, I was certain my corset was going to burst at the seams.

King Tenebris stood from his large, velvet chair. "If you would all please join my wife and I in the ballroom for dancing, we'd be delighted. We will also be joined by several other guests who were not with us for dinner. Please mingle and enjoy each other's company." He inclined his greasy black head, which was returned by low bows and curtseys from the rest of us. I stumbled a little as I rose, but overall, I had to give myself credit considering the boa constrictor wrapped around my middle.

I turned to face Will and Trent. "Well," I sighed, "the hardest part is over. It shouldn't be so hard to avoid him in the ballroom, I'd imagine."

Too late, I noticed Trent's eyes grow wide. "Who are we avoiding?" a velvety voice asked behind me. I didn't have to turn to know it belonged to King Tenebris.

I squeezed my eyes shut for a moment before pasting a false smile on my face. I turned around to see King Tenebris and Queen Isabella standing in front of me. I curtseyed once more, this time without the stumble. "An old boyfriend of mine," I lied. "Things didn't end well, and now that I'm joined by Tyler this evening," I reached back to pat Trent's arm, "I'd imagine it would be a bit awkward to run into him."

"Ah, yes," King Tenebris said. "Young love does have a tendency to end messily, doesn't it?"

I tried to contain my anger at his words. Yes, a murderer would think that, I suppose. Behind me, Will and Trent laughed good-naturedly. I glanced at Queen Isabella who stood half hidden behind Tenebris. To my surprise, she was looking directly at me with curiosity. Her eyes were beautiful but cold—they sent a chill down my spine. I quickly dropped my gaze.

"Will Longfellow," Tenebris stepped forward and took Will by the hand as he reached up to pat his shoulder. "It has been a few years. It's nice to have you join us again. Who are these young ones you have with you tonight?"

"This is my daughter, Bridgette," Will touched my back, "and her boyfriend, Tyler." He pushed Trent forward slightly.

"Is this the daughter you went home for?" Tenebris asked.

"No, no. Kayley is at home, with her mother."

Knowing how Will felt about the subject, I noticed his tone grow marginally more strained as he discussed Kayley with the man who refused to help her get better.

"That's too bad. You'll have to bring your wife with you next time. I'd love to meet her."

"Yes, she'd enjoy that very much. I'm sure you have many others you'd like to greet, so we'll leave you to it." Will bowed once more. Trent and I followed his example, then turned to follow the crowds out the large double doors, breathing a sigh of relief.

CHAPTER 27

THE DIARY

I glanced at my wristwatch—we were precisely on schedule as we left the hall. Katherine, Damion, and Trevor should be entering the palace any time now, dressed in uniforms like the servants wore. The palace grounds were protected from Travel, so we had to get creative in our ways to breach the castle. For the past two days, Trevor had been working to dig a tunnel from outside the perimeter walls that would come up in one of the staff supply closets in the basement. Elsie had sewn the costumes they'd be wearing based on Will's descriptions. From what I'd seen at dinner, they should blend in just fine.

We walked down the long hall to a magnificent archway which led into the ballroom. Once inside, we were met by a cacophony of music, dancing, and laughter. Beautiful women in their finest dresses were being spun around on the floor by men dressed in white, gray, and black tuxedos. Occasional red guard uniforms like Will's were sprinkled into the mix. We were shuffled off to the side as a couple came spiraling toward us, oblivious to our presence.

"The upper classes are pretty fond of dancing, I take it," Trent grumbled as he caught my arm, keeping me from tripping over my dress in our hustle to get out of the way.

"That's an understatement," Will agreed. Though he was evidently trying not to enjoy himself, there were traces of amusement in his face at the scene before him. "Don't you two have somewhere to be?"

I checked my watch. Less than two minutes until I was supposed to meet the others at our rendezvous point. "Well, I do. You okay here, Trent?" We'd decided Trent should stay with Will and keep an eye on him so that he didn't run off to alert any guards to our presence. He'd also be the lookout for any strange activity at the party scene.

"Just dandy," Trent said as a rather large man bumped him from behind.

"Sorry," I whispered. "I'll try to be fast."

"That would be appreciated."

"Be back soon." I stretched up on my toes and kissed Trent on the cheek.

"Be safe," he whispered as he squeezed my hand.

I slipped back out the large archway, with the excuse of looking for the restroom if anyone stopped me to ask where I was headed. I walked as casually as I could manage considering the amount of stress I was under, not to mention the corset digging into my flesh.

I moved swiftly toward the east wing under explicit directions Will had given me about the layout of the palace. There was a staircase located on the far eastern side that led up to the fourth floor—my target.

Once I reached the stairs, I assumed I was out of sight, so I used my speed to climb the steps, knowing it would be unlikely I'd be seen at the pace I could move. Once I reached the fourth floor landing, I swiftly ducked into the first hallway that was only a few yards ahead, then slipped through the brick wall into the first guestroom. From there, I moved through three more guest suites, a cleaning supplies closet, and a staff restroom before I reached my destination—a small storage closet in the library.

"Hey, Ava," Trevor's voice welcomed me as I materialized through the wall. "Nice of you to join us."

"Glad I could make it," I teased back. "Have you checked to see if the guards are really there like Will said they'd be?"

"I checked," Katherine's voice replied through the darkness. "There are four of them spread out along the north wall of shelves."

"Excellent. We all clear on the plan from here?"

"Yep!"

"Got it."

"I'm with ya."

"Great, whenever you're ready, Damion," I said.

"Lights out in three, two, one." With the wave of Damion's hand, the small crack of light from outside the closet door disappeared.

"Are you slowing time?" I asked Katherine, though I got my answer as I asked. My voice slowed and Trevor and Damion immediately appeared to be moving in slow motion. My ears

280

pressed down on me as even small hums and buzzing noises in the air were repressed, traveling at much slower speeds. Katherine, on the other hand, opened the closet door without any delay, and, thanks to my speed, I could almost keep up with her.

She jogged toward the south wall, and I followed as close behind her as I could manage. It was the strangest sensation to know I was moving at my fastest speed, yet to feel so sluggish. After a few twists and turns around bookshelves, lounge chairs, and tables, I could see the wall where the four guards stood, nearly frozen in their looks of confusion at the sudden loss of electricity. Slowly, they began to converge toward each other, as if to discuss what had happened.

Katherine approached the first guard, holding an open bottle of purple powder under his nose. The dust was supposed to knock out the person who inhaled it. After a moment's exposure, the guard collapsed to the ground, unconscious. Katherine hurried forward to the next guard until all four men lay unresponsive on the floor.

I caught up to her and gave her a thumbs up. We stepped in front of the middle set of shelves. I waited for Katherine to tap the sequence of books as Will had instructed. The code was supposed to open the secret door to the room beyond. Katherine did as she'd been told without success. She looked at me in confusion.

I motioned to myself, indicating I wanted to try. While I could move quickly, I couldn't speak quickly, since the sound waves I produced would still be slowed. Katherine, however, could speak at a normal rate since time hadn't been slowed for her at all. As a result, I was left to communicate through actions.

Will said the door was enchanted so that no magic could penetrate it, even my ability to move through solid objects, but I tried anyway, shoving myself against the books. Nothing happened. I tried a few times, continually running into the solid shelves.

I placed my hands on my hips to think. I was fairly certain Katherine had touched the sequence of books in the correct order but decided it was best to double check. *Fifth shelf, tenth from the right*, I thought, touching the spine of that book. *Seventh shelf, third from the left, then fourth shelf, sixth from the left.* Will had forced us to memorize *5,10R, 7,3L, 4,6L* as the code. I was impressed he'd remembered after all these years. Maybe he always dreamed of coming back and discovering the room's secrets. Maybe that's why it had been so easy to convince him to help us.

As I tapped the last book, the entire shelf radiated a faint gold light, then sunk back, revealing a black space behind. A sense of trepidation filled me—I had no idea what actually lay hidden behind these doors.

"What are you waiting for?" Katherine whispered. "Go!" She shoved my back, pushing me into the dark abyss, which somehow came to light as I entered the space.

The room was small and plain. Along the far wall, a desk and chair sat with a modest bookshelf on the wall to my left.

A pounding sound behind caught my attention. I turned to see Katherine attempting to enter the room, but she could not. A previously invisible forcefield rippled each time she connected with it in her attempts to enter the small room.

"Ava? Ava? Are you okay?" she cried as she pounded against the shield.

How odd. Couldn't she see that I was fine? I was only a couple feet in front of her and the room had come to light. I hurried back to her, hesitating only slightly at the shield, hoping it would let me re-enter once I left. I exited through it, feeling a small shiver as I crossed the threshold.

"Oh my goodness! I'm so glad you're okay! I thought you were lost in there, and I couldn't get through."

I turned back to see that the room was as black as it had been before I stepped in. Nothing beyond was visible.

Though Katherine had slowed time, we had no way of knowing how long it would be before the guards woke up or before someone came looking for them. We didn't have time to waste. I was frustrated I couldn't communicate this more effectively to Katherine, but I motioned to myself, then the door, then gave her a thumbs up.

"You're going back in?" she asked.

I nodded vigorously.

"Okay. Keep the door open though, just in case. And try not to take too long. Just grab the book and let's get out of here."

I gave her a thumbs up again, then ducked back into the room, which lit itself once more upon my entrance. I was relieved it had let me back through; my abilities must let me pass through the shield unobstructed.

Alright, time to focus. The diary was certainly somewhere in the small selection of books on the shelves. I scoured the titles but was disappointed to find they were all regular, published books— nothing handwritten at all amongst them.

With a sigh, I turned my attention to the desk; perhaps it was hidden in one of the drawers. I pulled the two drawers out on either side, but found nothing but pens, an empty notepad, and a small lion head charm. As my fingers connected with the charm, I was pulled into a memory it contained.

The setting hardly changed at all. I stood in the same small room behind a man who sat slumped in the desk chair in front of me. He exhaled in frustration, slamming the cover of the book in front of him closed. I edged closer to try and read over his shoulder and recognized the man as King Trinnen. The book was not one I'd seen among the others on the shelves.

Abruptly, King Trinnen slid the chair back and stood. If I had any more substance than a ghost in these memories, I would have caught it in the stomach. As it was, the chair went straight through me. He slid out the desk drawer, withdrawing the lion head charm, which he thrust into a divot on the side of the bookshelf. One of the shelves slid out, revealing a hidden compartment. King Trinnen shoved the book inside and pushed the drawer closed. The seams of the compartment hid easily in the wood grain. I could have stared at the shelves for hours and never noticed it.

With a huff, he walked the few steps to the room's door and pushed a lever to its side. The door slid back, allowing him to exit.

The scene disappeared, and I returned to reality. Knowing exactly what to do, I slid the lion head charm into the same notch King Trinnen had just placed it in. The head grew warm under my touch as the hidden drawer popped open, revealing an old, thin, leather book beneath. I pulled it out. Like the lion's head, it, too, felt warm to the touch, as if welcoming me.

Hurriedly, I flipped it open. I had a plan that the rest of the group didn't know about. Hiking up my dress to a black strap around my thigh, I pulled out my cell phone from the human realm. It was useless here for calls or texting, but I had Damion charge it up for me so that I could use the camera. I planned to take pictures of the pages rather than stealing the book so that if Tenebris returned to this room in the near future, he wouldn't be alarmed to the absence of the diary.

A quick scan of the diary's contents revealed a section labeled *Praesidium*. I stopped there and began snapping pictures of each page until I reached what appeared to be the end of the section, going a few pages further to be certain.

After I had the pictures I needed, I turned back to a paragraph that caught my eye: *Praesidium's Limits*. Quickly, I poured over the slanted scrawl.

Praesidium is well protected and cannot be removed from the wearer by any magical or physical means except by two individuals of the royal bloodline, united in their quest to override the will of the wearer. This safety measure has been implemented in case any wearer of Praesidium should abuse his powers or fail to act in the best interest of the kingdom. If such is the case, two members of the royal family can rightfully reclaim the power of Praesidium and bestow it upon a more worthy guardian.

Next to this paragraph of writing was a note, scribbled in very different handwriting.

Family is biggest threat—limit children to one in order to protect absolute power.

My heart dropped at the words I had read. In order to touch Praesidium, we needed two members of royal descent. Warren could not do it alone. No number of magical abilities would be enough to conquer it. The Miners' mission was hopeless.

I sunk back, leaning against the desk chair, feeling completely defeated as I realized what this all meant. There was no hope for Trent, Will, Kayley, or any of the Cyrun people. They were doomed to a life without choice. And worst of all—from what I'd read—it sounded very much like Praesidium had not been created to be abused as it was. I wondered at what point in Cyrus' history the royals became consumed with their love of power over the love of their people. Whose hand had written the scribbled note about family being the biggest threat?

Though I felt like doing anything but returning to a ridiculous party to celebrate King Tenebris, I knew there were several people who would be growing very anxious at my long absence. With

286

resignation, I returned the diary to its hiding spot and put the lion charm back in the desk. I ran out, past the guards who still lay collapsed on the floor, and to the spot where Katherine said she'd be waiting.

"All done?" she asked, excitement coloring her tone. "Did you get it?"

"I got what we need," I said, grateful that she'd returned time to its normal pace so I could communicate more easily. I hoped my disappointment wasn't too obvious to her. I didn't want to have this conversation right now. "We'd better use that powder to wake up the guards and get out of here."

"Right," Katherine said, reaching into her maid apron pocket. She withdrew a small flask with yellow powder inside. "The lady at the apothecary said to sprinkle this over the person and they'd wake within the minute." She handed the small bottle to me.

"Got it. I'll meet you back at the closet," I said, my voice still flat with my disappointment. Katherine's eyes flashed at my tone, but she took off without asking questions.

Hurriedly, I sprinted to the guards, standing over each one in turn and sprinkling them with the powder. Then I headed back to the closet, running into Katherine on my way. I ran with her at a normal pace for the remainder of the short distance. We entered the closet with Katherine panting heavily.

"How did it go? Was everything okay? Did you find the diary?" Trevor asked, his arms wrapping protectively around Katherine.

"We ran into a few minor hiccups. I couldn't enter the room for some reason, but Ava could. She said she's got what we need," Katherine answered.

"Yeah, I've got it. We all better get moving before we're caught. The guards will be awake any second now. I'm headed back to the party. Will, Trent, and I will be leaving as soon as we can. We'll return Will to his home and then be back to headquarters to fill you all in. Please be safe as you make your way back through the palace. The guards are going to be on high alert knowing that something weird has happened."

"We'll be fine," Damion said in his no-nonsense, business tone. "Time to move." He led the way out of the closet door with Trevor and Katherine at his heels.

Chapter 28

The Ball

I slipped through the closet's solid back wall into the staff restroom and was back to the main floor in less than a minute.

I returned to the ballroom, where Trent stood next to a dessert table looking distressed, as if he'd lost his puppy and was searching for it in the crowd. The kid was not the best under pressure. The mere sight of him helped ease the ache of disappointment in my chest. Next to him, Will stood casually conversing with another gentleman in a black tuxedo, a plate of chopped fruit in his hand.

I ducked behind a crowd of passersby so I could sneak up behind Trent. "Looking for something?" I whispered in his ear as I stood on my tiptoes.

Immediately, he spun around, grabbing me by the waist. He picked me up and whirled me around in a circle before he enveloped me in a bone-crushing hug.

"Umm, Trent?" I gasped. "I'm fairly certain the corset has already cracked my ribs. I don't think I can handle anymore."

"Oh, sorry," Trent said, loosening his grip so he could look at me. "Guess I got caught up in the moment." He gave one of those adorable half smiles that melted my heart. "So how did it go? Did you find... you know... *it*?"

I noticed Will had ended his conversation with the man he'd been talking to and stood behind us, listening. "Yeah, I did, so the sooner we can get out of here, the better." I didn't want to reveal any more information about what I'd discovered with Will listening in.

"I'm afraid we can't leave yet," Will interjected. "Nobody leaves before Tenebris has given his speech. We're probably at least a half hour away from that, so I'd suggest you make yourselves comfy and do your best to act natural."

"That's just fantastic," I said dryly. Waiting around in the heart of the enemy was the last thing I wanted to do.

"Might as well do something to help pass the time," Trent said, offering me his hand. "Would you dance with me?"

Despite myself, I smiled. "I suppose that's my best option to keep from going insane. But you should be warned—I've never actually danced before. Closest I've ever come is with my dad in the kitchen and he isn't the best teacher."

Will chuckled. "Yes, I can picture that easily. Your dad was always the light-hearted, care-free one of the family. Got himself into quite a few close scrapes because of it. You kids have fun but be careful." He looked at us significantly.

Trent waved him off. "We'll be fine."

He pulled me into the mass of swirling bodies, and I immediately felt intimidated by the grace with which everyone seemed to move. "You sure we should be out here?"

"Relax. We're fine. Nobody is going to notice us. Just try to forget about everyone else for a minute."

He put his hand on my waist, sending the familiar butterflies hammering in my stomach. He took my left hand and placed it on his shoulder, then grabbed my right hand tenderly. We began to gently sway to the music, and with every passing moment, I grew more relaxed. I was able to forget—for now, at least—that our hopes of defeating Praesidium lay in pieces. I pulled myself into Trent and rested my head on his shoulder, enjoying the way our bodies moved together.

"You really are the most incredible, beautiful girl I've ever met, Ava," Trent's low whisper tickled my ear.

I pulled back to look him in the face, seeing him for all he was to me—the man who'd rescued me from a dumpster, saved me from a gunshot wound, showed me the world I belonged to, and stood by me as I fought to free that world, without second guessing my crazy ideas. "And you are the bravest, gentlest, most handsome man I've ever met."

And with that, I stretched up onto my toes, reaching for his lips. Trent leaned in, closing the distance, and we kissed for an immeasurable moment. Though dancers swirled around us, it was as if the world had stopped for us, turning what was mere seconds into our own eternity.

When we finally broke apart, Trent smiled. "Now that's a feeling I could get used to. I was beginning to wonder what kind of moment you were waiting for exactly, but you were right—that was worth the wait."

I smiled too and leaned into his chest. We began to sway again with the music, holding each other a little more tightly, a little more peacefully.

Several songs passed without much conversation before the music came to a halt.

"Ladies and gentleman," a loud voice rang out over the crowd, "please stand for His Royal Majesty, King Tenebris."

The room broke out in wild applause; it was clear we were amongst the upper classes. I rolled my eyes. Trent nudged me and looked meaningfully down at his hands as he clapped enthusiastically along with the crowd. I pulled my palms together in a few short, forced rounds of applause before I dropped my hands. I waited for Tenebris to come out to the large podium, which stood at the top of the long, winding set of stairs along the south wall. The banisters were woven with gratuitous bouquets of flowers. Two large, golden doors stood at the top of the stairs through which I imagined Tenebris would emerge.

Just as the doors began to open, I found myself suddenly thrown off balance by a man who was moving hurriedly through the crowd, presumably to get a better viewpoint for the king's speech. He mumbled a hurried, "Pardon me," as he stumbled into me, pushing a scrap of paper into my hands as he went. Trent caught me, keeping me from falling to the floor as several annoyed guffaws from the surrounding crowd chastised the retreating man's figure. With curiosity, I glanced down at the piece of paper he'd slid into my palm.

Cheers erupted around me as Tenebris emerged through the grand doors. I used the distraction to quickly open the piece of crumpled paper and found the words:

Meet me at the angel statue in the north gardens.

--Mom

My heart stopped. *Mom.* Surely this note couldn't be intended for me, could it? My mother had died years ago.

"What is it?" Trent's low voice tickled my ear.

I held the note out for him to read.

"It's for you?" he asked, confused.

"I don't know. That man pushed it into my hands. Do you think it's some sort of trap?"

"Could be," Trent mused.

I deliberated for a moment. Dad had reaffirmed only a few days ago that my mother really had died, even though everything else he'd told me about Cyrus turned out to be false. Could it be that he'd lied to me twice? Or maybe he didn't know the truth himself. He had been banished to the human realm, after all. Any information he had came through somebody else. Maybe they'd lied to him. I knew I couldn't ignore even the slightest possibility of meeting my mother, even if it was a trap. Regardless, if someone was trying to lure me out to the gardens, wasn't it best to find out who and why?

"I'm going to check it out. I'll be quick, promise." I whispered to Trent as I began to move past him.

To my surprise, he didn't try to stop me. Instead, he said,

"Okay. Be careful. If you're not back in five minutes, I'm coming after you."

I nodded my acknowledgement.

As King Tenebris' loud voice echoed throughout the ballroom, I swiftly wove my way through the crowd, headed for the door.

Chapter 29

Memories

As soon as I exited the ballroom, I broke into a dead sprint, heading for the glass doors Will had described in his sketches of the palace floors. The doors should lead out to the gardens. I reached them in seconds, then proceeded out to the angel statue, which sat at the heart of the well-kept shrubs. It was visible above them, serving as a guide, though I was unfamiliar with the gardens previously.

My heartrate accelerated as I approached the statue, overwhelmed with the thought of meeting my mother, but also nervous that this was a set up. I slowed to a walk as the statue came into view. The angel stood in the center of a large pool with a stone ledge around the pool's base. Carefully, I peeked around the tall hedges that surrounded the pool's perimeter. There was no one in view, but a folded piece of paper sat on the pool's ledge with something small glittering on top of it.

Cautiously, I approached the paper and recognized the necklace which sat on it. It was the other half of the necklace I'd worn since birth. Dad said it had been a gift from my mom. The two roses twisted together in their stems, completing each other.

I picked up the piece of paper, glanced over my shoulder, then read:

The necklace should explain everything. I'll be waiting for you when you've finished.

I stared at the necklace, wary of touching it. Did the person who wrote this note—my mother or otherwise—know that objects could reveal their owner's secrets to me? Is that what the note meant?

I stood up with a huff, determined to leave the smoke and mirrors behind. I walked a few paces before my curiosity got the better of me. With a sigh, I returned to the pool's ledge and sat down. Hesitantly, I extended my hand out to touch the necklace, pausing just before my flesh connected with it.

One way or the other, it was probably best to know whatever secrets the rose contained. Squeezing my eyes shut, I thrust out my hand the rest of the way, feeling the cold metal of the charm as I did.

Instantly, I was sucked into a memory which took shape before my eyes. As the scene settled around me, I found myself in a quaint bookshop with about fifteen tall bookshelves standing in rows. A girl with long, auburn hair stood hunched over one of the lower shelves toward the front of the shop, cramming more books into the already crowded space. I immediately recognized her as my young adult mother, the rose necklace dangling from her neck.

The tinkle of a bell sounded, though the girl didn't turn to its noise, consumed as she was by her task. Carmichael entered the store's front door, a goofy smile on his handsome face as he crept up behind Rosaline. He snuck up behind her, then thrust out his hands, grabbing her waist, as he simultaneously let out a short, abrupt yell.

Rose jumped, straightening, as her hand flew to her chest. She let out a sigh of relief as she recognized Mike, who was laughing hysterically at her reaction.

"Michael!" she sighed with exasperation, swatting his arm. "That wasn't funny. You nearly killed me! My heart is pounding."

Mike chuckled. "It was kinda funny. But I'm very glad I didn't kill you, and I'm very sorry I scared you. Besides, I can think of better ways to get your heart pounding." He raised his eyebrows suggestively. Rose blushed and smiled, tucking a lock of hair behind her ear.

"Are you ready for this evening?" Mike asked enthusiastically.

"I suppose. I still don't understand why the king and prince are coming to Cashmere, of all places, but if it lends itself to a night of dancing with you, I guess I can handle it."

"Prince Trinnen is supposedly looking for a wife," Mike said as he leaned against the edge of the shelves. "I cannot imagine how lucrative the dress business must be right now. All the ladies are spending every last penny they ever earned on the finest dresses they can find to try and impress his Majesty," Mike rolled his eyes. "Anyway, I absolutely cannot wait for the entire province to see my lovely fiancée on my arm. Nobody is going to believe a woman as beautiful as you actually agreed to marry a goon like me."

Rose laughed. "That's completely absurd. But I am also

297

excited for more people to know about us. Maybe it will keep Burton and Oliver in line."

"Yes, yes, go on and remind me of the long list of suitors hoping I'll choke on my next chicken leg so they can swoop in and steal my girl, why don't you?" Mike sighed.

"Don't pay them any attention. I'm all yours and always will be." Rose stretched up to give Mike a kiss as the scene faded.

When the next memory took shape, I found myself in a setting very similar to the reality I'd just left at the palace, only we were outside in this instance. Many dancers held each other close, wearing their finest apparel, as they moved gracefully past each other in a swirling display of gaiety. Along the sides of the large wooden dance floor stood several tables full of delicious food. Most importantly, at the head of the dance floor stood a modest stage with two large thrones atop it. In one throne sat an elderly man wearing an ornate crown, looking utterly bored. I guessed he was Tenebris and Trinnen's father—King Simon. The other throne sat empty. I scanned the crowd for Trinnen. I found him near the foot of the stage surrounded by a group of giggling girls, clearly enjoying the attention they drowned him in.

Closer to where I stood, I caught sight of Rosaline in a shockingly brilliant green dress that hugged her elegant curves. Her auburn hair was pulled up, displaying the graceful bend of her exposed collarbone. She rested her head on Mike's chest who held her close as they swayed gently to the music. I inched closer to them, my heart melting at the sight of my parents, happy as they evidently once were.

The song ended, and I watched as Rose mumbled something to Mike who squeezed her hand before she briskly walked off. Whatever she said, Mike didn't seem alarmed. Perhaps she needed to use the restroom. I wondered idly what they'd use for restrooms out here.

Mike wandered over to a table filled with fruity looking drinks. He picked up a glass and downed it in one, large gulp. He then leaned casually against one of the pillars that held up the large, white tent, watching the crowd. I did the same, noticing the way every woman's head seemed constantly to turn in the direction of Prince Trinnen, despite the fact that nearly all of them were being twirled around the floor by other men, who seemed perturbed by their distraction.

I was lost staring at the maze of dancers when a loud crash caught my attention. I turned in the direction of the commotion to see Rosaline had fallen into one of the dessert tables. Her dress was covered in pudding and frosting. Next to her, Prince Trinnen was also covered in dessert. A large, stumbling crowd stood next to them. I gathered that the crowd had lost control and pushed Rose and the prince into the table. Probably a group of salivating girls were trying to get the attention of the prince and ended up trampling him instead. Rose simply happened to be in the wrong place at the wrong time.

The king was bored no longer. He immediately rushed off the stage to the place where his precious son stood. Guards also hurried to him, doing their best to clean him off. The band stopped playing, allowing me to hear what was being said.

"Please, stop, I'm fine," Prince Trinnen brushed off the concerned throng. "See to the lady, I beg you."

Immediately, the guards responded, turning their attention to Rose who seemed unsure what had just happened. Mike hurried over to her side, concern plain on his face.

"Are you okay?" he asked, grabbing a napkin and dabbing at the splotches of pudding smeared across her green dress.

"Yes, I'm fine. Just got caught up in the crowd," Rose sighed, also dabbing at her dress.

"I am truly sorry for running into you like that, my lady." Prince Trinnen was mostly cleaned up and bowed low to Rosaline.

Rose was quick to return the gesture and curtseyed. "It was not your fault, your Highness."

Mike, likewise, bowed, though the gesture seemed almost painful for him. "It might be best if you were a little more careful where you walk next time," he said as he straightened from his bow.

Prince Trinnen tried to hide the surprise from his face at being spoken to this way. He clearly bit back a retort and said instead, "Of course. I shall be more careful. And your name is?"

"I am Carmichael Longfellow of Cashmere and my lovely fiancée is the woman you just bathed in cream puffs."

Rose directed a subtle elbow into Mike's ribs and gave him a wide-eyed glance. She returned her attention to the prince. "My name is Rosaline Davenport. It's a pleasure to meet you."

My heart thrilled at even this small bit of new information—I'd never known my mother's last name.

Prince Trinnen seemed to properly notice Rose for the first time. His eyes scanned her beautiful figure—no less attractive with the stains of pudding splattered across the green silk—and widened at the sight he took in.

"Would you do me the honor of dancing with me, Miss Davenport, as an apology for my clumsiness?" Prince Trinnen extended his bent arm for Rose to take.

Rose looked at Mike, clearly unsure what to say. "Thank you, but there's no need. Apology accepted. I think I'd like to go home and change now." Rose turned to leave, Mike by her side.

"Stop!" King Simon's voice rang out. I glanced in his direction and noticed Praesidium cradled at the base of his throat. It glowed red at the command. Immediately, Rose and Mike froze in their step. "I insist that the lady obey the request of the prince," he said, obviously bothered by Rose's lack of enthusiasm at being asked to dance by royalty. Rose, her expression blank, returned to Prince Trinnen's side, taking his arm.

"It would be an honor," she said as she followed him out onto the dance floor. Mike—powerless to defy Praesidium—sank into a chair on the outskirts of the dance floor, resigned to watching his love dance with another man.

The scene began to waver, then fade. As it took shape again, I found myself in a familiar setting. I stood outside a small brown cottage with a pen of sheep in the distance. Mike and Rose stood on the front porch. A small lantern hung above them. I knew immediately what I was about to witness—my mother was going to break my dad's heart. I hesitated, unsure if I wanted to see this again. It was hard enough the first time.

Resigned, I moved closer, deciding there might be something new in this memory I hadn't seen or heard before. I was not disappointed. I immediately realized I'd come into the memory at an earlier point than I had the first time.

"Rose, I need you to tell me what's going on. You've been so distant these past few weeks. I don't understand what's changed between us. We were so happy before."

Rose's eyes were already filled with tears. "We were happy. We were so, so happy. But that's all changed now, Mike. Everything has changed."

"What do you mean? Nothing has changed for me. I feel the same way I have always felt about you, Rose. You're my life. You're my everything." Mike gently lifted Rose's chin to look her in the eye. She sobbed harder in response.

"He's chosen me, Mike." Rose's voice cracked. "Prince Trinnen has chosen me as the one he wants to marry. That is why I've been distant these past few weeks. He has been coming often to take me to the palace, to court me. I haven't had any say in the matter. His father has given him Praesidium now that he's chosen a wife. As soon as we are married, he'll be crowned king. There's no way to escape him." Rose's eyes raked over Mike as if begging for him to offer any other solution. Mike's face visibly broke into the tortured mask I'd seen the first time I'd viewed this memory.

"He chose... you? But why? He knew you were engaged to me! How could he choose you? He can't choose you! I won't let him!"

"You know as well as I do that we are completely and totally helpless. I cannot defy him. You cannot defy him. Oh, how I wish we could. He's forced me to come here tonight, to break things off with you. He left me no loopholes."

"No. This can't be. It doesn't work this way. I love you and you love me. We're meant to be together." Mike's eyes burned with the intensity of what he was saying. "He can't just force you to marry him. That's wrong! It's disgusting! I'll kill him myself!" Mike said, his face turning red amidst his anger and pain.

"Stop that. Stop that right now." Rose's voice was filled with urgency. "You can't get yourself into trouble over this, over me. Promise me right now that you won't intervene, that you won't try to stop this."

"I can't make that promise. I love you and I'll fight for you, Rose."

"I love you too, Mike. And if you really love me, you'll do what you have to do to protect yourself and to protect me."

"Oh, I'll do what I need to do to protect you from that monster, alright. You can bet on that."

"Stop it, Mike, I mean it," Rose looked into Mike's burning eyes with an intense pain of her own. "I have to go. I'm only making things worse by being here."

"No, Rose, don't go." Mike said desperately, grabbing for her. She twisted away from him.

"I'm so sorry, Mike. I really, truly am. I can't do this," Rosaline said, tears streaming down her face as she shook her head in dismay.

"Please, Rose, we can make it. I'll take you anywhere you want to go. We can get away from all of this. No one will be able to tell you what you can or can't do anymore. It can be just you and me. I promise." Mike's voice broke with the depth of his emotion.

"I wish it were that simple, Mike. I really do. I'm sorry, but I have to go now. Please don't try to follow me," Rosaline said, tearing the ring off her finger and slamming it into Mike's opened palm.

She turned to leave. Mike reached out and caught her arm. "Please, Rose, I'll do anything," he said with desperate eyes.

"I'm sorry," she sobbed as she stumbled down the steps into the night.

"I love you, Rosaline!" Mike called after her. "Please, no!" Mike's sobs rang out through the air. He turned and punched the lantern hanging by the door. The glass shattered, slicing his knuckles. He fell to his knees, cradling his head in his hands as he openly wept, blood pouring down his forearm.

The scene melted and reformed. I stood in the dank dungeons I'd visited in Will's memories where dad had been brutally beaten.

I prayed I wouldn't have to witness that horrible scene again.

The sound of haggard breathing caught my attention. I turned toward it and saw my father—broken and bleeding—on the floor of one of the dungeon cells. He looked like he was on death's door.

The dungeon door opened. I turned to see Rosaline slip through the crack, checking over her shoulder as she entered. She wore an elegant, baby pink dress, her hair carefully styled. She hurried over to the cell where my father lay, falling to her knees.

Her face crumpled in pain as she took in the sight of Michael on the floor. "Oh, Mike." Her hand covered her mouth in horror. "I am so sorry. So, so sorry. I told you not to fight for me. I begged you. I knew he'd do something like this to you."

Mike turned his head enough to see Rose. Unexpectedly, he smiled, though it appeared to take every bit of strength he had left. "You are so... beautiful," he sighed.

Tears cascaded from Rose's eyes, though she contained her sobs. "I am so sorry," she said again, reaching through the bars to him.

"It's not your fault. You told me not to," Mike gasped. "I just couldn't sit by and do nothing. I had to fight... for you."

"I wish you wouldn't have. Oh, how I wish you wouldn't have." Rose gently rubbed Mike's leg. "If I could change anything in my life, we never would have gone to that stupid dance. I never would have had the misfortune of meeting Trinnen. We would be happily married by now. Oh, how I wish." Rose gave Mike a pained smile through her tears.

"I'll find my way back to you someday, Rose," Mike whispered, the words difficult to make out. "Someday, we'll be free."

The dungeon door began to open again. Rose looked at it, startled.

"You have to hide!" Mike said, sitting up in his panic, his voice stronger than it had been throughout the entire conversation. "Quickly!"

Rose was already on her feet, running around a bend in the dungeon corridor. King Trinnen walked through the door with a blonde gentleman at his side. The pair marched up to the dungeon door where Trinnen let himself into the cell with a key. Without warning, he kicked Mike forcefully in the ribs. Mike bent into himself but didn't cry out, as if he was too exhausted to make any noise.

"You should know better than to try and steal what is your king's, peasant. Rosaline was mine the moment I set eyes on her. You were a fool to try and take her from the palace." Trinnen bent low over Mike's bleeding face. "Fortunately, I'll never have to worry about seeing your pathetic little face again. Enjoy the human realm."

He grabbed Mike by the hair and yanked him to his feet. "Jackson," the king addressed the man he'd brought with him, "you are ordered to leave this swine in the human realm. I expect you to report back when your task is finished." He gruffly shoved Mike forward into Jackson's arms and then stalked back up the dungeon corridor toward the door.

Jackson grabbed Mike by his left bicep and the two disappeared from view, Traveling to the human realm. Just as they vanished into thin air, Rose emerged from her hiding place, reaching out to the spot where Mike had just stood. She collapsed to the ground, weeping, rocking back and forth in her pain.

The sad scene before me transformed into one of utter panic. Rosaline sat completely naked in an oversized bathtub, her stomach bulging as if it would pop with the slightest provocation. A woman leaned over the edge of the tub at the end of Rose's bent legs, trying to coach Rose through her frantic breathing. I quickly understood that Rose was giving birth. Was I about to witness my own entrance into the world? How odd. I wasn't sure I wanted to stick around for this.

"Come on, Rose, keep pushing. You're doing great. Almost there." The haggard woman at Rose's feet was obviously trying to appear calm, but her wild eyes betrayed her.

"Ahhh," Rose grunted, her breaths coming in shallow gasps. "How much longer, Vi?"

"I can see a head," the woman responded excitedly. "Come on, Rose. Give me one more good push!"

Rose pushed as she screamed and the woman called Vi reached forward, catching a small child who emerged suddenly. I tried not to be too disgusted at how awful the baby looked—or how awful I looked, I guess. I cringed.

Rose and Vi smiled at each other as Vi snipped the umbilical cord and passed the baby to Rose.

"It's a boy," Rose breathed, her eyes alight with curiosity and love.

"You thought it would be," Vi responded with another adoring smile. "Good work."

Huh. Now I was really confused. Did I have a brother I didn't know about? This didn't make any sense at all.

Rose's expression changed to one of intense discomfort. "Violet, we're not done yet," she said with alarm.

"It's just your placenta. It's okay," Violet reassured her.

"No, we are not done yet!" Rose screamed, tensing up as she frantically passed the child back to Violet.

Violet ducked back down to examine Rose. "I think you're right. Another baby is coming!"

"For heaven's sake, no!" Rose cried. "I can't have two. What will he say? What will he *do*?"

"We'll worry about that in a moment. For now, concentrate." Violet shifted back into midwife mode. She frantically wrapped the crying boy in a blanket and left him in a small basket near the tub. She then turned her attention back to Rose who was again screaming in pain.

"You can do this. Keep pushing," Violet coached. Rose glared at her.

After another minute or so of strenuous pushing, Violet emerged once again with a baby in her arms. "It's a girl," she sighed as she passed the baby to Rose, whose eyes were filled with tears. Rose cradled the girl to her chest as tears continued to stream down her face. Violet bent over and picked up the boy from the basket.

"What am I going to do?" Rose looked up at Violet. "I can't have two. He'll do something to her—he'll kill her!" she moaned, her tears becoming even more intense.

"Shhhh, shhh, shhh," Violet tried to soothe Rose. "Surely King Trinnen would never do such a thing. This is his child, after all. He would never—"

"He would," Rose cut her off. "He most certainly would. He hates his own brother. He hates the constant challenge to his throne, his authority. He has already vowed to me that we will never have a second child. If he ever finds out about her, he will dispose of her. Believe me, nothing is beneath the royals and they have done it before."

"Oh, Rose," Violet stroked Rose's sweaty hair.

"Violet," Rose's voice dropped low and intense. She reached out and grabbed Violet's hand. "You must take her. Take her to your home. Keep her hidden. I will come for her as soon as I can—as soon as I think of a better plan. Please do this for me."

Violet looked into Rose's desperate eyes, considering. "You're sure about this?"

"It's the only option. Please," she begged.

"Very well. But please, Rose, think of something quickly. I don't know how long I can keep a newborn child without raising questions, and we both know we'll end up dead if the king should ever find out we kept a secret of this magnitude from him."

"I will. I promise."

"Would you like to name her before I take her?" Violet asked.

Rose smiled through her tears as she looked down at her new daughter's face. "Her name is Avalon Rosaline. Ava for short."

The two women smiled at each other as the gory bathroom scene began to fade away. My own breathing came in shallow gasps as I attempted to comprehend the implications of what I'd just seen, but before I could fully understand, I was thrown into yet another memory.

I immediately recognized this setting—I was on the light rail that went through downtown Denver. I'd ridden on it many times with Dad when we went into town. But Rose shouldn't be here—she couldn't be. Yet there she was, hidden on the last bench of the speeding car, clutching a small child to her chest. I noticed the other passengers watched her with curiosity. It was rather obvious from her posture and facial expressions that she was completely panicked.

"Next stop: 204 North Church Street," a voice announced over the intercom system. I watched Rose as she stiffly stood from her chair, holding the baby even more tightly as she wove through the crowd to the doors.

"Are you okay, Miss?" A man had reached out and grabbed her, showing his concern.

"I'm fine," Rose mumbled as she pressed on toward the door.

She exited the train, glancing around her before she took off at a brisk walk into the rainy night. Curiosity burning inside me, I followed.

We arrived at a small park I didn't recognize. Rose hid underneath the slide, bouncing her small child as she waited for something.

"Rose?" a familiar voice asked from somewhere out of sight. "Is that you?" I instantly recognized it as the voice of my dad—or the man I had always thought was my dad.

Rose let out a long breath before she stepped out from the cover of the slide. "Yes, it's me," she replied, her eyes raking over Mike hungrily. "Thank you for coming."

"You knew I would," Mike said, shrugging.

"I didn't, actually. But I hoped." Rose smiled at him through the rain.

Mike seemed uncomfortable with the comment. "Is this the girl?" he asked. He approached Rose and pushed back the blanket to get a glimpse of my baby face. My heart nearly melted as I took in my dad's soft expression. Despite what I may not have known about my past, this was the man who raised me, who loved me. This was my father.

"Yes, this is Avalon," Rose answered. "I don't have much time. They could be on their way right now. Please tell me, Mike. Will you do it? Will you take her?"

Mike looked back and forth between the baby and Rose. "I don't know the first thing about kids, you know. But yes, of course. Anything for you." He gave Rose a half smile. She cried harder in response.

"Come here, Rose," Mike said, grabbing the woman in an embrace with me cradled between their chests. "You can stay here with me. You don't have to go back." He hesitated. "Please don't go back." His voice broke as a tear cascaded down his cheek.

Rose stepped back as she said, "You know as well as I do that isn't an option. Please, just promise me that you'll take care of her."

"I promise," Mike said quietly, his voice pained.

"And promise you won't tell her where she comes from. She can't know—for her own safety."

"I know. I promise."

Rose looked down at the baby. "I love you, Ava. Forever and always." She kissed the baby on the head, then handed her over to Mike.

The scene faded to black. I found myself sitting on the ledge of the fountain back in the palace gardens, the rose charm clutched in my hand.

"What did you think?" a woman's voice asked from somewhere in the distance.

"Rose? Is that you?" I was fairly certain I recognized her voice, though it sounded older.

I heard a rustling from behind me. I stood quickly and turned toward it. A woman, dressed in red, emerged from around a tall hedge. Her face was heavy with makeup and her blonde hair curled down to her waist.

"Queen Isabella?" I asked, confused and afraid. So this had been a set up after all.

"Rose is correct," she said, edging toward me cautiously.

I hesitated, half-way convinced it would be best to run. What did she mean, 'Rose is correct'?

"I go by Isabella because Tenebris wants me to," the woman continued to explain. "I don't think anyone in the entire kingdom remembers my real name. They forgot, you see, because he wanted them to. Praesidium is a powerful object. But not powerful enough to make me forget. Fortunately, I am surrounded by many memories, just like you, Ava, though he wants desperately for me to be a different woman."

I tried to process this. "You mean to say you are Rosaline, my mother? And also the previous queen of Cyrus? Everyone told me the queen died in the rebel attack, along with Trinnen and their son."

Instead of answering me, she reached into the pool of water and splashed her face several times. As she looked up at me without the makeup distorting her features, I finally recognized her. Though she was older and had blonde hair, she most certainly was Rose.

Rose smiled. "That, again, is what Tenebris wanted everyone to believe. Instead, he married me. He always wanted everything that was his brother's, including his wife. They hated each other. Passionately."

"Are Trinnen and... my brother... really dead? Or is that also a lie?"

"I'm glad to hear you understand so well," Rose smiled kindly. "Yes, your father and brother are dead." Her face fell slightly with sadness.

"Please don't call that man my father," I said coldly.

Rose smiled sympathetically, then sat on the ledge of the pool, motioning for me to join her. I hesitated only momentarily before I sat next to my mother, marveling in that fact. I had long since given up hope of ever meeting her, yet here I was, staring into her eyes that matched mine so closely.

"I'm sorry. And I understand completely. It's very hard for me to have anything but bitter thoughts about him as well. As you've seen, he took everything from me. And Tenebris continues to do so. I do hope, though, that you can forgive me. And your brother."

"What was his name?" I asked softly.

Rose smiled. "His name was Kevin—a name Trinnen loathed. It was much too common for his son," Rose rolled her eyes. "But oddly, he let me have my way for once."

I smiled. I had a brother. A twin brother named Kevin. I was overwhelmed with regret that I'd never know him.

"You really loved Dad, didn't you?" I asked.

Rose smiled, not needing to clarify to whom I was referring. "More than you know. I still love him. And I love him even more seeing how well he raised you. I knew he would." She reached out and stroked my hair. I leaned into her soft hand slightly.

I learned something new in that instance—the touch of a mother was magical. Far more than any magic Cyril could gift. It was a power I'd never known, and I reveled in it.

"You deserve to be with him. And he with you," I said.

Rose smiled sadly. "That's something I've only dreamed of for twenty long years. I'm afraid it's not possible. Praesidium is too strong."

"It is strong. Most definitely. But I happen to know how to defeat it. And with the information you just revealed to me, it's suddenly become possible once more. I am the daughter of King Trinnen, after all."

Rose looked at me in confusion as my resolve to defeat my family's birthright strengthened within me.

King Trinnen was my father, which made me the rightful heir of Cyrus. The bloodline of Ganton ran through me. As such, I would be the one to destroy the long curse he'd placed on Cyrus those many years ago.

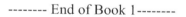

-------- End of Book 1 --------

Acknowledgments

My family has been wonderful in their support of this project. My husband, Ryan, has been patient with me as I've spent many hours lost in my writing and imagination. His excitement for my story truly helped me feel like this was something others would enjoy reading.

My parents, Kirk and Annalisa, were enthusiastic from the start, believing in my abilities even when I was unsure myself. I owe them more than can possibly be put in words.

My siblings, Spencer, Kiranne, and Jessalyn, provided wonderful feedback as my test readers. I'm thankful for the hours they spent helping me improve my writing. And, as always, I'm grateful for my angel brother, McKay, who watches over me.

My parents-in-law, Bill and Kathy, were also helpful readers, giving insight into parts they enjoyed and parts that could be improved. Their support means the world to me.

A huge thank you to my readers who gave my work a chance! I cannot express how much it means to me. You're the best!

Most of all, I thank my Heavenly Father who has given me all I have.

ABOUT THE AUTHOR

Janilise lives in Northern Utah with her husband, Ryan, and their many pets. She graduated from Brigham Young University with a degree in health education and history teaching. She loves running, camping, hiking, and doing anything outdoors. Her favorite place to be is anywhere with family.

To learn more about Janilise and to stay updated on her other writing projects, connect with her on her blog.

www.janilisewrites.weebly.com